CLAIMING
FELICITY

DISCOVER OTHER TITLES BY SUSAN STOKER

Ace Security Series

Claiming Grace

Claiming Alexis

Claiming Bailey

Claiming Felicity

Badge of Honor: Texas Heroes Series

Justice for Mackenzie

Justice for Mickie

Justice for Corrie

Justice for Laine (novella)

Shelter for Elizabeth

Justice for Boone

Shelter for Adeline

Shelter for Sophie

Justice for Erin

Justice for Milena (March 2018)

Shelter for Blythe (July 2018)

Justice for Hope (TBA)

Shelter for Quinn (TBA)

Shelter for Koren (TBA)

Shelter for Penelope (TBA)

Delta Force Heroes Series

Rescuing Rayne

Assisting Aimee (novella)

Rescuing Emily

Rescuing Harley
Marrying Emily
Rescuing Kassie
Rescuing Bryn
Rescuing Casey
Rescuing Sadie (April 2018)
Rescuing Wendy (May 2018)
Rescuing Mary (November 2018)

SEAL of Protection Series

Protecting Caroline
Protecting Alabama
Protecting Fiona
Marrying Caroline (novella)
Protecting Summer
Protecting Cheyenne
Protecting Jessyka
Protecting Julie (novella)
Protecting Melody
Protecting the Future
Protecting Alabama's Kids (novella)
Protecting Kiera (novella)
Protecting Dakota

Beyond Reality Series

Outback Hearts
Flaming Hearts
Frozen Hearts

CLAIMING
FELICITY

ACE SECURITY

BOOK 4

Susan Stoker

Montlake
Romance

Published by Montlake Romance, Seattle

www.apub.com

Amazon, the Amazon logo, and Montlake Romance are trademarks of Amazon.com, Inc., or its affiliates.

ISBN-13: 9781503954168
ISBN-10: 1503954161

Cover design by Eileen Carey

Printed in the United States of America

CLAIMING
FELICITY

Prologue

Megan Parkins put her pillow over her head to try to drown out the voices coming from the other side of the wall . . . but it was no use. She could hear her roommate, Colleen Murphy, and Colleen's boyfriend, Joseph, as easily as if they were standing right next to her.

"You're an embarrassment, Colleen. A complete and utter embarrassment. What'd I tell you before we left?"

"Th-That I should stay by your side."

"And what did you do?"

"I went to the bathroom."

"Did I tell you you could go to the bathroom?"

"No, but, Joseph, I really had to go."

Megan flinched at the sound of Colleen being struck. She squeezed her eyes together and clenched her teeth. She hated Joseph. With every fiber of her being. She'd told her friend over and over that he was bad news. That she should break up with him. But Colleen didn't listen. Defended Joseph, in fact, saying that his father had been really strict with him, and he'd learned discipline as a result. And now he was just teaching it to her. Besides, she claimed, he didn't mean it when he yelled at her . . . or when he hit her.

"I don't give a shit," Joseph went on. "If you have to piss your pants, you do it. The only thing I asked of you was that you stay by my side, and you couldn't even do that one simple thing."

"I'm sorry. It won't happen again."

"Damn straight it won't happen again," Joseph told her.

Megan heard him hit Colleen again. Then again. And a third time. Before she thought about what she was doing, Megan was on the move. She couldn't sit there and let Joe beat Colleen up again. Not after the concussion he'd given her the last time. If Colleen wouldn't help herself, Megan would.

She picked up the phone and quickly dialed 911. Whispering, Megan told the dispatcher what was going on and where they were.

The ten minutes it took for the cops to show up were excruciating. Joe continued to berate Colleen, punctuating his words with his fists. Megan wanted to scream at Colleen to stand up for herself, or to get the hell out of there, but she kept quiet. When Megan heard the sirens, she quietly left her bedroom and tiptoed past her roommate's room, down the hall, and to the front door. She was waiting for the pair of policemen when they arrived at the apartment and pointed toward Colleen's door.

Within moments, Joe was being interviewed off to one side by one of the cops, while the other tried to talk to Colleen.

Ignoring Joseph's intense gaze, Megan went over to her roommate.

"Can you tell me what's going on?" the police officer asked.

"N-Nothing. We were just having an argument," Colleen said meekly.

"How'd you get the mark on your face?"

"I fell the other morning in the bathroom. Knocked my head on the counter."

"You know that's not true," Megan interjected. "Last week Joseph hit you when you were ten minutes late getting to his apartment because of traffic."

Colleen was shaking her head before Megan had finished speaking. "No, I fell."

The officer looked between Megan and the battered, scared-out-of-her-mind woman in front of him. "Did your boyfriend hit you tonight?"

"No."

Megan ground her teeth together and shook her head. "Colleen, you need to get away from him. He's going to really hurt you one of these days."

The other woman stubbornly shook her head. "He loves me. We're fine. You need to keep your nose out of our business." She looked up at Megan for the first time since she'd entered the room. "You don't understand. He *loves* me. And I love him. We were just arguing tonight. That's it. All couples do it."

Megan cocked her head and looked at her friend. Other than the small mark near her temple from the week before, Colleen didn't have any other obvious marks to show that she'd been hit by her boyfriend. Any *new* marks anyway. But she wasn't putting weight on one of her legs and was holding one arm close to her stomach. Obviously Joseph had wised up and learned not to hit his girlfriend anywhere that would show.

"Don't do this," Megan pleaded in a soft tone so Joseph couldn't overhear her. "I heard him hitting you, Colleen. Please. Press charges. Get him out of your life."

It was as if Colleen didn't even hear her. "Officer, nothing is going on. My roommate misheard. We were simply arguing. That's it."

The cop sighed. "Do you want to press charges, Ms. Murphy?"

Colleen shook her head.

"Can *I* press charges?" Megan asked. "For trespassing, or assault, or *something*?"

"Do you have a restraining order against him?"

Megan sighed. "No."

"Unfortunately, if he didn't strike you, and you aren't the victim, then no. Stay here, I need to talk to my partner for a moment."

Megan nodded, and as soon as he turned away from them, she looked at Colleen. "Why are you protecting him? He treats you like shit."

"He loves me," Colleen insisted.

"He doesn't. That isn't love. Not a normal, healthy kind, at least."

"What would you know about love?"

"Well, I'm not an expert. But if a man told me he'd prefer I pee in my pants rather than leave his side, I'd drop his ass like a hot poker. Why can't you see how awful he is? We've been friends for two years. I've never seen you act like this before."

Colleen looked up and into her roommate's eyes. "I admit there are times when he's not the nicest, but you aren't around him all the time. He's the most romantic man I've ever met. He's super protective of me. We were on campus one time when a guy whistled at me, and he put his hand around the guy's throat and told him if he ever disrespected me again, he'd kill him."

Megan knew her eyes were huge in her face. "That's not romantic, that's crazy," she told her friend.

Colleen stubbornly shook her head. "No, I'm just not explaining it right."

"I think you're explaining it exactly right," Megan said dryly.

"His family is amazing. His mom died when he was little, and it's just him, his dad, and his uncles. His dad is strict, but they're all pretty hilarious. This huge Italian family. They have each other's backs, just like Joseph has mine. He's just stressed about school. He doesn't mean to hurt me. He's always so sorry after something happens."

"Oh, sweetie, all abusers are. They promise it'll never happen again, but it always does. It's just going to get worse. Please. Press charges. You deserve better."

Megan knew her friend was going to refuse by the stubborn glint in her eye. "No. I love him, and he loves me. We're going to get married and have at least three kids. I won't let you mess that up for me. I was going to wait until the end of the semester to move out, but it's obvious things between you and me aren't working out. If I can't have an argument with my boyfriend without you calling the cops on us . . . you're no friend of mine."

"Colleen, no, wait—"

"You heard her," Joseph said as he came up next to Colleen. He slid an arm around her waist and pulled her into his side.

Megan saw the way her friend winced at the movement, but she didn't protest.

"I've asked Colleen to move in with me. She agreed," Joseph told her, a gleam of triumph, and something else she didn't understand, in his eyes.

Megan turned to the police officers. "So you're just going to let him get away with this?"

One of them shrugged apologetically. "If she won't press charges and there aren't any new wounds on either of them, our hands are tied."

"Are you at least going to make sure this incident is recorded? So if she shows up dead, there'll be some record of my complaint against him?"

"There will be a record of the call," the other officer said. Then he turned to Joseph and Colleen. "Now, why don't you two go on and get out of here. Sir, you said you had an apartment in another building. We don't want to be called back here tonight."

"Thank you, Officer. Me and my girl'll get going right now. Can I press charges against *her* for making a false report?"

Megan's head whipped around to stare at Joseph in disbelief. "What?"

The officer nodded. "That's your choice."

"I'll think about it," Joseph said calmly. "Thank you for your assistance tonight. We don't want to cause any more issues. If my girlfriend needs an escort to collect her belongings at a later date, can we call the station?"

The police officers looked uneasy now, but one nodded. "Yes, if you think it's necessary."

"It's necessary," Joseph said. He turned his gaze to Megan. "My girlfriend's roommate is delusional and doesn't like that her friend has a loving boyfriend who looks out for her. She's crazy, and I don't trust her not to fill Colleen's head with bullshit about me and my family."

"You know it's not bullshit," Megan ground out.

"Enough. Go ahead and take your girlfriend to your place. Ma'am? If you can please come with me while Ms. Murphy packs a bag." The officer motioned to the doorway with his arm.

Megan looked toward her friend, hoping against hope she'd come to her senses, or at the very least defend her. But no. She was staring at her feet, not making eye contact with anyone.

"Colleen?" She waited, but her friend didn't look up.

"Ma'am?"

Knowing the cops would only wait so long, Megan said quickly, "If you ever need anything, I'm here for you. No strings."

"Officer?" Joseph said, anger in his tone.

"Come on, Ms. Parkins." Megan allowed him to lead her out of the room. When they were in the kitchen, Megan turned to him. "He's going to kill her. Isn't there anything you can do?"

He shook his head. "If your roommate doesn't want to press charges, there's not much we *can* do."

"So what . . . you have to wait until you find her dead body?"

The older man looked uncomfortable, but didn't answer. Simply stared down at her.

Megan sighed and leaned back against the counter. She crossed her arms over her chest and watched the hallway. Within ten minutes, Colleen appeared with Joseph still holding her waist and the other officer following close behind them.

Megan pushed off the counter and faced her friend, but didn't say a word.

Joseph led Colleen to the front door of the apartment, and right before they left, turned and made eye contact with Megan. "I underestimated you. It won't happen again. See you around." And with that, he disappeared out the door with Colleen silent at his side.

As soon as the officers left, Megan locked the dead bolt and raced to her room. She shut her bedroom door and locked that too. She backed into the corner of her room, behind her bed, and sank to the ground. The look in Joseph's eyes scared her to death. Megan generally wasn't afraid of much, but suddenly she was terrified of Joseph Waters.

She'd made an enemy tonight.

Chapter One

"Tell us how you found out about us again?" Logan Anderson asked.

Ryder "Ace" Sinclair was trying to look relaxed sitting across from his three half brothers. He'd introduced himself the night before, but now that his existence had had a chance to sink in, he and his brothers were having a more in-depth conversation. Finding out more about who the others were.

"My mom told me about how she met your dad when he was on a business trip down in Colorado Springs. She knew he was married, but it didn't seem to matter to either of them. When you find the person meant to be yours, there's no denying it."

Ryder ignored the growl of the middle triplet, Blake, and continued. "They were together a couple of times. My mom said she'd never been happier. But something happened here in Castle Rock, and Ace told her he couldn't see her anymore. Said it was for her own good. Broke my mom's heart. She found out two months later she was pregnant with me."

"Did she try to contact my dad? Ask him for money?" Blake asked.

Ryder grit his teeth and tried not to bite his new brother's head off at the implication of his words. "My mom didn't want a damn thing from Ace Anderson except his love. She adored him. Would do anything for him . . . including leaving him alone like he requested."

"So she knew about us?" Nathan asked. He was the youngest of the triplets, and hadn't asked too many questions yet.

Ryder nodded. "She said he admitted during one of the last times they were together that he had triplets. That he loved you guys more than anything. He told my mom leaving her was the hardest thing he'd ever done . . . even though he wanted nothing more than to be with her for the rest of his life."

There was silence around the table as the men absorbed Ryder's words.

He went on. "On her deathbed, she wanted to let me know that I had three half brothers. Told me where you were. Honestly, I think she felt guilty."

"About what?" Logan asked.

"My mom wrote your dad a letter. Told him about me. That I was his son."

"When?" It was Nathan who asked this time.

Ryder inhaled deeply. He thought his brothers knew this. He didn't want to be the one who told them, but it didn't look like he had a choice. "Right before he was killed."

"Fuck," Logan swore.

Nathan just looked at him with big eyes.

Blake pushed back from the table, his chair falling to the ground behind him. He paced back and forth. "I don't fucking believe this."

"She didn't mean to—" Ryder started, but Blake interrupted him.

"But she did . . . didn't she? She fucking got him killed."

"Easy, Bro," Logan said.

"My mother did *not* kill your father," Ryder bit out.

"Don't you mean *our* father?" Blake retorted immediately.

"Fine. Yes. My mother did not kill *our* father. *Your* mom did that. I don't know what happened. Maybe she found the letter my mom sent. Maybe Ace confronted her about it or told her he wanted a divorce. I don't know. But what I *do* know is that my mom died pining for the one man who ever loved her. She never got over Ace Anderson. Loved him to the very marrow of her bones. She kept his picture on our wall. Told me stories about how great a man he was. She never hid who he was from me. Even when we didn't have enough to eat, she never blamed him for leaving her. When she almost got attacked on her way home because she worked two jobs and didn't get home until way after it got dark, she didn't blame him for leaving. When I complained about not having anyone to come with me on Boy Scouts father-son nights, she didn't bad-mouth him. So fuck you for even insinuating that my mother had anything to do with his death." Ryder was practically panting in fury when he finished speaking. He thought he was done, but he realized that, no, he had a lot more to say.

"I made the decision to come up here and meet you three when I read in the paper about all that you went through with the Inca Boyz gang, and after some of my own research. I was curious about who my brothers were, but I wanted to look into what kind of men you were before I came up here and introduced myself to you. I wanted to hate you. Wanted to resent you for the life I led growing up. Me and my mom were poor. I never had new clothes growing up—we shopped at Goodwill. There were many nights I went to bed hungry. I wanted you all to know how good you had it with our father. But then I read that fucking article and realized that I probably had an amazing childhood compared to yours. Yeah, I was hungry, and we were poor, but all I knew was love. My mom never let a day go by when she didn't tell me how much she loved me. She didn't beat me. Didn't threaten me. I realized that I don't resent you at all for having my dad when I would've done anything to have at least *met* him. But if you think I'm going to sit here and let you talk shit about my mom, you're insane."

Ryder pushed to his feet, and he glared at Blake, standing on the other side of the table.

"We had no idea why our mom killed Dad," Nathan said quietly, without a hint of the emotion he was broadcasting clearly on his face. "We thought she finally just went too far one night. Blake, have you been through all of Dad's papers yet? Maybe the letter is in there?"

Blake shrugged. "It hasn't been a priority with all the other shit going on around here."

Logan met Ryder's eyes. "I'm glad you came. Unlike you, though, we didn't know jack shit about you or your mom before last night. I'm not going to say I think we'll all be best buds, but I appreciate how hard it must've been for you to come up here and meet us. I did some preliminary investigation into who you are last night, just as you did with us," Logan said.

Ryder wasn't offended in the least. "I figured you would. Satisfied with what you found?"

Logan eyed him for a beat before continuing. "Yes and no. You've got an impressive background, but there were a lot of holes, and things that don't quite add up."

Ryder couldn't help but grin. That was certainly one way to put it. He kept his mouth shut and didn't offer up any explanations for what Logan may or may not have deduced from his research into him.

Finally, Logan shook his head and said ruefully, "I should be more concerned about the lack of details in your background, but for some reason, I'm not." He stood and held out his hand to Ryder. "It's good to meet you."

Ryder took hold of Logan's hand and shook it. "Thanks. You too."

"You gonna stick around for a while?"

Ryder shrugged. "Wasn't really planning on it. Wasn't sure what kind of reception I'd get. I'm taking leave from work, so I've got some time, but didn't have any set plans."

"You have a job you can take an unspecified amount of time off from?" It was Blake who asked, the suspicion easy to hear in his voice.

"As Logan probably already told you, I work with a group down in Colorado Springs. We're hired out to work security." It wasn't exactly an accurate description of what he did, but it would do for now.

"That sounds . . . intriguing," Logan said.

Ryder nodded. "Spent some time in the military. Decided to use the skills I learned and got out."

Logan nodded. "I get that."

Ryder knew he did. He'd read that Logan and Blake had both done stints in the Army. Seemed like even though they were only half brothers, they had a lot in common. "You having any other issues with the Inca Boyz? I might be able to help with that," Ryder offered.

Logan shook his head. "After Nathan took care of the president, the gang pretty much broke up. Too much pressure from the cops, and no one wanted to step up and take up the reins."

"Good. Oh, and Nathan, good job on getting rid of that motherfucker without actually shooting his ass."

Nathan smiled. "Had lots of help from Bailey, her little brother, and Logan and Blake."

Ryder nodded and looked at his half siblings. He was proud of them. From what he'd found out about them, they'd all had pretty harrowing experiences with the gang, but they seemed to be flourishing with the women in their lives. They'd also done a hell of a job making their business, Ace Security, prosper in the short time it'd been in operation.

"If you have the time, I wouldn't mind you sticking around for a while. Get to know my wife and kids. They're your nephews, after all," Logan said, his eyes showing his sincerity.

Ryder went stock-still. Shit. He hadn't really thought about having nephews. Damn, it felt good. "I think I—"

He was interrupted by a door slamming open. A pretty woman, whom Ryder knew to be Logan's wife, burst into the room. She'd been there earlier, but had left, saying she had stuff to do.

"Cole just called. He said we all need to get over to the gym right now."

Logan was moving toward his wife before she'd finished speaking. "Why? What's going on?"

"I don't know!" she exclaimed, out of breath. "He just said something was going on with Felicity, and he needed us over there pronto."

"I'm sure it's nothing. But come on. Ryder, you want to wait here?" Logan asked.

"I'm going with you," he said firmly. He didn't know why. It wasn't like he knew who Cole or Felicity were. But for some reason he needed to tag along. Call it a sixth sense. Call it a premonition. But when the skin on the back of his neck itched, he'd learned to listen. He hadn't survived his stint in the special forces and through some of the mercenary jobs he'd taken to start ignoring it now.

Shrugging as if it didn't matter to him one way or another, Logan said, "Okay. I have a feeling our talk here isn't over, but we can get back to it later. Blake, you good?"

The other man nodded once and headed for the doorway. Nathan followed.

Ryder brought up the rear and followed his brothers out of Ace Security's offices and toward a gym he'd noticed on one of his trips up to Castle Rock. Rock Hard Gym. It was located in the same downtown square as his brothers' business, along with a coffee shop, some law offices, and other random stores.

Ryder took a deep breath as they reached the door to the gym. He'd thought his half brothers had purposely been ignoring his existence. He had no idea they didn't know anything about him or his mom.

They walked past the front desk, past a large room filled with weights and other cardio machines, and down a hallway that held offices.

Grace Anderson opened one of the doors, and they all filed in.

Ryder took one look at the woman in the room, and his breath caught in his throat.

Chapter Two

Felicity Jones glared at her business partner, one of her closest friends. She and Cole had made an agreement when they'd first opened Rock Hard Gym. He would legally own the gym on paper, but she was an equal partner, as she'd ponied up a good amount of the cash to get the gym going. She'd thought there was an implied agreement that anytime she wanted out, he'd pay her back the money she'd put in. But now he was refusing. Not only that, but he was demanding more information.

Why did she want the money?

Why did she want to leave Castle Rock?

What wasn't she telling him?

All very perceptive questions, and things she wasn't ready to talk about. Not with him. Not with anyone. Not now, and not ever. It was for their own good.

But then Cole had gone and called Grace. And Felicity knew without a doubt she'd bring reinforcements—namely, her husband and his brothers.

It wasn't fair.

But what about her life had ever been fair?

When the door to the office opened, Felicity wasn't surprised to see Grace and her husband enter. And Blake and Nathan. She had no idea who the other man was, but she barely glanced at him. She turned to frown at Cole.

"Great. Now it's five against one. You think intimidation will work? You should know me better than that."

The unknown man pushed through the others to stand by her side. "Five against two."

Felicity gaped at him. "Who the fuck are you?"

He held out his hand as if they were in the middle of a formal gathering. "Ryder Sinclair. And you?"

Felicity's hand was moving before she could call it back. Manners her mom had instilled in her at an early age were hard to overcome. "Felicity Jones."

The second Ryder gripped her hand, Felicity knew she was in trouble. His hand was warm, but not sweaty. He didn't squeeze her hand too hard, but used just the right amount of pressure as he shook her hand. But more than that, the second he touched her, goose bumps raced down her arms. She had the feeling that if she threw herself into his arms, he'd keep her safe. She couldn't take her eyes off his hazel ones. He looked familiar. She stiffened. Shit, had she met him before? "Have we met?" she blurted as she tried to drop his hand.

Instead of looking offended or put out by her question, he merely shook his head and refused to let go. "No, we haven't met . . . much to my disappointment. But we know each other now."

Felicity felt a strong urge to burrow into his chest and let him take care of her. He was taller than she was by a couple of inches, the perfect height for her head to rest comfortably on his broad shoulder, but she straightened her spine and used her free hand to pry his fingers off her instead of throwing herself into his arms. She was an island. Couldn't rely on anyone. Not if she wanted to keep them safe.

"Whatever, Casanova." She turned to the best friend she'd ever had and raised her eyebrows as if to ask, "What the fuck?"

Grace smirked at her in return and crossed her arms over her chest. Then she turned to Cole. "What's Felicity done now? Why are we here?"

Felicity opened her mouth to forestall anything Cole might tell them, but he was faster.

"She wants her half of the business in cash and is gonna bolt if I give it to her."

There was silence in the small office for a heartbeat before Grace gasped. "What? Leese, you can't go. I need you. You're Ace and Nate's godmother."

"I didn't say I was leaving," Felicity protested weakly.

"But you didn't say you were staying either," Logan wisely deducted.

Felicity scowled at him, having no clue what to say. They were all looking at her with disapproval, which cut her to her core. But she couldn't stay. She'd stayed way too long as it was. The horrible feeling inside her was why she hadn't ever tried to make friends before. Why she moved around as much as she did. She knew it would hurt to leave Castle Rock, but hadn't known how badly.

"I don't know why Cole is making such a big deal out of this. It's not like he doesn't have the money."

"Swear to me right now that if I give you the money, you won't leave," Cole ordered.

Cole was taller than everyone in the room, and Felicity hadn't ever been intimidated by him, but she couldn't look him in the eye and lie.

"I won't leave."

Her words seemed to echo in the room.

Felicity looked at the scarred desk across from her. She remembered the day she'd found it. She'd been driving around Castle Rock and had seen it on the curb with a "Free" sign next to it. She'd immediately called Cole and made him come and haul it away. She'd spent hours sanding it down and fixing it up. It seemed to fit here. Battered and broken, but just needing some TLC to be perfect.

She looked up when Cole stepped up to her. He took her chin in his fingers and forced her head up to his. He wasn't hurting her, but he wasn't letting her go either. "Look me in the eyes and say it so I believe you."

Felicity swallowed and opened her mouth, but the man at her other side got there before she could.

"Take your hands off her." His voice was low and deadly.

Cole's hand immediately dropped, and Felicity turned her head to look at Ryder. He was pissed. And she had no idea why. She took a small step away from him, not wanting to be anywhere near him if a fight broke out, but he wouldn't let her. His arm shot out, hooked her around the waist with an unbreakable grip, and hauled her back so she was right next to him.

Felicity opened her mouth to protest his high-handedness, but the second she was next to him again, he dropped his hand. It was as if he wanted her next to him so he could protect her, not because he was an asshole. It made no sense, but that was the vibe she got. As irritated as she'd been at his presumptiveness the second he dropped his hand from around her, she felt almost bereft of his touch.

"I wasn't hurting her," Cole bit out.

"Don't care. No one makes her do anything she doesn't want to do," Ryder retorted.

Felicity eyes went from one man to the other as they volleyed back and forth.

"Felicity doesn't do anything she doesn't want to," Cole said after a second.

"Damn straight."

"Look, you might be related to the Andersons, but this doesn't involve you," Cole told him.

"The fuck it doesn't," Ryder shot back.

Cole's eyes narrowed, and the two men glared at each other.

"Um . . . he's correct . . . Ryder? Is that right?" She was finally putting the pieces together about the man standing next to her like a pissed-off guard dog. Ryder Sinclair. No wonder he looked familiar.

Half brother to the Anderson triplets. The half brother they hadn't known existed. He'd showed up the night before, and Grace had called to let her know all about it.

Grace had wanted to talk more last night, but Felicity had seen the envelope in the mail she'd picked up from the post office, from *him*, and had told her friend she couldn't talk anymore. The words on the note were burned on her brain.

Hey, sweetheart. Did you think you could get away from me? I told you I was an expert at Hide and Go Seek, but you just never learn. I'll be seeing you soon.

Honestly, she'd expected him to find her way before now. She'd been in Castle Rock for five years now. But the note had still been a shock, and her first instinct was to run. As far away as she could get. But Cole wasn't cooperating. All her money was tied up in the gym. She wouldn't get very far with the two thousand bucks she had in her account at the moment. That wouldn't even cover the cost of a new identity. Nope, she needed the fifty thousand she'd contributed to the gym.

Before moving to Castle Rock, she'd been extremely frugal, saving every penny. She'd met Cole one day when they'd literally bounced off each other while running in the park. Felicity had gone around a bend in the path and couldn't stop herself before plowing right into him. They'd both laughed, and from that first day, they'd been close.

They had an instant connection, not a romantic one, but one more like brother and sister. And since she'd never *had* a brother or sister, it felt good. Really good. Good enough for her to decide to take a risk and settle in Castle Rock. Put down roots—little ones, but roots nevertheless.

One night, not too long after they met, they were sitting in his apartment, drunk as skunks, and Cole told her about his dreams of owning his own gym. He described it so vividly, Felicity could easily picture it. Slowly over the next few months, Felicity had gotten swept up in Cole's excitement.

Felicity had thought about the money she'd saved up. She'd been on the move for so long, she'd forgotten how nice it was to have friends. To have dreams. Plus, she was tired of running. So she'd offered Cole her life savings so he could achieve his dream. It had felt good. She loved working side by side with him. Loved making the gym a safe community place where everyone, no matter how in shape or out of shape they were, could come and work out. But now she desperately needed that money back.

"Yeah, I'm Ryder," the man next to her said, answering her earlier question.

Felicity shook her head and told herself to concentrate on the conversation. She needed to set him straight. Show him the Felicity the world expected to see. "Right, Ryder. I appreciate you wanting to make sure I'm good, but I don't need you or anyone else fighting my battles for me. In case you haven't noticed, I can take care of myself."

Instead of backing off at her caustic tone, he actually took a step closer. His gaze was piercing, and she felt as if he could read her mind. See how scared and freaked out she was inside.

"Be that as it may, you don't have to anymore. And as I told Cole, no one touches you without your permission."

"He's my friend," Felicity said. "He's allowed."

Ryder shook his head.

She'd opened her mouth to reply with an extremely juvenile comeback when Cole spoke up.

"He's right. I'm sorry, Felicity. But I know you. When you won't look at me when you're talking to me, you're lying. Look me in the eyes and tell me that if I give you the fifty thousand, you won't disappear."

Felicity turned to her friend and looked up at him. He was standing near her, his tattooed arms crossed over his chest. He was frowning down at her, but his eyebrows were raised as if daring her.

She opened her mouth to lie, but the words got stuck in her throat. She couldn't do it. Couldn't lie to him.

The words that came out of her mouth were soft . . . and tortured. "It's time for me to go."

"You can't go!" Grace exclaimed.

Felicity's shoulders slumped. Leaving would tear her heart from her chest, but she wouldn't put Grace, or her sons, in danger, not when her friend had just started living free for the first time in her life.

The walls began to close in on her. Closer and closer. It got harder to breathe, and she began to pant. Air. She needed air.

As if he could read her mind, Ryder put his arm back around her waist and pulled her into his side. He led her over to a small couch in the corner of the office and sat with her. He put his hand on her nape and forced her to lean over and put her head between her knees.

"Breathe, love. Breathe."

Felicity could hear the others expressing their concern, but only peripherally. She concentrated on the feel of Ryder's large calloused hand on the sensitive skin of her neck. She reached out with one hand and grabbed hold of his jeans at the calf as she tried to suck oxygen into her starved lungs.

She heard the shuffling of feet and Cole warn, as if he were a thousand miles away, "Don't hurt her."

Then Ryder's emphatic response: "Never."

Then a door shut, and Felicity couldn't hear anything but her labored breathing.

"Relax." Ryder's hand moved from her neck to her back as he caressed her. "In and out. Slow down your breaths. You can do it . . . there you go . . . good. I've got you . . ."

It was ridiculous, but his words helped. A lot. She felt her lungs expanding with precious oxygen, and as the man she'd just met for the first time today continued to murmur nonsense in her ear, she got control over herself.

Sitting up, Felicity ran a hand through her short hair. She hated her hair, but cutting it off was what she needed to do in order to hide . . . at least she thought it had been. But she supposed now that she'd been found, she'd have to pick a different color and grow it back out. She'd gotten used to her black hair, but it didn't matter anymore. Black, red, purple . . . apparently she could be found no matter the color.

"You okay now?"

Felicity nodded her head automatically. No. She wasn't better. She'd never be better. "Yes, I'm better," she lied.

Ryder chuckled from beside her. "Your mouth is saying one thing, but your eyes are saying something else."

She turned to face the man next to her for the first time since her panic attack had started. "You got them all to leave . . . can you please get Cole to give me my money?"

"No." His answer was immediate, and final.

Felicity's eyes closed in despair. Why she'd thought this man would help her, she had no idea. But the crushing disappointment spread through her chest.

"Look at me," he ordered.

Felicity shook her head.

"Please. Look at me," he repeated. "As I told Cole, I'm not going to force you, but I'd like to look at your beautiful blue eyes when I say what I need to say."

Goose bumps broke out on Felicity's arms at his words. Taking a deep breath, she brought her eyes up to his and braced for whatever it was he felt he needed to say.

"Thank you, love. I'm going to help you. I want to know who has frightened you so badly that I can see the fear shining out from your eyes. I see right through the image you project to the world. To others you're a take-no-shit chick—from the tattoos on your arms to the sassy attitude you throw. But I see a woman who is scared to death, one who needs someone to hold her and tell her everything will be all right. I'm going to fight those demons for you, love. Not only fight them, but obliterate them.

"That's why I'm not going to tell Cole to give you the money you need to run. Running won't solve your problems. But *I* will. I'm going to make it so you're free. Free to be whoever you want, not who you think you need to be."

Felicity could only stare at him. His words were conceited, but spoken with a conviction that she desperately wanted to cling to. For some reason, she believed him. If she let him, he could probably take down the monster after her, once and for all.

But that was a big if.

Chapter Three

Ryder sat at a table in the coffee shop across from Rock Hard Gym and sipped his coffee. Black. No frou-frou shit for him. His eyes were glued to the door across the street as he listened to Logan.

He'd been staying in a local hotel for the last week, but that was going to end soon. It wasn't a matter of money, but because of the itch on the back of his neck. Felicity was in trouble. He could feel it down to the marrow of his bones. But he couldn't help her if she didn't talk to him.

Ever since he'd told her he would take care of her problems, she'd been avoiding him. Wouldn't meet his eyes and fled his presence as soon as she could. But he wasn't deterred. No, the best things in life came to those who waited.

And he would wait her out. For as long as it took.

Felicity Jones was his. He didn't question it. It just was.

He'd seen a lot of bad things in his life. Had done things that would make people call him a monster. But Felicity was his reward. His reward for all the shit in his life.

The second he'd looked in her eyes, he'd seen through all her lies.

The bravado.

The toughness.

She was hurting. Badly. And he was dying to know why. Dying to fix it. To make the hurt he could see clearly in her eyes go away.

But it was more than obvious she didn't want to expose any of her vulnerabilities. He wanted to demand answers to the million and one questions he had, but knew it would make her more wary of him than she already was.

"You never did say what it was that you do down in the Springs," Logan said not quite nonchalantly.

Ryder tore his eyes away from the doors of the gym and met his brother's. "I'm a private investigator."

"No shit?"

"No shit."

Logan didn't say anything for a moment, then asked, "That all?"

Ryder wanted to smile, but refrained. His brother wasn't dumb. Not in the least. "Nope."

"Didn't think so. I won't ask, because it's obvious that you won't answer."

Ryder grunted as he took another sip of his coffee. His eyes went back to the window.

"Nathan's been doing some poking around. Says you were only in the Army for a couple of years before you got out."

Ryder nodded. "Went in straight out of high school. Wanted to make some money to send back to my mom, to make her life easier. Was in for two years before another opportunity came up."

"Interesting," Logan said, trying a bit too hard to sound disinterested. "The usual hitch is four years."

Ryder didn't respond, but held his brother's eyes for a beat before turning to look out the window at the door to Rock Hard Gym once more.

"I don't know what's going on with Felicity, or you, for that matter, but don't you hurt her. She's the toughest chick I know. And if it wasn't for her, me and my Grace wouldn't be where we are. I wouldn't have my sons," Logan said after a minute.

Ryder turned his gaze back to Logan's. "You think Felicity's tough?"

Logan's head cocked and his brows shot up. "You don't?"

"She's scared out of her fucking skull, and she's this close to bolting." He held his thumb and index finger up, almost touching.

"She might be scared, but that doesn't mean she's not tough. When Grace was taken from me, Felicity stood by my side and did what she could to help her out. If she had two minutes alone with Margaret Mason, Grace's mother, I'm afraid of what she would've done to her. She's got a backbone of steel."

Ryder shook his head. "It's all a facade. You *have* to see it. I've been here a week, and it's as clear as day to me. All you have to do is look into her eyes, and you can tell she's broken inside."

Logan shook his head. "Not to me. Talk to me. Tell me what I've missed."

Ryder put down the coffee and sighed. "I haven't looked into her background. But I don't need to have her background to know she's a woman on the run. With her coloring, it's obvious that her jet-black hair came out of a bottle, which makes me wonder if she's trying to disguise her appearance. Her eyes never stop moving; she's constantly scanning her surroundings, as if looking for danger. She lives above the gym she co-owns, so I'm assuming she doesn't pay rent and didn't have to fill out an application. I overheard Grace complaining, good-naturedly, that Felicity doesn't have any bills—paid cash for her car, doesn't have a credit card. Her cell phone is one of those pay-as-you-go jobbies. And last, but certainly not least, she's a silent partner in that gym. Cole said she didn't sign one paper. And now she wants fifty Gs in cash."

The napkin Logan had been using was now clenched in his fist. "So what can we do?"

"You want honesty?"

"Always."

"Let me handle it."

Logan was shaking his head even before Ryder had finished speaking. "She doesn't even know you, man. She's not going to trust you."

"It's why she *will* trust me," Ryder retorted. "Think about it. Grace is her best friend. She's godmother to your kids. She loves you and your brothers like family. She wants to run to *protect* all of you. She's not going to tell you shit. To keep you out of whatever it is that's haunting her. Me? I'm an outsider. She'll tell me."

"You're awfully sure of yourself," Logan observed.

"It's because I'm right. I'm not going to hurt her," Ryder told his brother, bringing the conversation back full circle. "The last thing I want to do is hurt one hair on her head."

"I wasn't talking physically," Logan said. "I'm not as unobservant as you think. In all the time I've been back in town, she hasn't dated. Cole said he's never seen her with a man since he's known her. Five years is a really long time to go without being with someone."

Ryder didn't argue. It *was* a long time. He knew firsthand. He hadn't been with anyone since he'd gotten out of the Army and started his new life. Being with someone meant giving his enemies a way to get to him. He hadn't ever wanted to open that door, but it had been blown wide open with his trip up to Castle Rock. He knew introducing himself to his brothers meant changes in his life, but he'd been ready for them. He was almost thirty. He wanted what his brothers had. A wife. Kids. Family. He'd been alone for so much of his life, and now he had not only three brothers, but three sisters-in-law and nephews as well.

And Felicity.

His enemies had a pretty huge fucking bargaining chip now, and he wouldn't give them a chance to use it. No fucking way. He needed to talk to his handler soon, officially tell him of his plans to be done with Mountain Mercenaries, although the man probably already guessed. But not until Felicity was safe.

"I'm not going to hurt her," Ryder repeated firmly. "Not physically. Not mentally." He looked his brother in the eyes. "She's mine, Logan. I knew it the first time I laid eyes on her. I'd kill for her. No one puts their hands on her without her permission ever again. No one."

"You've killed before." It wasn't a question.

Ryder didn't respond but met Logan's eyes with an unblinking stare.

After a long pause, Logan said, "I want to know whatever you find out."

"I got this," Ryder told him.

"I have no doubt, but I owe Felicity more than I could ever repay. She was Grace's friend when she had no one. She got her out of her parents' house and away from them. If what you say is true, I need to help."

"It's true."

"Then let me help. Let *all* of us help. We might not be as good as you are, but we're no slouches. Let Alexis and Nathan see what they can ferret out online. Let me and Blake help keep watch over her when you can't. Cole can only stay by her side so long. Don't shut us out. She's like family."

"She'll *be* your family by marriage if I have anything to say about it," Ryder said definitively.

"Felicity is already my sister in all ways that matter," Logan said firmly. "I'm having a hard time being pissed at you for staking your claim because from where I'm standing, Felicity needs a man like you to have her back. But let us fucking help, dammit."

Ryder nodded. "When I have more information, I'll let you know. But you should know, I have my own backup as well."

"But they're not here. They're in Colorado Springs," Logan guessed—correctly.

"True."

"But we *are* here. We're going to help," Logan told him.

"You're a pain in the ass," Ryder commented dryly.

"So Grace tells me. This settled? You'll keep us informed?"

"Yeah. As soon as I find anything out, I'll let you know."

"Good. Oh, and Ryder?"

"What?" he asked, exasperated. "Jesus, I think I might just miss being an only child if you keep this badgering up."

Logan's lips quirked up into a smile, but then he tilted his head to the window and said, "If you want to find anything out today, you might want to get going."

Ryder's head whipped around, and he saw Felicity walking quickly down the sidewalk toward the parking lot and her PT Cruiser. He was up and moving in a moment. He heard Logan chuckling behind him, but all his attention was focused on Felicity's hips as she headed away from him.

Felicity turned the key in her little PT Cruiser, and just as she was putting the car in gear, the door on the passenger side opened, and a man fell onto the seat next to her.

She screamed and scrambled for the handle of the door, trying desperately to get out.

"Jesus, it's me, Ryder. Fuck. I'm so sorry, I didn't mean to scare you."

Felicity turned wide eyes to the man next to her and tried to catch her breath. She closed her eyes and concentrated on lowering her heart rate. "You scared me to death."

"I know. I'm sorry. But you know . . . I could've been anyone. You obviously thought so too. You should be more vigilant."

Felicity took a deep breath, opened her eyes, and ordered in as harsh a voice as she was capable of right that second, "Get out."

"Nope. I'm comfortable right here," Ryder said, shutting the door and crossing his arms over his chest.

She almost snorted out loud because he didn't look comfortable. Not in the least. She wasn't that much shorter than he was, but for some reason seeing him scrunched in the little seat next to her made her want to laugh.

But she couldn't laugh. She needed to get rid of him. Felicity wasn't an idiot. She knew Ryder had been following her around for the last week. Knew he wanted to talk to her, get her to tell him what she was running from, but she couldn't. All she wanted was to be left alone . . . wasn't it?

She couldn't deny his words last week felt good. Really good. She *wanted* to be free. Hated looking over her shoulder all the time. But she couldn't risk his life. Or Grace's. Or anyone else's. No, leaving town was the best thing for everyone. She didn't really need the money Cole was holding hostage. She'd left Chicago long ago with less cash than she had now, and she'd managed. She was stalling because for the first time, she didn't *want* to go. She liked Castle Rock. Loved her friends. Enjoyed her job at the gym even if it wasn't what she'd envisioned herself doing back when she was in college.

"Seriously, Ryder. Get out. I'm just going to the store. You can continue stalking me when I get back."

"I could pick some stuff up," he told her evenly.

"I mean it. I don't want you here."

His voice dropped. "Tough."

"I can take care of myself. I've been doing it a long time," she argued.

"I know you have, love, but now you don't have to."

"Argh . . . do you have a comeback for everything?"

"Yup."

Felicity glared at him for another beat, then sighed and gave in. She refused to admit to herself that she felt safer with him around. Nope, he'd never leave her alone if she did that. Only one thing had happened in the last week—an old newspaper clipping about her college roommate's death had arrived in the mail. She knew exactly who'd sent it. He was up to his usual tricks . . . slowly and surely attempting to freak her out, to make her feel less and less safe. She had no doubt

31

he'd escalate his little gifts in the coming weeks. She almost preferred he just make his move and be done with it, but she knew he wanted her to suffer first.

Sighing, Felicity put the car in gear and backed out of the parking space. Making sure to look both ways for anything or anyone that might be suspicious before she pulled out, they were finally on their way.

"When did you move to Castle Rock?" Ryder asked.

Felicity stiffened. It looked like the inquisition was starting immediately. "About five years ago. Give or take a few months." When he didn't respond or ask anything else, Felicity risked glancing over at him. He was staring out the front of the vehicle, and she could see his jaw clenching.

For the first time in ten years, she wanted to spill her guts to someone. Ryder made her want to lower the shields she'd put up when she stepped foot out of her mom's house, and let someone in. She opened her mouth to say something, but closed it a second later. No, she couldn't risk it. Couldn't risk *him*.

It was stupid. She didn't know Ryder. Didn't care about him. Since she wasn't emotionally attached to him, he could help her, and if something happened to him, she wouldn't care . . . right? Inwardly, she sighed. God help her, she *did* care about him. Even after such a short time, she couldn't deny his protectiveness was intoxicating and flattering. Not to mention he was freaking gorgeous.

He was muscular and built; he obviously worked out. His brown hair was constantly messy, as if he frequently ran a hand through the strands. He had a five o'clock shadow on his square jaw, and his nose was just crooked enough for her to think he must have broken it at one time. His hands were large, with calluses on them. She remembered that from when she'd shaken his hand last week and when he'd touched her neck. His shoulders were broad, and she had a feeling he carried quite a load on them . . . with no problem.

But most of all, she was drawn to the way he made her feel. He didn't treat her as if she was Wonder Woman, but neither did he make her feel weak. Ryder Sinclair was more alpha than any man she'd ever met, and that was saying something, considering she'd been hanging around the Anderson brothers and Cole. But instead of getting her dander up and making her want to take him down a peg, it made her want to let him stand in front of her and face the dangers in her life for her. Even though she knew Joseph was out there somewhere, watching her, she didn't feel nearly as freaked as she should. Because of Ryder.

The grocery store Felicity liked to go to was up in Denver. It carried organic and specialty food that she couldn't get in Castle Rock. She gave Ryder credit—he didn't ask where they were going as she pulled onto the interstate and headed north, he just sat next to her in silence, letting her have her space . . . for now.

They spent an hour walking around the store together. He teased her for her purchases, and she made fun of him for buying nothing more than a dozen doughnuts, a box of granola bars, and a bag of almonds.

"Is that what you've been eating?"

He shrugged. "Not much space in the hotel. Besides, I've been eating at the coffee shop a lot."

"What? Why there? They don't even have real food. Just muffins and stuff."

He met her eyes dead-on and said, "Because it's across the street from the gym, and I can keep an eye on you from there."

She stopped in the middle of the aisle and stammered, "Ryder . . . you . . . why?"

He leaned toward her and said softly, "Because I told you I'd make sure you were free of whatever is haunting you. And the only way I can do that is to keep you in my sights."

Felicity bit her lip and struggled to find the words to express what she was thinking. Unlike most people, he let her think. He didn't fill the silence with empty words. Finally, she looked up at him and said, "You can't make me safe. No one can."

It was more than she'd admitted about her personal life in a really long time.

As if he understood how much of a concession it was for her to say even that, he slowly brought his hand up and ran his palm over her short, spiked hair. His eyes followed his hand and came back to her face when he gripped the back of her neck in a tight, but comforting, grip. "I can make you safe." It sounded like a vow.

"You can't."

"I can," he insisted. "When we get back to Castle Rock, invite me up to your apartment. We'll talk. I'll give you my résumé, my *real* résumé, the one no one but my handler knows. Then you can decide if you trust me to keep you safe or not."

"Your handler?"

His brows went up, as if in a challenge.

Felicity felt herself giving in. She wanted to stay in Castle Rock. But she wanted to protect her friends more. Her leaving wouldn't guarantee their safety, a fact that she admitted to herself for the first time. He could go after them as a way to get to her after she left. Could she trust Ryder? She didn't know, but she was just selfish enough to give him a chance.

"Okay."

"Okay." He applied pressure to her neck, and she willingly let him pull her forward. Right there, in the middle of the store, filled with yuppies and parents on the hunt for food they deemed "safe" for their children, Ryder wrapped his arms around her and held on tight.

Felicity ducked her head and laid it on his broad shoulder. She wrapped her arms around his waist and let him hold her. For the first time since she was twenty years old, she leaned on someone else. It felt good. Too good. But she couldn't manage to tear herself away.

"I told you once, and I'll tell you again. I'm gonna fix this for you, love," Ryder said quietly.

"I don't think you can," she mumbled.

"I can. And I will."

He said it with such conviction, she almost believed him.

Chapter Four

Ryder stood behind Felicity as she nervously fumbled with the lock at her apartment door and frowned. There were so many things that were security issues, his fingers twitched with the need to fix them. Her door wasn't terribly sturdy, as it was simply another door in the interior of the gym. There was a stairwell in the back hall of the gym that led to a skinny hallway on the second floor of the building that needed more lighting. Felicity explained that the other rooms were used for storage, for the most part, which someone could easily hide in. She'd explained that a small apartment was built into the space when the blueprints were drawn up.

It was obvious Felicity wasn't comfortable having Ryder in her apartment, but she'd just have to get over it. She didn't know it, but letting him into her private space was akin to agreeing to be his. She wasn't a woman who trusted easily, and being invited into her apartment seemed intimate. It shouldn't have felt so right to step inside her place, but it did.

He could smell her scent stronger here. She always smelled good, especially when he'd held her in his arms in the middle of the grocery store, but here it was ten times stronger. Lilacs. It was just one more thing about her that didn't "fit" her outward appearance.

As he'd pointed out to Logan, she wasn't tough at all. She was broken. And Ryder knew it because he'd been just like her at one point. The first time he'd killed a man, he fell into a pit of despair so deep he didn't think he'd ever be able to pull himself out. And to compensate, he'd put on a mask and created a new persona, just as Felicity had.

But he'd only worn his tough-guy image for a year before he'd shed it around his teammates and friends. Friends who truly understood what he was feeling. Felicity had been wearing her take-no-shit exterior so long, there were only glimpses of the tender woman underneath. But Ryder had seen them. Loud and clear. And it was *that* woman he wanted to know. Wanted to be his. He just needed to chip away at her tough outer shell one bad memory at a time.

They brought the grocery bags into the kitchen, and he handed her items as she put them away. They worked together in a companionable silence. After everything was stowed in its proper spot, she turned and waved her arm around the small apartment, which could be seen from the galley kitchen. "It's not much."

And it wasn't.

It was clinical.

Depressing.

There wasn't one personal touch in the small space.

The walls were a boring white. There were no pictures. No splashes of color. No girlie pillows on the black sofa in the middle of the living area. There might've been DVDs inside the cabinet next to the television, but Ryder doubted it. No books. No piles of mail sitting around. He might as well have been in his hotel room for all the personality the place had. It was hard to believe she'd been living there for as long as she had.

He shrugged. "It's fine."

Felicity rolled her eyes. "Do you want something to drink?"

"What do you have?"

She went to the fridge and opened it, as if she had no idea and had to look to see. "Water, beer, and V8 juice."

Ryder raised his eyebrows at the industrial-size water dispenser in the corner of the kitchen.

She shrugged. "I drink a lot, and Cole told me I should just order one of the dispensers we have sitting around the gym for myself up here. So I did. When I run out, I just grab one of the water jugs from downstairs. It's easier, and cheaper, than constantly buying smaller bottles."

"Water's fine," Ryder told her when she finished her explanation.

She nodded and grabbed a glass, filled it up from the dispenser, and handed it to him. She poured one for herself as well and leaned back against the counter. "So . . . you wanted to talk?"

Ryder took a sip of the water, then nodded. He held out his hand without a word.

Felicity looked at his hand, then up at his face, then back to his hand.

He stood stock-still, waiting for her.

Just when he thought she was going to brush by him and ignore his gesture, at the last second she lifted her hand and placed it in his.

Ryder felt his dick twitch in his pants, but ignored it. Her small show of trust went straight to his heart. She didn't trust easily, if at all. Her taking his hand wasn't exactly spilling her guts, but it was a start. He could work with it.

Closing his fingers around hers, he led her into the other room. He gestured to the couch, and she sat. He followed suit, sitting right next to her. So close their thighs touched. She went to scoot away from him, but he squeezed her hand. "Stay?"

She took a deep breath and nodded.

Resting their hands on his knee, he got right to it.

"When I was nineteen years old, I was a private first class in the Army. I was on patrol in a city in Iraq. Our job was to walk around, get to know the locals, show them that we weren't any danger to them, earn their trust. I didn't mind it. The kids were my favorite part. We couldn't communicate that well with each other, as they didn't know

English, and I didn't speak their language either, but we communicated with hand gestures and facial expressions. They were innocent and so easily amused. Children here in the States have every electronic gadget imaginable. They're entertained by television and cartoons. They get Happy Meals and fast food whenever their parents will relent and buy them for them. These kids had nothing. Maybe a ball. Sticks and rocks. But they were as happy as any kids I've ever seen. Their faces would light up when they saw us. They'd follow us all over the village."

Ryder took a deep breath. He'd never told anyone this story before. His handler, Rex, knew what had happened, probably from reading the official report from that day. He'd mentioned it once in passing, but hadn't asked any questions, and they hadn't discussed it at all.

Felicity squeezed his hand. She didn't say a word, but that small nonverbal movement said more than she knew. He needed her compassion to continue.

He didn't look at her, but went on. "One day we were patrolling as usual, and I noticed a little girl who always greeted us wasn't there. Zariya was ten. She had beautiful black hair that came down to the middle of her back. It was always a mess, tangled from blowing in the wind. She let me braid it once, after we'd walked through the entire village and had fifteen minutes to kill. It was soft. So soft. It reminded me of my mom's hair. She taught me to braid, and the time we spent together in the mornings when I braided her hair was something I missed when I left home." Ryder took a deep breath before continuing. "I asked one of the boys where Zariya was, and he pointed to an alley with a lot of doors. The squad had been down it, but we hadn't seen or heard anything unusual. Me and my friends went where the boy had pointed, wanting to say hello to the happy little girl. When we approached one of the doors, we heard crying from inside. Not hesitating, we knocked, then entered."

Ryder stopped. This was harder than he thought it'd be. He didn't know if he could continue. Didn't know if he could bare his soul to

Felicity like this. He wanted her to trust him, but had second thoughts about telling her this story. Suddenly he didn't think she'd feel safe around him if she knew what he'd done that day.

"Was it bad?" she asked softly.

"Yeah." His voice cracked on the word.

"Tell me," she urged.

Ryder cleared his throat. He'd come this far, he might as well finish it. "We walked in and saw the place was a mess. Trash everywhere, and it stunk. Like the worst body odor you could ever imagine. But the thing that stuck out to me was a pile of black hair on the dirt floor in front of us. I couldn't comprehend what I was seeing, but I knew it wasn't good. We heard whimpering from nearby, and we all moved that way. Two of my friends were in front of me, and they stopped in the doorway. I pushed past them, and it took me a moment to understand what I was seeing.

"It was Zariya. The bastard had shaved her head. Bald. Probably to punish her for something she'd done. He was in bed, on top of her. She was whimpering and crying, but he didn't even care. My buddies and I were pissed, and one took hold of my arm and tried to pull me out of the room. I remember staring at him as if he was crazy. We couldn't leave her there. Not like that. Then he pointed to the side of the room. To a white dress. A fucking wedding dress. Zariya's parents had allowed her to be married to a man at least four times her age. And he was raping her."

Ryder heard Felicity's gasp, but he didn't stop. Couldn't. "I snapped. My buddies said that she was married and we couldn't interfere with local customs. They were going to let that man continue to hurt her. Night after night. Not caring that she was only a little girl. I didn't give a shit if that was all right in their culture. Didn't care that I might start an international incident and hurt relations in that village. I walked right up to that fucker and blew his brains out. I tore him away from Zariya and reached for her. I wanted to comfort her, needed to tell her that everything would be all right, but she freaked. Screamed her head off. Scrambled to get away from me. Curled up into a little ball in the corner of the room and refused to look at me.

"Before that, she'd been following me around for weeks, smiling, holding on to my jacket as we walked around the village. Not once had she ever been scared of me. Not once, Felicity."

"What happened to her?"

Ryder whipped his head around to look at Felicity. "What?"

"What happened to Zariya?" she asked again.

Ryder sighed and brought a hand up to run it through his hair. "I don't know. I was dragged back to base and put in isolation when I wouldn't calm down. Then they shipped me to Germany and back to the States."

Felicity looked horrified. "What?"

Ryder shrugged. "I was knocked down two ranks to private and was told that if I brought up the 'incident' again, I'd be dishonorably discharged. I was ashamed of losing control and didn't want to have to tell my mom what had happened. So I dropped it."

"Assholes."

Ryder once again looked at Felicity in surprise.

"I mean, really?" she went on. "That guy totally deserved what he got. And I can't believe your buddies didn't do anything. I mean, they could've made up a story about how the guy attacked you or something. They knew what he was doing, and they let you take the fall. That's not cool. And then not to go back and help poor Zariya . . . and get her out of there and to the States? And not to tell you what happened to her? After you saved her? Fuck. Maybe we can ask Alexis if she can find her. No, I know, she can ask that guy who's been teaching her how to hack if *he* can track her down. She said that he's got all sorts of military contacts. How old would she be now? Twenty-one? Twenty-two? I'm sure—"

Ryder put his hand over Felicity's mouth and smiled at her. She glared up at him, sparks shooting out of her eyes.

"As fucking happy as I am to see an emotion in your eyes besides fear, love, I don't want to find her." He moved his hand away from her mouth, brushing the pad of his thumb along her bottom lip as he did. She opened her mouth to protest, and he quickly explained himself. "Iraq is a world away from here. The fact of the matter is that she was probably hustled out of there by her parents. They probably pawned her off on another man, just as old as the one I killed, as soon as they could. I hate it. So fucking much, but there's nothing I can do."

"But, Ryder . . ."

"No, love. My point in telling you that story wasn't to distress you."

"Then what *was* your point?" she asked, clearly disgruntled.

"That was the first man I killed, but it wasn't the last."

She was silent for a long moment before saying, "He deserved it."

"He did."

"And I bet the others did too."

Her tone was matter-of-fact. It wasn't a question. She wasn't looking for verification of her statement, but he gave it to her nevertheless.

"They did."

His job with Mountain Mercenaries had been a godsend. Exactly what he'd needed as an outlet for his bitterness and anger. He tracked down awful human beings who needed to be taken out . . . and he did what needed to be done. He wasn't ashamed of what he did for a living, but he wasn't exactly proud of it either. But if he wanted Felicity to trust him with her secrets, he needed to trust her with his own.

Felicity licked her lips, and Ryder wanted nothing more than to taste them. Taste her. But now wasn't the time. He wanted everything from her before he'd let himself touch her.

The fear was back in her eyes as she said, "He's powerful."

Ryder knew who she was talking about. Whoever was after her. "I expected as much."

"And rich. And used to getting what he wants."

"Yeah, bullies usually are. Let me help protect you. Let me in."

"I'm scared."

To hear her admit it was everything. She'd hidden behind her tough exterior for a long time, so her admitting she was frightened was the first step toward her trusting him. Allowing herself to be vulnerable around him. Her words were a tiny crack in the impenetrable shell she'd worn for so long to protect herself.

"I know you are. And I'll spend the rest of my life trying to make sure you're never scared again. But I need a name. Just a name for now, love."

She loosened her hand from his for the first time, and as much as Ryder hated to let her go, he did. She needed her space, and he'd give it to her . . . but not too much. He didn't move from her side. He moved his now free hand to her thigh and simply let the warmth from his body seep into hers.

If he wanted her to open up to him, it was only fair he did the same. He'd opened the door to his soul a crack with the story about Zariya, but he needed to throw it wide open. Let her know exactly who he was and why she could trust him. Why she *should* trust him.

"I was approached when I was back in the States at my Army base. I was doing some bullshit job as punishment when I was contacted by a man who said he'd heard about what happened and had investigated me. He said he needed someone like me, who wasn't afraid to do what needed to be done, to join a special group. I was hesitant at first, but after going to Colorado Springs and meeting the other men who would be on the team, I agreed. He got me out of the rest of my Army commitment, I didn't ask how, and I became a mercenary. I became a part of a close-knit group who went where we were told, when we were told. At first I wanted to know the details of every job I went on. Why the man I was hunting was bad. Why he needed to die. And every time a bit of my soul died when I learned why. Sex slavers, kidnappers, terrorists, stalkers, murderers . . . they were all bad men, love. Every single one. I had no problem killing them. After a while I stopped asking why. I trust my handler, Rex, that much."

Felicity wasn't looking at him now. Her head was turned, and he could see her pulse hammering in her throat. He forced himself to continue. She needed to accept his past. In order for them to work, she needed to come to terms with it. Just as he had long ago.

"I won't apologize for what I've done. For what needed to be done. Ultimately, I couldn't save Zariya, but I could save others like her. Children were reunited with their parents, wives were returned to their husbands and families, people were given peace from the nightmares that plagued them. I can do the same for you, Felicity. I've got the resources and friends who do what I do, who will help me. But here's the truth . . . I'm done being a mercenary. I've served my country, in public and private ways, but I'm a liability now."

Her eyes came to him at that. "A liability?"

"Yeah. The last thing I want is for someone to use my family against me—I think you know exactly what I'm talking about. When it was just me and my mom, I could keep that relationship on the down low, but my circle is bigger now. Way bigger. And that circle now includes you. The last thing I want is to make you safe only to expose you to additional danger because of my job."

"Can you . . ." Her voice petered out.

"What, love? I'm an open book to you. I've told you things I've never revealed to another soul. You can ask me anything."

"Can you just . . . quit? I mean . . . it doesn't seem like that's something you could just decide to walk away from."

"I can. And I will. This isn't the Mafia, Felicity. Everyone on the team knows at any time they can be done with it. It's one of the reasons we all agreed in the first place. The bottom line is that once I rid you of whoever is putting that petrified look in your eyes, whoever broke you, I'm done with that life. I know this is hard for you. You've been on your own for a long time. Held everything inside a long time. All I need is his name. I'll take it from there. After that, anything you want to tell me comes at your own speed. I'll never pressure you for information . . . unless it's absolutely necessary to protect you."

Felicity moved then. Not away from him, as Ryder thought, but toward him. She simply leaned over and fell into him. His arms came up and caught her. She rested her head on his shoulder and put her face against his neck and sat there, her arms at her sides. Not hugging him, not saying a word.

The only movement Ryder made was to encircle her with his arms. He'd sit there for days if that was what she needed.

It was an hour before either of them spoke again. He'd leaned back against the cushions of the couch, making them both as comfortable as possible. He'd thought Felicity had fallen asleep, as her steady, warm breaths against his skin had been rhythmic and even for the last thirty minutes.

But she wasn't.

It was only two words.

Two words that would change both their lives.

"Joseph Waters," Felicity whispered into the quiet of the room.

Chapter Five

The next day, Ryder made a phone call.

"Hey, Gray, it's Ace."

"Ace! Where'd you run off to? Haven't seen you around The Pit in a while. Black and Arrow are jonesin' to challenge you to a game of pool too."

Ryder smiled. It was nice to be missed. They'd seen too many instances in their line of work of people disappearing who weren't missed until months had gone by. He wasn't the most social of men, but even though he'd only been gone for a little more than a week, Gray and the others had noticed. "I had something to do up in Castle Rock. Listen, I need a favor."

"Anything." Gray's answer was immediate and heartfelt.

They were a ragtag group, but they could trust and rely on each other with no questions asked. They'd had each other's backs more than once. They weren't a sanctioned special forces team, but they sure acted like it when they were on a mission. "I need as much information as you can find on a Joseph Waters. I don't know where he's from, what he does, or even what he looks like."

"Shit, man, I thought you were going to give me a challenge."

Ryder couldn't help but grin at Gray's sarcasm. He could imagine the tall man leaning on his cue in the pool hall with a disgruntled look on his face. For a man who was six-five, and whom everyone gave a wide berth because of his perpetual scowl and very muscular physique, he had a knack for becoming invisible while on jobs. It was weird, but no one ever seemed to see him when he was in stealth mode. But he was no computer genius—that would be Meat.

"Talk to Meat. He loves this shit. If I get more info, I'll get it to you guys."

"You got *anything* else?" Gray asked.

"My woman is scared to death of him. If I had to guess, he's stalking her. She's been on the run for years. Changed her appearance, operates with only cash, and is willing to give up being a godmother to adorable twin boys to bolt once more. Inquiry needs to be discreet," Ryder warned. "By the way she's acting, I'm guessing the asshole already knows where she is, but I'm not willing to risk her life in order to get more information."

"Your woman?" Gray asked.

"My woman," Ryder confirmed firmly.

"She's been on the run for years?" Gray asked.

And this was why Ryder called Gray instead of any of the others. He had a soft spot for women. Rex knew this and frequently assigned the large man to jobs where a woman or child was in danger. It motivated him to get the job done as fast as possible. Ryder didn't know Gray's history, but had no doubt it involved a woman.

"Yeah. My guess is anywhere from five to ten years."

"Her name?"

"Felicity Jones."

"That her real name?" Gray asked.

Ryder sighed. He loved Felicity's name . . . hated to think that it might be made up. But now that he thought about it, Felicity probably wasn't her birth name. "Not sure, but probably fake."

"I'll talk to Meat. See what we can come up with. You need backup? Should I call Rex? Arrow and Ball are here playing pool with me. They could come up if you needed extra eyes or ears."

Ryder shook his head even though his friend couldn't see it. "No, I'm good for now. You heard of Ace Security?"

"Of course. They're those brothers who single-handedly took down the Inca Boyz. They're new in town, right? Just started last year?"

"Yeah, that's them."

"Wait . . . Ace . . . Ace Security . . . what aren't you saying?"

"They're my half brothers."

"No shit?"

"No shit."

"Damn," Gray breathed. "You weren't kidding when you said you didn't need backup. From what I've read, they're pretty badass."

Ryder chuckled. "They can hold their own . . . but they aren't like us."

"It sounds like you've got a lot to tell us," Gray said.

"I do."

"You bring Miss Felicity down here soon. I want to meet her."

"Not sure that's the best idea."

"Actually, it's a great idea. If this Joseph guy knows where she is, the best place for her to be is smack-dab in the middle of a bunch of mercenaries who can protect her."

"I can protect her. No matter where she is," Ryder growled.

"Easy, Ace. I didn't mean nothin'."

Ryder took a deep breath. He knew he was overreacting, but the mere thought that his good friend didn't think Felicity was safe didn't sit well.

"Yeah, sorry. I'm a little sensitive when it comes to her."

"She's it for you, huh?"

"Yup."

"She know about what you do?"

"Some."

"And she didn't freak?"

"No."

Gray whistled low. "Hang tight and don't let her go, Ace. Any woman who knows our background and doesn't immediately run is a keeper."

"I'm not letting her go," Ryder told his friend.

"Good," was Gray's simple response. "I'll talk to Meat, put out some feelers. See what we can find. Stay in touch."

"I will. Thanks, Gray."

"No thanks necessary. You want me to talk to Rex about your future availability?"

"Not yet," Ryder told him. If things worked out with Felicity and he needed to step away from the jobs, he'd tell their handler himself.

"Later."

"Bye, Gray." Ryder clicked off the phone and put his cell back into his pocket. He'd spent the night at the hotel last night, but no more. Felicity was in danger, and he wasn't letting her out of his sight for another night. She was freaked. Way freaked. Which meant she probably had a reason.

He shut the door to the hotel room and swung his duffel bag over his shoulder. He needed to spend more time with her, get her to trust him more. The more she realized he wasn't going anywhere and would protect her with his life, the more she'd open up to him . . . at least he hoped so. He didn't *need* information in order to protect her, but it would make his job a hell of a lot easier.

Ryder strode into Rock Hard Gym and lifted his chin at Cole, who was manning the front desk.

Cole eyed him for a beat, then asked, "You find out what's bothering Felicity?"

It wasn't the place to talk with all the people walking around, but Ryder needed to give him something. He'd seen the way Cole and

Felicity acted around each other. They were friends, which was a good thing. If the other man had showed any inclination to want Felicity as more than a friend, he would've had to set him straight. Ryder wouldn't let anyone get between him and the woman he wanted to make his. But since it was obvious they *were* just friends, Cole could be a powerful ally to help keep Felicity safe.

"She's scared. Petrified."

"Felicity?" Cole asked. "That woman isn't scared of anything or anyone."

Ryder was getting tired of people not seeing the real Felicity. "She's tough, I'll give you that, but I'm telling you, she's on the verge of bolting even if you don't give her the money. It's clear as day if you take the time to look."

Ryder knew he'd crossed a line when Cole's eyes narrowed and his lips pressed together. "You've been here, what . . . a week? I've known her for five years, man. *Five years.* We're best friends. If she was scared of something, she would've told me."

Ryder mentally shrugged. Looked like this would be the place to talk to Cole, after all, since he wasn't going to let it go. "Look at her," Ryder ordered, using his head to indicate the wall of windows where Felicity was standing. She was in the room with the weight and cardio machines. It was a busy morning—most of the treadmills and half of the ellipticals were occupied. Members roamed the room using the various weight machines and doing sit-ups on the pads strewn around the area.

Felicity had her hands resting on the wall behind her, at the small of her back, and her eyes never stopped scanning. They flitted from one person to another. Assessing. Scrutinizing each and every person. Someone dropped a weight nearby, and Felicity jumped and took three steps away from where the noise came from before stopping herself. She laughed, but it was easy to see, even from this distance, that it had been forced.

Cole turned back to Ryder. "She could be spooked because of everything that's happened recently with the Inca Boyz."

They both knew the man was grasping at straws.

"Maybe. But my guess is that her request for the fifty thousand coincided with whatever she's running from catching up with her."

Cole's hands fisted. "Someone's after her?"

Ryder shrugged one shoulder. "That's my guess."

"Why wouldn't she tell me? Or Logan, Blake, or Nathan? We can protect her. She doesn't have to run."

"When all you've ever done is run, it's easier to do what you know. What's worked in the past," Ryder said.

Cole went to step around the reception desk, but Ryder stopped him. "No. You cannot confront her about this."

"The fuck I can't," Cole muttered.

Ryder stepped in front of the other man, physically blocking him.

"Get out of my way," Cole bit out.

"I've got this."

"Whatever. You don't even know her."

"I know her better than you do, and I've only been here a week."

"Fuck you. You just want in her pants, and then you'll be gone."

Ryder ignored the barb for now. Cole would learn exactly what Felicity meant to him in good time. For now, he needed to stop the man from doing the one thing that would certainly make Felicity bolt.

"Underneath that badass exterior is a woman who is scared out of her mind. She's smart, way smarter than she lets anyone know. She has a quote on her forearm that says, 'We can't solve problems by using the same kind of thinking we used when we created them.' Do you know who said that?"

Cole shook his head.

"Albert Einstein. I looked it up last night. Why would she choose *that* quote if it didn't mean something to her? Her black hair is cute, but it's not her natural color."

"I don't even want to know how you know that," Cole said, his eyes flashing over to the window once more.

"Stop being an asshole and listen to me. I haven't slept with her. If you took half a second and paid more attention, you'd see it. She's got bright-blue eyes. Pale skin. Light eyebrows. Not to mention blonde arm hairs. If that ebony hair was natural, it's likely the rest of her would be darker as well. She's trying to disguise the real her. Have you been up to her apartment?"

Cole's eyes were on Ryder now. He nodded.

"And did you see it? Really see it?"

"She's a neatnik. Everything has a place—that's how she likes things," Cole said.

"Right. But she has not one personal item in her place at all. It's sterile. As though if she left, no one would know anything about her. There aren't any pictures of her godchildren. If she and Grace are such good friends, where are the pictures of the two of them?"

"I . . ." Cole began to speak, but his mouth simply opened and closed as if he didn't know what to say.

Ryder leaned forward. "I am *not* going to hurt her, Cole. I'd sooner cut off my own arm than cause her one second of pain. But she needs help, or she's going to bolt. She'll cut you and the rest of her friends off without a second glance, and you'll never hear from her again. I'm going to figure out who she's running from, and I'll kill him if I have to. It won't be the first time."

Cole's eyes narrowed. "Who *are* you?"

Ryder smiled. "I'm Logan, Blake, and Nathan's half brother."

Cole shook his head. "No. I mean, yes, you are, but you're in a whole different league from them. I shouldn't be happy that someone who freely admits to killing wants one of my closest friends, but for some reason I believe you when you say you won't hurt her."

"I *won't*," Ryder told the other man. "And you should know, I've never felt like this before. Never. She's special, and I'm going to do whatever it takes so she can live the rest of her life without fear. Here in Castle Rock with her friends."

"You don't live here," Cole noted. "Assuming your job is down there in the Springs."

Ryder simply shrugged. "I'm done with my previous occupation."

"Just like that?" Cole asked with raised eyebrows.

"Just like that. The second I made the decision to come up here and meet my brothers, I knew I'd be making an occupation change. And meeting Felicity just solidified that. I won't risk her, or my family, being exposed to the kinds of people I would have to deal with if I stayed. Not to mention, I'm not willing to spend weeks, and sometimes months, away from her."

"You're serious."

"Deadly." Ryder's eyes flicked to where Felicity had been standing and saw that she was on the move. Toward them. He needed to wrap this up and make sure Cole knew how serious the situation was. "I don't know who is after her . . . yet. But don't let her out of your sight. If I'm not around, be on her like white on rice."

"Your brothers know about this?"

"Not yet, but I'll be talking to them too. Bottom line is that if she doesn't feel safe, she's not safe."

Cole nodded. He didn't look happy, but for now he seemed to be following Ryder's lead. He'd take it.

"What are you doing here?" Felicity asked Ryder harshly as she came up to the two men.

Ryder didn't let her prickly attitude faze him. He wrapped an arm around her waist and pulled her into him. He kissed the side of her temple and said, "You're here, so I'm here."

She rolled her eyes and tried to push his hand off her waist. With no luck.

"I'm working."

"I see that," Ryder said.

"Cole, Mr. Hunt could use your assistance with the weights. I can take over here."

"Sure. Later, Ryder."

"Later."

As soon as Cole was out of hearing range, Felicity turned to Ryder. "What was that?"

"What was what?"

"I saw you guys. You were intimidating Cole. Stop it. You can't act all he-manny around my friends."

"He-manny?" Ryder asked with a laugh.

"Stop laughing at me."

Ryder's smile disappeared in an instant. "I'm not laughing at you. I would never laugh *at* you, love. With you, yes. But not at you."

The uncertainty in her eyes almost did him in, but Ryder held her eyes with his, hoping she saw the sincerity in them.

She sighed. "I just . . . I need that money."

Ryder moved then. Put a hand on either side of her head and leaned into her. "No, you don't. You don't need to run. I told you before, and I'll keep saying it as often as you need me to in order to truly understand it. I'm going to fix this for you."

"You can't."

"I can. And will."

Tears welled up in her eyes as they stared at each other. As much as it hurt Ryder to see the tears in her eyes, he took solace in the fact that she didn't yank herself out of his grip, but she didn't lean into him either. She would. Eventually.

"I need to go and talk to my brothers," he said.

She dug her nails into his biceps. "Not about me."

"Love, they need to know."

"No." She shook her head wildly.

Not thinking, only wanting to reassure her, Ryder leaned forward and caught her lips with his own. She stilled under him and gasped.

He was only going to give her a small kiss, but couldn't stop himself from taking advantage of her shock. His tongue surged into her mouth, and after only a small pause, she hurriedly twined her tongue with his.

Ryder groaned at the first taste of her. He could taste the coffee she'd had that morning as well as a hint of her toothpaste. He wanted more, way more, but standing in the foyer of her gym wasn't the time or place.

He reluctantly pulled back and grinned at the look of lust in her eyes. He much preferred that to the fear he usually saw. He pulled her forward and kissed her forehead. He held her to him for a moment. Then he eased back and said, "I know it's hard letting people in, but I'm not going to run up and down the streets of Castle Rock with a sign that says, 'Felicity Jones is in trouble.' These are your friends, love. My brothers. I know you've been dealing with this by yourself for a very long time, but you aren't alone anymore. You agreed to let me help you last night."

"But . . . I didn't . . ." Felicity stopped and took a big breath. "I don't want anyone to get hurt because of me."

"We won't."

"You don't understand," she protested.

"I do. More than you know. He hurt people you were close to in the past, didn't he?"

Felicity nodded. The terror was back in her eyes. Ryder wanted nothing more than to replace it with passion again, but there was time for that later. "He's met his match with me, love."

"He killed my mom. I don't have proof, but I know it was him." Her words were tortured and whispered.

"Fuck," Ryder said, then brought her into his embrace. Her reasons for wanting to run and not put anyone else she loved in jeopardy suddenly became crystal clear. He didn't press for details because he sensed how difficult it was for her to share even that little bit. Hopefully later she'd feel more comfortable in telling him more. For now, she just needed comfort. His comfort.

Ryder lowered his head so his lips were at her ear. "I'm so sorry, Felicity. *So* sorry. But that's all the more reason for me to end this. You know who I am, what I've done. I told you last night. So trust that he's not going to hurt me. And if I tell my brothers, Grace, Alexis, and Bailey won't be hurt either."

Felicity pulled back and looked up at him. She didn't say anything for several seconds. Finally, she nodded. Once.

That was all he needed. "Good." He kissed her forehead once more, then stepped away from her. "Stay here. You'll be safe here with Cole."

"You talked to him?"

"Some. Not a lot." Ryder knew she wanted to protest, but she bit her lip instead and nodded. God, the trust she gave him was intoxicating and humbling at the same time. "I'll be back for lunch."

"Okay."

He turned to leave.

"Ryder?"

He craned his neck around to see her. "Yeah?"

"Thanks."

"You don't have to thank me, love. I'm doing this for me as much as I am you."

Her brows came down in confusion. "You are?"

He smiled then. "Yup. The sooner I get this taken care of, the sooner I can get you to agree to marry me." And with that bomb, he spun around and left the gym with a huge smile on his face.

Joseph Waters walked slowly on the treadmill in the back corner of Rock Hard Gym. He'd learned a lot from his father and uncles over the years. How to track people, how to intimidate and use threats to get what he wanted, but most important, how to blend in and not be seen. He'd perfected the art of makeup and disguises to go almost anywhere undetected. As long as he looked like he belonged, he could go anywhere. Be anyone.

Disguised as a much older man, he kept his head down, but his eyes were up as he watched Megan. He needed to gather as much information as possible before he made his move.

His father had told him time and time again to forget about her, but he couldn't. He'd waited too long to find her, wasted too much time and money tracking her down. He should've gotten rid of her stupid mother years ago. It had been so easy to stake out the old bitch's funeral. He knew Megan would show up. It was easy to spot her, despite the tattoos and black hair. He was a master of disguises—hers didn't even give him a second's pause. He'd been waiting too long to get his hands on her for a simple disguise to work.

Joseph watched as Megan warily glanced around the room, and he grinned. Yeah, he'd spooked her with the little note and newspaper article he'd left her. Good. She *should* be spooked. When someone dropped a weight and she jumped, he couldn't stop the chuckle from escaping. Making her miserable was so much fun.

His grin disappeared when she stalked out of the room to the front reception area and began to talk to two men there. He knew who Cole Johnson was, and he didn't even register on his give-a-shit meter, but he didn't know who the other man was. At first glance, Joseph knew he was going to be a problem, though. As a man who dealt with violence on a daily basis, Joseph recognized a kindred spirit when he saw one.

When the man leaned in and kissed Megan, Joseph actually growled.

"Are you all right?" a man in his twenties asked from nearby.

Joseph forced himself to smile and waved at the concerned bystander. "Just caught something in my throat, young man. I'm good. Thanks."

"Sure thing."

Joseph looked through the windows on the other side of the room once more. He saw how Megan clung to the mystery man. How she looked up at him, trusting him to keep her safe. Oh hell no. She wasn't safe. Not even close. Joseph turned off the treadmill and picked up the small towel. He carefully dabbed at his face as if he was perspiring, making sure not to smear his makeup while hiding his smile. Maybe he'd fuck with this man first. Fucking with him would mean fucking with Megan. Two birds with one stone.

He liked that. Liked it a lot.

Chapter Six

Ryder sat at the table in the back of Ace Security and looked around at his half brothers. He didn't exactly have a lot of information to share with them about Felicity's situation, but he was hoping they'd agree with him that she needed watching over. As much as he wanted to be with Felicity twenty-four/seven, he knew that simply wasn't going to be possible. She'd hate it, and the last thing he wanted was to make her feel as if she was suffocating.

"Tell us what you found out about Felicity," Logan ordered, getting right to it.

For the next fifteen minutes, Ryder went over what he knew about her situation, which admittedly wasn't a lot. He told them Cole was watching her at the moment and was briefed on the basics of her situation as well.

When he was done speaking, Logan asked, "Are you sure about all this?"

"Absolutely."

"Why?" Blake asked. "I mean, you don't know her. You've only been here a little over a week. What makes you think you know Felicity better than we do?"

Ryder did his best to keep his anger in check. The question was valid, but it was the defensive way Blake delivered it that made his hackles rise. "I know I'm younger than you guys, but I've seen way more in my twenty-eight and a half years than you ever will in your entire lives."

"Me and Logan were in the Army. We were deployed," Blake barked out. "Don't treat us like we're innocent little boys who don't know anything about the world."

Ryder fixed his gaze on his brother. "Have you ever broken the lock on a CONEX container to find fifty-three naked women inside, locked in cages stacked on top of each other? Have you ever had to kill a woman by breaking her neck because it was more humane than letting her bleed to death from the rusty coat hanger that had been shoved between her legs by the so-called abortion doctor she'd been forced to go to? Have you ever raided a Korean brothel and had to carry out bleeding and traumatized little girls age five to ten who had been raped every day, several times a day, for as long as they could remember?" Ryder leaned forward over the table, not taking his eyes from Blake. "Have you ever had to tell a mother that you found her kidnapped twelve-year-old daughter—dead from a bullet to the head after a rescue attempt went bad?"

The room was deadly silent after Ryder stopped speaking. The only sound was the ticking of a clock on the wall.

"I'm no stranger to evil, or fear," Ryder said flatly. "And I absolutely will not hesitate to kill anyone who tries to, or has, hurt the innocent. I've done it before, and I'll do it again in a heartbeat. The look in Felicity's eyes reminds me of the women I've seen who have been traumatized so badly they've pushed it deep inside to try to deal with it. Felicity's good at hiding that trauma, but it's there. I suspect something's happened recently to bring it back to the surface. To make her want to run again."

"Again?" Nathan asked.

Ryder tore his eyes from Blake's to look at his other brother. "Yeah. She's been here five years. I'm guessing she wasn't planning on staying here as long as she did. But she met Cole, and Grace, and decided to stay."

"A few months ago, she took a trip to Chicago," Blake said quietly, his tone much less acidic than it was a few moments ago. "She wouldn't tell Grace or Alexis or anyone why she was going."

Ryder brought his gaze back to Blake. "Chicago?"

"Yeah. She drove there and back," Logan said. "Grace begged her to fly, as it would be faster and safer, but she refused. Said the drive would do her good. Let her clear her mind or some shit."

Ryder's mind raced. "It takes an ID to fly nowadays. She have one?"

Logan nodded. "Of course. A driver's license."

"You've seen it?" Ryder asked.

"Uh . . . well . . . no, but she has to have one. She's got that PT Cruiser she drives everywhere," Logan said.

"She's currently living above the gym," Ryder mused. "She didn't need an ID for that, as Cole knows her. She doesn't use credit cards, does she?"

"I've never seen her with one . . . have you?" Blake asked his brothers.

Nathan and Logan shook their heads.

"Right. She could've bought the car with cash, and she doesn't fly."

"Grace always complains when Felicity drives them somewhere. Says she drives like a ninety-year-old half-blind grandma," Logan said.

"I think, based on that, we can assume she's never gotten a speeding ticket. She lives under the radar, totally," Ryder concluded.

"Fuck," Logan swore. "How could we have missed this?"

Ryder immediately shook his head. "You had no reason to think she was in any trouble, and you're not around her all the time. Besides, you had your own women's situations to deal with. Felicity has had years of practice hiding in plain sight."

"You've been here a *week*, and you figured it out," Blake said. "We've known her for over a year and never put two and two together."

"People who are trying not to be found get really good at being invisible," Ryder said easily. "Their lives depend on it."

"So . . . what do you need from us?" Nathan asked.

"As I said, something has spooked her. I have a feeling whoever she's been running from has found her. I don't know if he's here in Castle Rock yet or not, but we can't take that chance. All it'll take is one minute of inattention, and he could get to her."

"Do you think he wants to kill her?" Blake asked, sounding much more invested in the conversation now.

"I honestly have no idea," Ryder said. "I mean, if that's all he wanted, I have a feeling she'd already be dead."

"Then what does he want?" Logan asked.

"What do all bullies want?" Ryder asked rhetorically. "They want to see their victims suffer. It feeds their ego. They need to feel superior. They feed off the fear of the people they're picking on. It doesn't matter if the bully is eight, or seventy-eight."

"We sure have experience with that," Blake muttered. "That describes Mom to a T."

"So he's gonna fuck with her before he moves in for the kill," Logan stated.

Ryder's lips pressed together in annoyance, and he nodded. "That's what I think."

"The more he fucks with her, the better our chance to catch him," Nathan stated.

Ryder wanted to yell at the other man, but unfortunately, knew he was correct. "Right. As much as I hate it, there's not too much we can do to keep him from playing his games, but we *can* make sure Felicity knows we've got her back."

"Twenty-four-hour surveillance is going to take a lot of time," Logan noted.

"I'll pay whatever it costs for Ace Security to take this one," Ryder said immediately.

Logan's face turned red, and he glared at his brother. "Fuck you. That's not what I meant. Shit, Felicity is like our sister. We would never try to profit off her situation. All I meant was that we'll need to rearrange some of our cases. Take less on until this asshole is caught."

"Sorry. I didn't mean to piss you off," Ryder said sincerely. "But I think it'll take less time than you think. I'll be with her at night, so no one has to worry about that. During the day, when she's working at the gym, Cole can keep his eye on her, and if she needs to run errands or hang out with any of your wives, one of us can be nearby."

"What about video surveillance? I know there's a few exterior cameras at the gym, but I don't know about interior ones," Blake asked.

"Cole has said more than once that he absolutely isn't down with having cameras inside. He doesn't want the members to feel as if they're being spied on," Logan said.

"I'll talk to him," Ryder said. "Maybe just a few aimed at the entrance. We don't want to invite this asshole to have free rein."

"Will Felicity know about all this surveillance? I can't imagine she'll be okay with it," Nathan said. "If she's anything like my Bailey, which I think she is, she's gonna balk at the restrictions."

Ryder was shaking his head before Nathan had finished speaking. "No, she won't say anything about it, because deep down she's scared to death of whoever this is getting to her. And yes, I'm not going to hide anything from her. It's her life, she deserves to know."

"You'll be with her at night?" Logan asked, his eyes narrowed.

Ryder could tell he wanted to say more, to ask about his intentions, but he didn't give his brother the chance. "Yeah. I'm not going to let her out of my sight. I've given her a week to get used to me, but I'm done with that."

"And if she's not okay with it?" Logan pressed. "Look, she's Grace's best friend. You're my brother, but I won't let you, or anyone else, fuck her over, especially if you're just looking to scratch an itch."

Ryder wanted to be upset, but he couldn't be. Logan was just looking out for Felicity. It was actually a relief that she had such a staunch support system. He looked his brother in the eye as he said, "The first time I laid my eyes on her, I was fascinated. Yeah, I'm attracted to her, but it was more than that. I've never felt like this about a woman before in my life. Do I want her in my bed? I won't lie. Yes. But when we get together, it'll be her choice. And I'm going to do whatever I can to make her want me in her life as much as I want her in mine."

"And if, when all this is over, she realizes it's just been gratitude she feels toward you? That you were nice to have around to make her safe, but she doesn't want anything to do with you once whoever this is after her is taken care of?" Nathan asked in a calm and even tone.

The question had seemed to come out of left field from the quieter brother, but Ryder saw a kinship and understanding in the other man's eyes that he hadn't seen from Blake or Logan. "Bailey didn't feel that way after Donovan was taken care of . . . did she?"

Nathan shook his head. "No."

"Right. To answer your question, if Felicity doesn't want anything to do with me after I take care of whoever is after her, it'll suck, but I won't pressure her."

Nathan nodded.

"How can we help besides helping keep an eye on Felicity?" Blake asked.

Ryder met his eyes in relief. The relationship between them wasn't exactly buddy-buddy, but the man had bent enough to work with Ryder to keep Felicity safe. It was enough.

"For now, that's what I need help with. I've got my team working to find the man who is after her."

"You know who it is?" Logan asked.

"No, but I have a name. Joseph Waters." Ryder waited and could tell that it didn't ring any bells with the men around him. "And after talking to you guys today, I know more than I did yesterday. Namely, Chicago. If you think of anything else that might be useful, I need to know. It might be something she's said in passing, but every little thing can help."

"Why can't you just ask her to tell you everything? It would be faster."

Nathan was shaking his head before Logan finished speaking. "That's not how it works. If Felicity is anything like Bailey, she's kept her secrets for so long, it's almost impossible to talk about them openly. Ryder needs to earn her trust. Make her feel safe."

"She might not have that kind of time," Logan insisted. "We need intel."

"I told you, I've got my team working on it," Ryder said.

"Your team. Who is this mysterious team of yours?" Logan asked, crossing his arms over his chest and leaning back in his chair.

Ryder debated telling his brothers who he really worked for. There was a chance they hadn't heard of them, but there was also the chance they *had*. He'd already told them about some of the missions he'd been on, so they'd figure it out sooner or later anyway. Deciding being up front was the way to go, he said, "Mountain Mercenaries."

Blake whistled long and low.

Logan simply nodded his head.

Nathan stared at him with wide eyes.

"I think it goes without saying that I'd appreciate it if you kept that to yourselves."

"Of course," Logan said immediately. "We've heard nothing but good things about the work you and your team have done. Should've guessed who you were after hearing your little speech earlier."

Ryder shrugged. "I'm proud of what I've done, of the bad guys I've taken care of, but it's not exactly something I go around talking about. My cover for anyone who looks or asks is that I work as a private investigator, which isn't exactly a lie."

All three men nodded.

"We're small potatoes compared, but if you need any help trying to find information, we're happy to help," Logan said.

"Taking down the Inca Boyz isn't small potatoes," Ryder countered. "I'll keep you guys informed of anything I find out and will let you know if we need assistance." He stood. "I need to get back over to the gym. Make some phone calls, pass along the Chicago thing."

The others all stood as well. Everyone shook hands.

Blake held Ryder's hand for longer than usual. "I'm trying not to let my hard feelings about our dad's actions affect my feelings about you. I'm struggling, but I'm trying."

His words made Ryder like him all the more. "I understand. If it makes you feel any better, my mom said Ace struggled with the affair. I truly believed he loved my mom, but ultimately he decided that he needed to honor his vows."

Blake nodded, and the two men dropped their hands.

Ryder left Ace Security feeling better than when he'd arrived, especially now that he had more eyes on Felicity. He strode to his car to grab his duffel. Felicity needed to know he wasn't going to back out on her now. That he'd be sticking by her side until whoever was after her was no longer a threat.

He stopped and stared at his Nissan 370Z. It was a slick sports car, one that could easily catch up to, or outrun, bad guys, but not too flashy to stand out in a crowd. At the moment, however, it wasn't in any condition to catch up to anyone.

All four tires were flat.

Ryder's teeth clenched in fury. He didn't care about the tires; replacing them was merely a nuisance. It was the words etched into the side panel of the car that infuriated him.

"Not a chance in hell, motherfucker," Ryder murmured as he stared at the words.

Mind your own business

Chapter Seven

In her apartment, Ryder sat across from Felicity and watched her eat out of the corner of his eye. It had been a week since the incident with his car. She'd been horrified and had apologized a hundred times, and he'd finally had to tell her that if she said she was sorry one more time, he'd have no choice but to turn her over his knee and paddle her ass as *she* wasn't the one who vandalized his car.

He wouldn't have, there was no way he would ever strike her, but she didn't know that. She turned red, bit her lip, and nodded. Score one for him.

He did have to admit, however reluctantly, that the mysterious stalker had done him a favor, as Felicity hadn't even blinked when he'd told her he'd be staying in her apartment with her from then on out. The relief in her eyes spoke volumes.

But she wasn't doing well. She wasn't eating much—currently she was moving the food around her plate more than she was consuming it. And while he was staying in her small apartment with her, she was still as closed off as ever.

She wouldn't let him into her bedroom, not even to check the lock on the window or to clear the room whenever they returned after being out. The more she refused to let him see what was behind her bedroom door, the more he wanted to know. He had a feeling he'd learn more about who Felicity was simply by getting a peek at her private space.

But it was more than obvious she needed a break.

"Blake invited me over to his house today to look through our dad's papers. I thought you might come with me."

Felicity's eyes swung to his. She cocked her head. "Why?"

"Why what?"

"Why would Blake do that? He doesn't exactly like you. And why would you think I'd want to come too?"

Ryder held her gaze. "It's not that he doesn't like me; he's not happy with the choices our dad made. The fact that our dad broke his vows, even though he didn't have a good marriage, crushed him. At least that's what Logan told me."

"So why invite you over to look through Ace's stuff?"

"I'm not exactly sure. But to answer your second question . . . Grace dropped off the babies for Alexis to look after for a couple of hours. I thought you might like to spend some time with them."

Her eyes dropped to the food she was pushing around her plate. "I should stay here. Cole's been working like a dog, and I feel like a slacker."

"He doesn't mind, you know that. Besides, if you left town, he'd have to work a lot more than he is now. What does it matter?"

That got to her. She smacked her hand down on the table next to her plate. "Would you stop throwing that in my face every other second?"

Ryder leaned forward, glad to see the spark of anger in her eyes. It was much better than the fear and defeat that had been there for the last week. "No. I won't. Not if it makes you think about what you'd be giving up if you left. How much you'd be missed. You aren't some random stranger here, Felicity. You're needed and loved. You leaving would devastate everyone."

Ryder watched as her fist clenched around the fork she was holding. For a moment he thought she might throw it at him. But after a couple of seconds, she relaxed her grip and looked up at him. The devastation in her eyes was easy to see. "I can't go, and I can't stay. I'm stuck."

Ryder immediately moved to her side. He squatted down next to her chair and put one hand on her thigh and the other on her cheek. "You aren't stuck, love. You're right where you belong. *He's* the one who doesn't belong here."

She closed her eyes and breathed hard through her nose, pressing her lips tightly together. Ryder got up on his knees and leaned into her. He ran his nose along her jawline. He heard her gasp in surprise, but she didn't pull away from him.

He made his way up her jaw to her ear. He nuzzled it, then brought his lips up to the lobe. His tongue came out and lightly licked. When she jerked in surprise, but still didn't pull away, and instead dropped her shoulder, giving him more room, Ryder grinned. He took the lobe between his lips and sucked.

She moaned, and one of her hands grabbed his forearm.

Wanting more, so much more, Ryder forced himself to loosen his lips. He brought them up to her ear and whispered, "I haven't pushed. Haven't told you how beautiful you are in your flannel pajamas and how much I love the smell of lilacs you dab onto your skin every morning. Haven't broken into your bedroom to get to you when you have those nightmares every night. But I want to. I want that right."

"Ryder," she said softly, the yearning easy to hear in her voice.

He pulled back and looked into her ice-blue eyes. "I see you, love. You don't have to be anyone but who you are with me. You don't have to hide. You've hidden yourself from that asshole for so long, you've forgotten that you don't have to keep the real you from your friends. From me. From the people who love you."

He hadn't come right out and said that he loved her, but the sentiment was there.

"I'm scared."

He knew she didn't mean scared of whoever was after her.

"You have nothing to be worried about."

"I'm not like the woman you see."

Ryder laughed. He couldn't help it. When her brows drew down in irritation, he reined himself in. "Felicity, I know who you are."

"You don't," she insisted.

"I know you hate green beans, but love peas. You hate working out, but you do it every morning because it's what you think people expect from you. You can't cook worth a darn, but it doesn't stop you from trying. You love flowers, birds, and pastel colors, but you pretend you're too tough for that shit. You have these tattoos on your arms to try to make yourself seem impenetrable, but then you cover them up with long-sleeve shirts when you go somewhere that you'll be around people other than your friends. You love babies and want your own someday. I know you do your best to pretend like you like living like this, in a sterile and blank canvas without any pictures or decorations, but I have a feeling behind that bedroom door is the real Felicity Jones."

She stared at him and swallowed hard before saying, "Felicity Jones doesn't exist."

"She does," Ryder said softly. "She's sitting right in front of me."

Felicity shook her head. "No, she's a figment of my imagination."

"Listen to me," Ryder ordered. "I don't know what name you were given at birth, but the person sitting here in front of me, the person who I want more than anything I've ever wanted before in my life, is you. Felicity Jones might not be who you used to be, but she's who you've become. Good or bad, our pasts are what they are. They shape and mold us. Can I be honest with you?"

A small smile appeared on her face. "Like you haven't already been?"

He grinned back, then got serious. "I probably wouldn't even have looked twice at the woman you used to be. She wouldn't have interested me in the slightest. But Felicity Jones does. She has me wrapped around her little finger so tightly I'll never be the same."

He held her eyes, willing her to understand. To believe.

"Megan Parkins," she whispered. "That's who I used to be. Young and ready to take on the world. Then I butted into someone's life. Tried to help her when she didn't want my assistance. And it was the worst decision I've ever made. It ruined my life."

Memorizing the name to give to his team, Ryder placed his hands on either side of Felicity's head and speared his fingers into her short hair. "You could no more let someone get hurt on your watch than you could let one of Grace's babies cry and not pick him up. And that decision you made ultimately led you to me. While I hate that you've been on your own for as long as you have, and that you don't feel safe, I am infatuated with the person you are today. Felicity, Megan, Henrietta, or Michelle freaking Obama. I don't care what you call yourself, the woman sitting here in front of me is who I want."

He gave her a chance to protest. To push him away. But she did neither. Instead, her hands came up and clutched his T-shirt. Ryder leaned in, slowly, still giving her time to reject him. Reject his touch. But she licked her lips and leaned into *him*.

It had been a week since he'd last kissed her, but he remembered every second of that first kiss as if it had just happened. He hadn't thought anything could top it, but he was wrong. This kiss was the best he'd ever experienced. Ryder had a feeling that every touch of his lips to hers would top the one before it. He wanted a lifetime of her taste on his lips.

Her head tilted, giving him more room, and he didn't hesitate to take advantage. His tongue speared through her lips, tangling with hers, memorizing her feel and taste. One hand moved to her nape to hold her against him, and the other trailed down her body and came to rest on her breast, right over her heart. He didn't grope her, merely wanted to feel the beat of her heart under his hand.

They kissed for several minutes. Neither willing to be the first to pull away. Felicity participated in the kiss the same way she did every-thing else . . . with all she had. She didn't meekly sit there and let him kiss her—her tongue pushed against his and learned every inch of his mouth. When he growled, she moaned right back. She took what she wanted.

And it was hot as hell.

Ryder felt her heart thumping under his hand, and he wanted noth-ing more than to pick her up and throw her down on the couch he'd been sleeping on for the last week and show her without words that she belonged to him. That he'd keep her safe. That he'd kill anyone who dared hurt her. But the vibration of her phone brought him back to his senses.

It rattled against the tabletop with every text that came through.

Ryder pulled back and ran his hand over the top of her head. He licked his lips and tasted her on him. His cock was rock hard, and it took everything he had to remove his hand from her chest and reach for her phone. He handed it to her without breaking eye contact.

She blushed, but accepted the cell. She looked down and chuck-led. "Alexis is impatient. Says that if I'm not over at her house in fifteen minutes, she won't be responsible for what she does to Grace's babies."

"She's not much of a kid person?" Ryder asked.

"No, it's not that. She loves kids. But I think sometimes having the twins is a bit overwhelming for her."

"Then we should get over there and let you give her a hand," Ryder said softly.

She nodded, but when he stood up, she asked, "Um . . . Ryder?"

"Yeah, love?"

"What are we doing? We can't start something with *him* out there."

"We already have." And with that, Ryder turned his back on her to grab his jacket. If she thought she was going to backtrack and pretend he hadn't gotten under her skin, she was mistaken. That kiss hadn't been an I'm-testing-things-out-to-see-if-I-might-like-you kiss.

It was a claiming.

Chapter Eight

"What is up with the two of you?" Alexis asked quietly two hours later.

Felicity looked down at the baby in her arms so she didn't have to look at Alexis and shrugged. "What do you mean?"

"Don't play dumb, girl. You and Ryder have been stealing glances at each other all afternoon.

"It's complicated," Felicity told her.

"It's really not," Alexis argued.

"It is. Besides, I haven't known him that long."

"I knew the first time I saw Blake that he was the man for me," Alexis said without a trace of self-consciousness.

Felicity gaped at her. "You did?"

"Yup. And he only saw me as an annoying younger chick who he had to work with."

"There's no way. He loves you."

"He does," Alexis agreed. "*Now*. But when he first met me, he thought I was a rich spoiled brat who was fucking around and only wanted to work at Ace Security for some reason he didn't know or understand."

"Wow. What changed?"

Alexis shrugged. "I guess he got to know me. Saw how much I enjoyed what I did. That I wasn't going to up and quit." She flipped her light-brown hair behind her shoulder and smirked. "Then he took a look at all this"—she indicated her curvy body with a hand—"and couldn't resist."

Both women chuckled.

"It's different with me and Ryder. I think he's just . . ." Felicity's voice trailed off. She didn't know *what* Ryder was. "He's one of those guys who wants to make sure everyone is safe. He doesn't like injustice."

Alexis's eyes narrowed as she eyed Felicity. "That might be true, but that is *not* why he's giving you fuck-me eyes."

"Alexis!" Felicity admonished and covered Nate's ears. "You can't say things like that around the babies."

The other woman laughed. "They're like five months old. They have no idea what I'm saying. And don't change the subject. I know what I see. And if you think he's only sticking by your side because he wants to get the bad guy, you're insane."

Felicity snuck another look over at Ryder. He was sitting next to Blake, and they were both bent over a stack of papers, flicking through them. Every now and then they'd exchange words, but for the most part, they were concentrating on whatever it was they were looking for.

Just as she looked over at him, Ryder looked up, catching her eye. He smiled at her and mouthed, "You okay?"

She nodded and forced her gaze away from him back to little Nate in her arms. The baby was adorable and sound asleep. Both he and his brother had been fussy when they'd arrived, but after a bottle and some snuggling, they were sleeping once more.

"He can't go more than a couple of minutes before checking on you," Alexis said softly.

"He's going to get hurt because of me," Felicity said, looking at her friend.

"No, he's not."

"He is. I'm poison to be around. I shouldn't be here. I—"

"Look at him, Felicity," Alexis ordered.

Without thought, she did as she was ordered. Alexis kept talking, soft and low so the men couldn't hear her.

"He's strong. He's going to find that asshole harassing you and make it stop. And don't get mad—Blake only told me the basics. Ryder is the kind of man who would happily stand between you and the world. Give him a chance, and he'll change your life in so many wonderful ways. He knows what he's doing. I don't know his history, but Blake told me the other night that he's truly one of the best in the security field. And that means a lot coming from him—Ryder isn't exactly his favorite person. So if he says he's good, he's good."

Felicity turned to Alexis. "I want to, but—"

"No buts," Alexis whispered. "Help him do his job, Felicity."

"How?"

"Talk to him. Tell him everything you can about whoever is after you. Why he's after you. Everything."

"But if I tell him everything, he won't like me anymore."

Alexis shifted baby Ace in her arms and scooted closer to Felicity. "Bullshit."

"Alexis. Language!" Felicity admonished again.

The other woman chuckled. "When I first met you, I was so intimidated by you. I thought you were some sort of motorcycle chick who ate those weaker than you for breakfast. But you hardly ever swear, and sometimes I think you're nicer than Grace is . . . and that's saying something. Seriously, Felicity. That man doesn't give a shit what's in your past. All he sees is you, and he likes what he sees."

Her words were so close to what Ryder had said earlier that day that Felicity flinched.

Alexis continued. "I'm so in love with Blake, I don't know what I'd do without him and can't remember my life before him. When I was in trouble and the Inca Boyz had me, the only thing I could think about was holding on for Blake. I knew he'd move heaven and earth to get to me. You can't be afraid to live life, Felicity. Yeah, you've got more troubles right now than the average person, but life isn't guaranteed. You could die in a car crash tomorrow. Or Ryder could. You only have one life to live."

Felicity stared at Alexis. "How'd you get so smart?" She whispered.

"Experience."

Ryder couldn't stop himself from glancing up at Felicity every couple of minutes. He couldn't get their earlier kiss out of his mind, and it seemed that she couldn't either. He'd catch her looking at him every now and then, and every time he did, she'd blush.

He wasn't sure it was the best idea for him to bring her to his brother's house when he knew Blake wasn't exactly fond of him, but Ryder wasn't going to leave her side, not if he could help it. And he thought Felicity spending some time with Alexis and her godbabies might be good for her.

And it seemed it was.

She was visibly more relaxed.

And he couldn't believe how amazing she looked with little Nate in her arms. He hadn't really thought about having children, but seeing Felicity holding a baby did something to him. Made him want what his brother had. He wanted a family . . . with Felicity. Ached to see her round with his child. She'd make an amazing mother, and he wanted to experience every second of it with her. Morning sickness, hormones out of control, even the birth. He wanted to be right at her side the first time they heard their child take his or her first breath.

"I think I found it!" Blake said enthusiastically.

Ryder almost dropped the stack of papers he'd been holding at Blake's loud exclamation. Shaking his head to try to get his head back into what they were doing, he went to stand behind Blake.

His brother was holding an envelope as if it contained anthrax instead of a simple piece of paper.

"That's my mom's handwriting," Ryder confirmed. When Blake didn't move to open the letter, he asked, "Want me to do it?"

Blake shook his head. Alexis came up next to him and awkwardly put her arm around him since she was still holding baby Ace. "Blake?"

"It's just that . . . he was *married*. He shouldn't have done it," Blake said softly.

"Your dad was miserable," Alexis consoled. "With three babies at home. I'm sure your mom was making his life hell. You can't blame him for looking elsewhere for affection."

Blake looked up at Alexis. "I'd *never* cheat on you, Lex. I don't care how many crying babies we had at home."

Alexis put her hand on Blake's face. "I know you wouldn't. But then again, I would never hit you. Scream at you and throw a cast-iron pot at your head." Her words were affectionate and soft, but laced with steel. "You can't judge people until you've stood in their shoes. I know you loved your dad, and experienced some of the same abuse he did, but you aren't him. You can't judge him based on our marriage."

Blake sighed and looked back down at the letter in his hand. Then up at Ryder. "You seen this?"

Ryder shook his head. "No. My mom only told me she wrote him, not exactly what she said." He felt more than saw Felicity come up beside him. She stood next to him, supporting him, without saying a word.

Blake hesitated for a beat, then opened the flap of the envelope and pulled out a piece of paper. He unfolded it and laid it flat on the desk in front of him.

All four adults gasped at what they saw.

The cursive lettering on the page was feminine and neat, but it was the word scrawled diagonally across the page that had surprised them all.

BITCH

No one said anything for a couple of seconds, then Ryder said dryly, "*That's* not my mom's handwriting."

Blake picked up the letter and said, "Most of this is still legible." Then he began to read.

Ace,

I know you're probably surprised to hear from me, but I couldn't leave this earth and not contact you. I've felt guilty for years for keeping this from you, but I knew you did what you thought was the right thing. I've never blamed you for leaving me, in fact, it only made me love and respect you more.

We have a son, Ace. I found out I was pregnant two months after you left. I don't know how it happened, we were always so careful, but I don't regret having him.

I named him Ryder Ace Sinclair. He knows about you. I didn't hide who you were from him while he was growing up, except where you lived. He looks so much like you it sometimes makes my heart hurt looking at him. He graduated at the top of his high school class and did a stint in the Army. He works in security now, keeping people safe. I'm so proud of him, and I know you would be too.

I don't expect you to do anything at this point. I don't have much longer to live, cancer, but I'm not writing this letter to get your pity. I don't regret one second of our time together. There wasn't ever anyone who lived up to my expectations when it came to a man. You set the bar too high.

Maybe someday, if you think it's safe, you'd consider meeting Ryder? He knows everything now. I talked to him last night.

I still love you, Ace. I never stopped. I hope you're happy, it's all I ever wanted for you.

Love,

Patricia

Ryder took a deep breath. His mom's love for Ace was loud and clear in her letter. He'd known she loved the married man she'd had an affair with that resulted in his conception, but he hadn't *known*.

He stole a glance over to Felicity. Now he understood. He had no idea how his mom had the strength to let Ace Anderson go. There was no way he could watch Felicity walk out of his life. Especially knowing she was living in an abusive relationship. No way.

As if she'd heard his thoughts, Felicity brought her eyes up to his. "She let him go *because* she loved him so much."

Ryder's heart felt as if it stopped beating for a moment, then kicked into gear again, double the speed it had been. Felicity was right. Whatever Ace Anderson had said to his mother when he left had kept her away. She'd done it because she loved him. With all her heart.

"My mom found this," Blake said in a weird tone as he stared at the letter with the awful word scrawled across it. "I recognize her handwriting." He turned the envelope over and fingered the postmark. "This arrived the day my dad was murdered."

Ryder sucked in a breath. *No.* Without thought, his hand clamped on Blake's shoulder. He didn't know what to say, but he wanted to let his brother know he was sorry, so very sorry.

Felicity shifted behind him, and Ryder realized she was reaching out to take baby Ace from Alexis. As soon as Alexis's arms were free, she kneeled down next to Blake and wrapped her arms around him.

Blake buried his head in Alexis's hair, and they held each other.

"Come on," Ryder told Felicity. She was holding both babies now, and he steered her away from the desk and the grieving couple. Ryder's head was spinning with the knowledge he'd just learned as well. He couldn't help but feel guilty. He didn't have anything to do with his mom writing the letter or what his father's wife had done, but still . . .

"It wasn't your fault," Felicity said, as if she really could read his mind.

"I know, love. It's just so sad," Ryder returned.

He settled them both on the couch, then reached out and took Nate from her arms. The little guy was heavier than he looked. Ryder then leaned over and pulled out his phone. The information they'd gleaned was huge. Blake needed his brothers' support.

An hour later, Logan, Grace, Bailey and her brother, Joel, and Nathan were all gathered in Blake's house. It was a tight fit, as the house wasn't huge, but no one seemed to notice.

Felicity was sitting on Ryder's lap on the couch, and Grace was sitting next to her with baby Ace in her arms. Logan was pacing next to the couch, bouncing an irritable Nate in his arms. Blake was sitting in a large easy chair with Alexis in his lap, and Nathan was sitting on the love seat with Bailey at his side. Joel was sitting cross-legged on the floor at their feet.

"So, we think Dad got this letter, and Mom found it?" Logan asked.

Blake nodded. "That, or Dad showed it to her."

"Why would he *do* that?" Nathan asked. "He knew better than anyone how she would've reacted."

No one answered his question for a beat. Then Grace spoke up. "What if he showed it to her hoping she'd get mad enough to divorce him? Or at least tell him to get out? I mean . . . he obviously knew she was violent, but maybe he realized how much he loved Ryder's mom and wanted Rose to do something drastic so he could leave."

"She did something drastic, all right," Alexis said in a quiet voice.

"Or he got the letter and was going to hide it, so she never saw it, but Rose found it anyway," Bailey added. "Then freaked out and confronted him about it."

"Regardless, who hid it back in all of Dad's papers, and why?" Logan mused, still rocking and pacing with his restless son.

"I should've looked through his stuff earlier," Blake lamented.

Ryder's head spun. He hated seeing the men he'd come to respect so confused and heartsick. "Does it matter?" he asked in a lull in the conversation. "I mean, what happened is done. We can't change it. I wish my mom didn't write the letter, then maybe you guys would still have your dad."

"If she didn't write the letter, we wouldn't have come back to Castle Rock," Nathan said matter-of-factly. "Grace would possibly still be under the thumb of her parents; Blake, you and Alexis wouldn't have met; and Bailey could've been hurt badly by Donovan." His eyes dropped to Joel, making his point without actually saying a word. Then he looked back up at Ryder. "And we wouldn't have met our half brother. I'm sorry it happened. I hate that Dad never got to meet our women or his grandkids. But we can't change the past."

"Nathan, you have always had a way with words," Logan said softly, sitting on the arm of the couch. Grace reached over and put a hand on his knee in silent support.

Blake sighed huge and looked over to Ryder. "I'm sorry I've been a dick."

Ryder stared at his brother in shock. His words seemed to come out of left field.

"I was so disappointed in Dad and the fact that he'd broken his marriage vows, I didn't think about much else. But really, Mom broke them first. There was no love, honoring, or cherishing in her relationship with Dad. It's stupid that I was upset with him when Mom was the one who constantly hurt us growing up. Not to mention she murdered him, for God's sake. But Dad *was* honoring his vows by giving up your mom, and ultimately died as a result. Yeah, he cheated, but with three babies, and a wife who didn't treat him as she should, it's no wonder he looked elsewhere for affection. But when push came to shove, he sacrificed his own happiness to come home. To come back to where he was denigrated, yelled at, and beaten. But he did it for us. He sacrificed his happiness for us."

"He protected us as best he could," Logan mused.

"I never thought he did that good a job of it," Blake admitted.

"Remember that time when we were little and wanted to go trick-or-treating? Mom didn't want us to go, saying it was a stupid holiday, but he hurried us out of the house and told us to have fun," Nathan added.

"We came back, and he had a black eye and was limping badly, but he still sat on the floor with us and watched as we went through all our candy," Blake said. "I've been bitter that he didn't do more to protect us, but when I really stop and think about it, he was always standing between us and Mom. Yeah, there were lots of times when she still got to us, but Dad did what he could to take the brunt of her anger."

Ryder sent a silent prayer up to his mom, thanking her for being loving and generous. They'd been poor, but he'd never known anything but tenderness from her. "When my mom told me about the affair, and about our dad, she wasn't bitter at all. I couldn't understand it at the time. I asked why she let him go so easily. She told me that it wasn't easy, but that he went back to your mom because of you guys." Ryder looked each of his brothers in the eye.

"He left my mom, and a life free of abuse for you guys. He had to protect you. My mother said he flat out told her that. And that was why she never attempted to talk to him again. She understood. It hurt, but she understood. She didn't tell me about the letter, but I know she thought that since you guys were older, and no longer in need of protection, it would be okay to write him."

Ryder heard Felicity sniff. Her head was resting on his shoulder, and she had a death grip around his waist. The other women were also crying, and the men looked more sad than pissed.

The emotions in the room were high, but there also seemed to be an air of relief.

"This sucks," Blake said. "But, I'm glad we know. I've always wondered what happened. I mean, Mom was always a bitch, but I couldn't figure out why she went from simply being abusive to murder."

"Should we bring this to the cops?" Alexis asked. "I mean, Rose did kill Ace, after all."

"No," Blake said immediately. "It won't change anything. They're both dead; we need to let Dad rest in peace once and for all. He made mistakes, I don't think any of us can deny that, but what's done is done."

At that moment, baby Ace let out a loud fart.

The room was silent for a moment, then Joel blurted, "Nothing like a baby fart to break the tension."

Everyone laughed, and just as Joel stated, the tension in the room was broken.

Grace got up to change her baby's diaper, and Alexis and Bailey wandered into the kitchen to refill drinks.

Logan, Blake, and Nathan went into the office to look at the letter once more, and Joel got up and started working on his homework at the kitchen table.

Felicity went to get out of Ryder's arms, but he tightened his hold on her. "Are you okay?"

She nodded. "Why wouldn't I be? I should be asking *you* that."

"I'm good."

Felicity put her hand on his cheek. Ryder had never seen her look so mellow. "It's not your fault," she told him.

"I know. I'm not happy that her letter was apparently the impetus for Rose to kill Ace, but I know I didn't have anything to do with it."

"Good. Why don't you go in there with your brothers," she said with a tilt of her head, indicating the office.

"I think I will. You okay out here?"

She rolled her eyes. "Yeah, Ryder. I'm good. I'll just go in and help Alexis and Bailey in the kitchen."

Ryder widened his eyes in mock horror.

"Shut up," she giggled, then smacked him on the shoulder. "Let me up, you big brute."

With a grin, Ryder helped her stand. He liked this side of her. Liked their easy-going teasing. Too much of their time together had been intense; he wanted a lifetime of teasing and joking around with her.

When Ryder and his brothers came out of the office an hour later, he felt much better about his relationship with his brothers. None of them were happy with what they'd learned, but with knowing came a certain amount of peace. The Anderson brothers, because they realized that their father had chosen to stay in an awful marriage to protect them; and Ryder, because of the forgiveness they'd extended to his mother for her role, however unintended, in Ace's murder.

Ryder stopped short at the sight that greeted him when he walked into the large open living area. Grace was fast asleep on the couch with one of the twins snoring on her chest. Bailey was holding the other baby, and she and Alexis had their eyes glued to some reality show on television.

But that wasn't what caught Ryder's attention. It was Felicity sitting at the table with Joel. Their heads were together, and she was showing the boy something on a piece of paper. They were so engrossed in what they were doing, neither saw Ryder approach.

"So that's the easiest way to divide fractions. I agree that multiplying them is much more fun, but if you follow those steps, you can easily do the division," Felicity was telling Joel softly.

"Cool! You're just as smart as Nathan," Joel told Felicity, his eyes staring up at her in awe.

She chuckled. "I don't know about that. But math is fun. I like it. Numbers make sense. They always work the same way, there's always a right and wrong answer. You can't say that about English or a lot of other subjects."

Joel nodded vigorously. "Yeah, that's what I think too. Sometimes I don't understand how to do stuff the way my teacher explains it, but Nathan always helps me when I get home. But you made it even easier to understand than he did last time we tried to do this stuff. Thanks!"

Felicity ruffled his hair and said, "You're more than welcome."

Ryder cleared his throat.

"Hey, Ryder," Joel said, "is Nathan done? I want to show him how Felicity taught me to work these fractions!"

"Yeah, he's done. Just talking with his brothers about everyday stuff."

"Cool. Thanks again, Felicity!" he called, and was off like a shot.

Ryder eased into the seat he'd left and looked down at the scrap paper on the table in front of him. It was covered in fractions and math problems. He looked over at Felicity and said, "Math, love?"

She bit her lip and nodded, but didn't elaborate.

Ryder reached for her arm and straightened it on the table in front of him. With his fingertip, he traced the cursive words on her forearm. "We can't solve problems by using the same kind of thinking we used when we created them. I love this."

"Albert Einstein," Felicity said softly.

"I know."

"It . . . it's about more than math," she admitted.

Ryder's heart melted. "I figured as much." He continued to run his finger up and down her arm, not commenting on the goose bumps that rose as a result of his touch.

Felicity took a deep breath and looked up at him. Instead of seeing fright in her eyes, he saw determination.

"I need your help, Ryder."

"You got it, love."

"It's my college roommate's boyfriend, he—"

Ryder put his finger over her lips. "Not now, and not here."

Her brows came down in confusion. "But I thought you wanted me to tell you everything."

"I do. But I want to make sure you feel safe when you do it. I don't want there to be any interruptions either."

"I feel safe now, and what kind of interruptions are—"

As she was speaking, Joel burst back into the room. "Felicity! Nathan says good job! He's impressed that you know fractions!"

Ryder lifted his eyebrows at Felicity, as if to say, "See?"

"That's great, Joel."

"We'll talk later, love," Ryder told her, then leaned over and kissed her temple.

With every day that went by, every day he spent with her, Ryder was discovering another facet of Felicity's personality and true self. He knew she was smart, but seeing her work so easily with Joel had solidified it. He couldn't remember how to divide fractions if his life depended on it.

He just had to continue to be patient. She'd given him her real name and had said she'd tell him her story. Nothing in his life had felt as good as Felicity's trust.

Late that night, after a fun dinner with his brothers and a hilarious game of Cards Against Humanity—played while Joel was occupied watching a movie—Ryder led Felicity into the now-closed gym. They nodded at the lone cleaning woman who came in each night to disinfect the locker rooms and make sure all the workout machines were wiped down.

Ryder kept hold of Felicity's hand as they walked down the hallway, past the offices, to the stairs that led up to the second floor and her apartment. Felicity was half-asleep on her feet, but even so, as soon as they entered her space, she dropped his hand and headed for the kitchen.

She went to the water cooler, and poured herself a large glass of water. Ryder had seen her do the exact same thing each night before she went to sleep.

"You do that every night," he observed quietly. "Why?"

She shrugged. "It's good for me. I didn't always eat very healthy, and I realized the best thing for me is water. I try to drink at least two liters every day. Sometimes I do, and sometimes I don't. But I find if I drink a full glass right before I go to sleep, it makes me feel better. Cleaner." She shrugged. "It's probably all in my head, but water was always free, and it was the one thing I could do to help keep myself healthy when I couldn't afford to buy the best food. Drinking water was way cheaper than seeing a doctor if I got sick."

Ryder walked toward her and took her head in his hands. He leaned down and kissed her tenderly, feeling the coolness of her lips from the water.

"What was that for?" she asked.

"Because you're amazing."

Felicity blushed, but for once, didn't contradict him.

"You're tired," he observed unnecessarily.

She nodded.

"Okay, get on to bed. I'll make sure we're locked up tight. You gonna let me check your room tonight?"

She shook her head.

"You know that nothing in there would make me leave . . . right?"

Felicity sighed. "I know . . . I'm working up my nerve to let you in my personal space. It's the one place in the world where I feel like I can truly be myself."

Ryder kissed her forehead. "I'm in no rush, love. I'm happy enough that you're not protesting me staying here in the first place." He inclined his head toward the couch where he'd been sleeping.

"You could sleep in the guest room, you know. I realize there are two cribs in there for Nate and Ace, but there's also a twin bed."

Ryder was shaking his head before she'd finished the sentence. "Thank you, but no. If I can't be right at your side making sure you're safe, I'll settle for sleeping out here, where I can be between you and anyone who might break in and try to get to you."

She stared up at him with wide eyes for a moment before closing them and sighing. When she opened them a second later, they were filled with tears. "No one has made me feel as safe as you do."

"Go on to sleep, love. I'll see you in the morning."

"I want to tell you . . . but . . . I'm not ready. It's stupid because I was going to talk to you earlier, and I know my time's running out because he's here. Watching me. I can feel his eyes on me almost all the time. I should just tell you because I know you'd be able to help me."

Ryder tightened his hands on her head. "No pressure, Felicity. He won't get his hands on you while I'm here."

"Thank you."

"Don't thank me. You don't ever thank me for being by your side. For wanting to be here."

Her lips quirked upward.

"What? Are you laughing at me?" Ryder asked, much happier to see her smiling than crying.

"It's just that . . . you can be so *stern* at times. But I've seen you hold your nephews and talk to them so tenderly, it's hard to reconcile the two."

"I told you what I did for a living," Ryder warned. "Don't mistake my tenderness for you and my family for weakness."

She got serious. "I wouldn't. I think it's that dangerous side that makes me trust you implacably. The fact that I know you've killed before and would probably kill for me makes me feel safe."

"There's no *probably* about it," Ryder said matter-of-factly.

They stood there for several seconds staring at each other before he sighed and took a step away from her. "Finish your water and go to bed, love. Tomorrow's a new day. We'll play it by ear."

She nodded, finished the rest of the water in her glass, and set it in the sink. She brushed past him and headed for the closed door to her room. She turned at the last minute and looked back at him.

"Good night, Ryder."

"Good night, love."

Joseph Waters, disguised as a woman several decades older than he was, slowly ran the mop over the floor in the gym. He kept his eyes on the hallway Ryder Sinclair and Megan had gone down. It had been easy enough to get rid of the weak old woman who had been cleaning the gym. He hadn't planned on killing her, but the stupid cunt hadn't stopped screaming even when he'd held a knife to her throat.

She wasn't even close to being the first bitch he'd killed, and she wouldn't be the last. Most of the time, women would shut right up when they felt his blade at their throat, but not her. All he'd needed was the set of master keys she had to Rock Hard Gym. Bathrooms, locker rooms, offices and, most important, the apartment on the second floor. Not that he needed them. He'd been taught by one of the best lock pickers his dad had employed. He could pick almost any kind of lock in less than a minute. But the keys certainly made things easier.

It had been simple to check out Megan's apartment before she and her protector had gotten home. He'd taken his time, gotten a feel for who she'd become in the years he'd been looking for her. Joseph had seen enough for a plan to start forming in his head for how he was going to bring her to heel.

A gleam entered his eye, and he robotically ran the mop across the floor as he imagined her chained up, scared, and spread out for his use. Yeah, Megan Parkins would rue the day she dared call the cops on *him*.

And now that he'd been inside her apartment, he knew exactly how he'd get to her.

But first he'd play.

He smiled as he put the mop back into the closet. Megan and Cole would find out soon enough that their regular cleaning lady wouldn't be able to continue in their employment.

He'd made several copies of the keys she carried already and could enter and exit the building at will. The stupid janitor had given him the code to the alarm after only one small cut on her neck. He hated weak women. He much preferred they stand up to him before he broke them.

He smiled as he let himself out of the gym. He'd be back. This was going to be fun.

Chapter Nine

Felicity heard Ryder on the phone the next morning as she lay in bed. She heard him say her real name, the one she'd revealed the day before. She wasn't surprised. She'd known when she'd told it to him that he'd be reporting it to his friends. Instead of feeling nervous or scared about it, though, it felt . . . freeing.

For the first time in ten years, she didn't have the urge to constantly look behind her. Oh, she knew Joseph was out there somewhere. He wouldn't have sent her that note or the newspaper article if he didn't want her to know he was near. It wasn't his way to pop out of the bushes with a gun. No, he liked to torment. To scare. And he was damn good at it. He'd found her right after she'd left Chicago, and it had been traumatizing enough for her to figure out how to acquire a new name and try to disappear for good.

She couldn't hear Ryder's exact words anymore, he must've moved into the kitchen, but she could still hear the low rumble of him talking. Felicity's eyes roamed her room. Keeping everyone out had become second nature, a part of protecting herself. If the living area was pristine and barren, her bedroom was the exact opposite.

She had a picture of her and her mother on the table next to her queen-size bed. Books lay in disarray on the floor, as she didn't have a bookshelf to keep them on. She'd kept a few of her old physics textbooks, and they were interspersed with crime thrillers, how-to-live-off-the-grid instruction manuals and, of course, her sci-fi books.

After she'd gotten her latest tattoo, she'd overheard a group of college girls talking about her, saying that she looked scary and how she probably had posters of motorcycles and guns on her walls. It was the impression she wanted to give strangers. She'd purposely done her best to change the image she projected. She'd always been the good girl—the nice one—and look where that had gotten her.

The short hair, the muscles, the tattoos—it was all to transform herself into the opposite of who she once was. But . . . it hadn't really worked. She still felt like the same person inside. She didn't like people to be scared of her, didn't like to constantly be snarky and closed off. It hadn't kept Joseph from finding her. Hadn't kept him from killing her mom. All it had done was make her feel more alienated from everyone around her.

But who was she, really? Her bedroom was the one place in her life where she could be herself. Truly herself.

On her walls were cheap posters and pictures she'd picked up in discount stores and from Goodwill. A poster of Monet's *Woman with a Parasol*, a watercolor of a field of bluebonnets that she'd picked up when she'd been hiding in Texas, a piece of notebook paper tacked up on the wall with a picture drawn by Joel of an alien being shot by an astronaut, a newspaper clipping with the story about Grace's mother going to jail, complete with a picture of Margaret Mason in handcuffs being led into the courthouse, and an eleven-by-fourteen portrait in which she and Grace were standing with their arms around each other at Grace's wedding. They were both laughing hysterically, their heads thrown back, huge smiles on their faces. It was one of Felicity's favorite photos. She'd never seen Grace so happy before then.

Then there was her bed. She'd collected embroidered pillows from the thrift shops in the area and had even scored a queen-size quilt that looked handmade. It had pastel squares all sewn together to make a huge multicolored daisy. Her mother hadn't made it, but she liked to pretend she had.

Her sheets were the one thing she'd bought new. They were top of the line, high thread count, and so silky smooth against her body, it felt as if she was lying on a soft, puffy cloud. She had lugged with her the first stuffed animal her mom had ever given her when she'd run away so many years ago. It was a giraffe whose neck had to have been sewn back on at least ten times over its lifetime, but it was precious to Felicity, and literally the only thing she had left of her old life.

Overall, her room was a lived-in, comfortable mess, and Felicity knew Ryder would take one look and know for a fact that her tough bravado was merely a facade. But he already knew. He'd told her as much. For the first time, she didn't mind the thought of letting someone in. Letting *Ryder* in.

Grace knew she liked to read science fiction, but not how much she loved physics. Or that she'd been well on her way to a career in that field. Felicity had to be the strong one in their relationship—constantly pushing Grace to get away from her parents. She hadn't been able to let her best friend know how scared she herself was.

Then when Grace had gotten together with Logan, she bragged to him and his brothers about her badass best friend, and Felicity hadn't wanted to burst her bubble. She liked the respect she saw in their eyes when the Anderson brothers looked at her.

But somehow Ryder had seen right through the shield she'd had up and broken right past it. She knew it was only a matter of time before she told him everything. She wanted to. She just had to build up the nerve.

Felicity rolled out of bed and headed for the attached bathroom. Cole wanted to talk to her today about some marketing ideas for the gym, and she had some other errands she needed to get done. As much as she wanted to hide out in her room, she knew she couldn't. Life went on. Even when stalked by a psycho asshole.

"Yeah, her name is Megan Parkins. I told you already that she's most likely from Chicago. Have you gotten anything on the name Joseph Waters yet?"

Ryder's friend, Meat, said, "Not yet. But having her name will certainly help."

"I'm going to call Rex," Ryder said. Calling his handler wasn't something the mercenaries usually did. Rex usually got in touch with *them*, not the other way around. But Ryder wasn't willing to sit back any longer than necessary. Not when it meant Felicity would be in danger. All the Mountain Mercenaries knew their handler had connections. Deep and sometimes scary ones. It was how he got his intel about what missions to send them on.

If Meat was having trouble finding Joseph Waters and what his connections were—because it was more than obvious he had them—then perhaps Rex could assist.

"That's a good idea," Meat said. "I've found a couple of men named Joseph Waters in Chicago, but none seem like they'd be your guy. Rex has contacts he can use to delve deeper."

Ryder nodded even though his friend couldn't see it. "Yeah, that's what I thought too. I appreciate your help, though."

"Anytime. As soon as I have a dossier written up on Megan, I'll encrypt it and send it."

Ryder bit back the immediate protest that sprang to his lips. He knew he needed more information, but he wanted Felicity to be the one to talk to him. Getting the information in the official report that they used before heading off on a mission seemed . . . wrong. But all he said to Meat was, "Thanks. I'll talk to you later."

"Later, Ryder."

As Ryder clicked off his phone, he thought about the situation. He'd felt eyes on him just as Felicity said she had over the last week.

It was as if the asshole was simply biding his time. And that meant he was patient . . . and therefore way more dangerous than a spontaneous, impulsive, crazy asshole.

Most stalkers didn't have the wherewithal to control their urges to possess, or hurt, their prey. Joseph seemed especially threatening since he had to have seen Felicity with him. Had to know Ryder was protecting her. Him being at her side would make whatever Joseph had planned more difficult. Getting to Felicity would be more complicated. Ryder wouldn't, and couldn't, underestimate the man.

"Good morning."

Ryder turned and smiled at Felicity. She stood at the entrance to her small kitchen. Her dark hair was sticking up in spikes all around her head, and she was wearing a gray baseball shirt over a pair of jeans. She'd gone heavy on her makeup, but he could still see the dark circles under her eyes that she'd tried too hard to conceal. He hated that she wasn't sleeping well, but truth be told, neither was he. It wasn't the lumpiness of the couch that had him tossing and turning all night, but the thought of someone somehow slipping past him and getting to Felicity.

"Morning, love. You look beautiful this morning."

She blushed, but gave him a small smile.

"What's on the agenda today?"

Felicity brushed past him and reached for the refrigerator door handle. She opened it and pulled out a V8 juice. She unscrewed the top and eyed him as she took a long sip. Finally, she asked, "How long are you going to do this?

"Do what?"

She waved her hand. "Sleep on my couch. Monitor my every step."

"As long as it takes."

She put the bottle down on the counter and frowned up at him. "You don't know him, Ryder. He'll wait you out."

"Then he'll have a very long wait. I have no intention of going anywhere."

"You can't stay up here forever. You have a job down in Colorado Springs."

"Actually, no, I don't," Ryder countered. "I told you before, I'm a liability now. I have too many connections. The thing that made me so good at my job was that I was a loner. I didn't have anyone in my circle. Yeah, I had my mom until she passed, but not a lot of people knew about her."

"You're quitting?"

"Yup."

Felicity looked confused. "But . . . you need to do something, right?"

"Not for a while. I got paid very well for what I did. I've got plenty of money. In fact, I was hoping you might go house shopping with me at some point."

Felicity shook her head as if she hadn't heard him right. "What? A house? Here?"

"Yeah. Here."

They stared at each other in silence for a few seconds. "You're *moving* here?" she asked quietly.

"Yes, Felicity. My family is here. I want to watch my nephews grow up. I want to get to know my brothers better. And you're here. You have your gym, and your friends are here."

He thought she might get emotional after hearing his intention, but he'd expected tears. Not the huge smile that spread across her face.

"You're moving here," she stated.

"Yeah," he confirmed.

"I want that," she said firmly. "I've never felt about someone the way I feel about you. I want to see where we can go. But I need to get this asshole making my life a living hell to fuck off first."

He smiled back at her. "As much as I like this new attitude, I'm a bit confused by it," He admitted. "What brought on the change? Last night you were scared and unsure about me being here still. Now you're not. Why?"

"I thought about everything after I went to bed last night."

"Everything?"

"Yeah. Everything. Joseph. My mom. How I got here to Castle Rock. Grace and what she went through and how happy she is now. Alexis and Blake, and even Bailey and Nathan. Hell, Joel has been braver than I've been recently. And I got mad. That asshole doesn't have the right to do this to me. He doesn't have the right to ruin my life. But the thing is, he only ruins my life if I *let* him. When I was twenty, I wasn't experienced enough to know how to fight back. Then, all I knew was running and hiding. But since I don't have to hide anymore, Joseph knows where I am, and I like living here, I decided that I would do whatever it took to help you help me."

"Come here," Ryder ordered, holding out an arm.

Without hesitation, Felicity took the few steps to get to his side. She snuggled into him, and he closed his arms around her. He kissed the top of her head, then vowed, "You won't regret this."

She picked up her head and looked up at him. "I know I won't. Ryder?"

"Yeah?"

"You're gonna make love to me, right?"

He about choked, but he immediately said, "Absolutely."

She dropped her cheek back to his shoulder and nodded. "Good. It's been a long time for me, and honestly, I wasn't sure I'd ever trust anyone enough to let them get that close to me again. But even though we haven't known each other that long, I trust you more than I have anyone in my entire life."

Ryder took a deep breath. "It's been a while for me too, love. And you know, I hope, that I trust you the same way. I wouldn't have told you about Zariya if I didn't."

"I know. I thought about that last night too. I'm not saying I'm ready to drag you to my bed right this second, but I wanted you to know that I'm going to do everything in my power to fight back this time. If Grace could do it, and have her happily ever after, I can too."

They stood wrapped in each other's arms for a long moment, then Ryder palmed her nape and urged her back. When she looked up at him, he said, "All you have in your fridge is egg whites and V8 juice. Feel like going out for breakfast?"

She smiled up at him and nodded. "Yeah, I can do that."

"Good." He didn't push her to tell him everything right that second. For now, Ryder needed to make sure Felicity felt safe, that she knew she not only had him, but his brothers as well, at her back. Now that he knew they were on the same page when it came to a relationship, the urgency to have her under him had lessened.

But knowing they'd eventually get there had eased the caveman inside of him. She was already his; the lovemaking would come.

They didn't make it to breakfast. When they'd gone downstairs, Cole had informed them that he'd received a call from the electric company wanting verification that they wanted to end their service. As they were discussing it, the alarm company called with the same request.

By the time lunch came around, they'd heard from two other companies who wanted to verify the cancellation of services, and when they'd made a preemptive call to check on their lease, they found that the owner of the building had also been informed that they would be shutting down the gym.

It had taken all day to clear up the misunderstandings. At first Felicity assumed it was just a simple mistake with the electric company, but as time went on, and as more and more companies contacted them about severing services, the ball of fury in Felicity's gut grew. As she'd told Ryder that morning, she was no longer scared—she was furious.

She had no doubt Joseph was behind everything. He'd done the same thing to her before. Except then she hadn't found out that the landlord had rented her apartment to someone else until it was too late. The electricity had shut off one day, and when she'd called about it, she'd been informed that they had a record of her canceling it because she said she'd be moving.

Ryder had hovered around her office as she and Cole dealt with the various businesses and reassured them they were not going anywhere as well as put in safeguards to prevent the same thing from happening in the future. Ryder had gone out and gotten them both lunch and had placed the sandwiches on their desks without a word.

When six o'clock rolled around, Ryder came into the office and declared that she was done for the day.

Cole had agreed. "There's nothing more we can do today when everyone's closed. I'm pretty sure we got ahold of everyone important. The water delivery and laundry service will continue. I haven't been able to get ahold of the cleaning service, but when Mrs. Hanley shows up, *if* she shows up, I'll have a talk with her and verify that we want to continue using her services. Thanks for your help today, Felicity."

She stared at him for a beat. "Uh . . . we're partners, Cole. Of course I was here."

"I thought you decided you wanted your money and were out?" he fired back.

Felicity couldn't get pissed at him. She *had* told him that. "I changed my mind."

"For good?"

"For good."

"Can I please put your fucking name on the business now?"

She stared at him in shock. He sounded pissed. Really pissed. "I . . . It's still not a good idea."

"The fuck it's not. If you think I haven't known you could up and disappear on me one day, you're insane. Every day I woke up wondering if today was the day one of my best friends would be gone. Every day I feared having to make this gym work without you. I started this place up knowing I might one day have to do it alone, but I dreaded that day with everything in me. I like working with you, Felicity. Everyone loves you around here. If you left, I'm not sure I'd have the enthusiasm to keep this place open."

"She's not leaving," Ryder answered for her.

Cole's gaze met Ryder's, then he nodded and looked back at Felicity. "I still want your name on the paperwork."

"Okay." The look of relief in his eyes made her stomach hurt. She'd never meant to hurt her friend. Had thought he'd be better off without her. Hell, she'd thought he'd jump at the chance to buy her out. "But not yet. When all this is over."

"Fine. But I'm holding you to it."

Felicity nodded. "Okay."

"Okay."

"Come on, love. You need to eat. And you haven't had enough water today. Let's go upstairs."

She nodded and took hold of Ryder's hand as she stood.

He led her upstairs as he had the night before and held open her apartment door. She walked in and stopped so suddenly, Ryder bumped into her. She would've fallen, but he grabbed her hips to keep her steady.

"What? What's wrong?" Ryder asked, the easy-going persona long gone.

"Someone's been in here," Felicity whispered.

In a flash, Ryder shifted her until she was behind him, his arm out, preventing her from getting around him. "How do you know?"

"There's a picture frame sitting next to the television that isn't mine."

"Anything else?" Ryder barked.

Looking around him, Felicity examined the room. She slowly shook her head. "No, what I can see from here looks normal."

Ryder walked slowly and cautiously to the television and the picture frame. Using his long-sleeve shirt as a kind of glove, he picked it up and brought it back to Felicity.

"Who is this with you?" he asked.

Felicity looked at the picture, and her breath caught in her throat. When she could speak, she said, "It's me and my old roommate, Colleen."

Ryder turned the picture so he could see it. His only comment was, "I like your black hair better."

She snorted. It wasn't what she expected him to say. Not in the least. He wasn't happy, that was clear. His neck was red, and his jaw was clenched tight, but he was trying to lighten the mood—for her. If she hadn't already been sure she wanted this man, that would've done it.

"No one came up here today. I'd stake my reputation on it."

"We were gone for a lot of the day yesterday," Felicity said unnecessarily.

"I can't believe I didn't notice this last night or this morning," Ryder murmured, obviously upset. "Go sit at the table, love. I need to check the rest of the apartment. You okay with that?"

Knowing he meant he'd be looking inside her room, Felicity immediately nodded. If she was going to sleep with this man, she needed to let him in. *Completely.* That meant inside her sacred space as well as inside her head.

Ryder put the frame on the kitchen counter as he passed it, escorting her to the table as if she couldn't make it there on her own. Once she was seated, he knelt at her side.

Felicity stared at him. Here was the deadly man she'd only heard him speak about. In the small time she'd known him, she hadn't seen this side. Oh, she'd seen him upset and concerned, but nothing like this. More than six feet of pissed-off male. It actually made the muscles in her body relax. This man wouldn't let Joseph hurt her. No way.

"You okay?" he asked.

"Yeah."

"It's okay if you aren't," he insisted. "It won't change the way I feel about you. The way I see you."

Felicity put her hand on his forearm. "If you weren't here, I'd be a mess. I hate that he got inside my space, but you'll protect me."

"Damn straight."

She couldn't quite smile, but she could feel the urge. "Go on, Ryder. I'll be right here. Make sure he's not lurking under my bed or something. I'll check my room after and see if he's left me anything else."

Ryder reached out with a hand as quick as lightning, pulled her face up to his, and kissed her with a short, but incredibly intense meeting of his lips to hers. Then, without letting go of her head, he pulled back a fraction of an inch and declared, "I won't let anything happen to you."

He'd said it over and over, but it never failed to make her feel better. "I know," she reassured him.

Then he nodded, let go, and stood, all in one motion. Without a word, he pulled a handgun out of a holster somewhere on his body, Felicity had no idea from where, but she wasn't concerned about the fact he'd been carrying. It was one more thing that reassured her about the big man who'd somehow attached himself to her.

As he stalked down the short hallway to check out the rest of the apartment, she made a decision. She'd tell him everything. All of it. Tonight.

Joseph lay on his bed, smirking. He wished he'd installed a few cameras in her apartment. He would've given anything to see her reaction to the photo he'd left for her. There was something very exciting and arousing about being in her apartment when she wasn't there. He'd taken his time, looking in every cabinet and drawer, inspecting the apartment, learning about his prey.

And without a doubt, Megan Parkins was his prey. She'd pay for her interference . . . eventually. In the meantime, it was fun to mess with her. The electricity and other services were mere inconveniences. He knew she'd be able to get those straightened out easily. But the picture had to have freaked her out. He once again thought about how scared she had to have been when she realized he'd been in her space.

His hand moved down his body and slipped under his sweatpants. Joseph stroked himself, imagining what Megan had looked like when she saw his gift. Maybe she'd even cried. He loved it when bitches boo-hooed. He closed his eyes as he thought about all the plans he had for Megan.

Ryder would be a nuisance, but nothing he couldn't deal with. He released himself from his pants and sighed in pleasure. He continued to run his hand up and down his length. He got more and more excited the more he thought about what he had in store for her.

She'd be freaked.

Scared out of her mind.

Ready to do whatever he said.

The smirk spread on his face as his hand moved faster and faster.

As he orgasmed, he imagined the look of horror and absolute terror on her face when she realized what he'd done. When she realized that she couldn't outsmart him this time. That she'd never escape him again.

Chapter Ten

"Rex? It's Ace."

"What's wrong?"

Ryder's lips twitched. Figured his handler would immediately know something was up. "I have a situation that I could use your help with."

"Shoot."

"Right around the time my mom died, I found out I had three half brothers. They live in Castle Rock, and I came up to meet them. Stepped right in the middle of a situation."

"What kind of situation?"

Ryder liked that his handler didn't beat around the bush. "One involving a woman who has become very special to me, and a stalker who has gotten too close for comfort. He broke into her apartment tonight."

"You need her locks changed right now? Or will the morning work?" Rex asked without hesitation.

Ryder sighed in relief. He knew he could ask his brothers for a locksmith recommendation, as they most likely had some connections in the area, but Rex offering to take care of it right now meant he could concentrate on making sure Felicity was all right sooner rather than later. "Morning will be fine. I'm not leaving her side tonight, so she'll be okay until morning."

"What else?"

"Joseph Waters. It's who Felicity says is after her. From Chicago. Meat did some checking, but hasn't come up with anything concrete."

"I'll get with Meat, see what he's found, then see what I can come up with."

"Appreciate it."

"You might have turned in your resignation, Ace, but you're still a part of this team and always will be. You need anything, especially if it concerns your woman, I'll be pissed if you don't call."

And with that, the elusive Rex disconnected the call.

After hanging up, Ryder thought, not for the first time, how lucky he was to be a part of such a close-knit group of men. He knew it wouldn't have mattered if he'd called Ro, Ball, or any of his other friends—they all would've been on their way up to Colorado Springs in a heartbeat if needed. They might not all work together on every mission, but Ryder knew without a doubt any one of the other men would lay down his life for him, as he would for them in return.

Ryder turned from the water cooler at a sound behind him to see Felicity standing in the entrance to the kitchen, looking unsure. Her short, black hair was sticking up in disarray, and her eyes were puffy with dark circles under them.

He clenched the glass of water in his hand tightly. He hated Joseph Waters with all he had in him. The man was a coward, and Ryder hated cowards. Oh, he didn't like anyone who preyed on those weaker than they were, but he hadn't come across anyone as manipulative, sneaky, and sadistic as Joseph in a long time.

He forced himself to relax, and took two steps to Felicity's side. He held out the glass of water he'd poured for her, and she reached for it. She smiled up at him, but Ryder saw right through her bravado. She'd held it together extremely well as he searched her place, made his call, and encouraged her to get ready for bed. But he could see she was at the end of her rope. Physically and mentally.

"Thanks," she said softly, and brought the glass up to her lips.

He waited until she'd drunk half the glass, then put his hand on the small of her back. "Time for bed, love."

She took a big breath, as if shoring up her courage, then asked, "Are you coming too?"

He eyed her critically.

Yeah, he wanted to be with her in her room, but it had to be her choice. And not because she was scared of Joseph Waters.

"He's not coming back tonight," Ryder said softly, meeting her gaze with his own intense one. "He can't get in through the windows, they're too high up. The only way anyone is getting into this apartment is through the front door. And even if that happens, I'll be here to keep him from getting to you. I can sleep on the couch just as I have every night."

"I know," she said immediately. "I have no doubt whatsoever that if Joseph came through that door, I would be in absolutely no danger because you're here. At one time in my life, I wasn't afraid to ask for what I wanted. No, to demand it. But as the years have gone by, I've gotten more and more reluctant to do that. And it pisses me off. It's ironic. I used to be the girl next door. Ready to take on the world. The harder I tried to be a badass, covering myself in tattoos, acting tough, dyeing my hair . . . the meeker I've become. It's as if I've let Joseph win."

Without looking, Felicity put the glass of water she'd been holding on the counter and pressed herself closer to Ryder. He didn't even try to hide his body's reaction to her closeness. His erection pressed against her stomach. When she didn't pull away, but reached up and put both her arms around his neck, he immediately tugged her all the way into him so they were touching from their thighs up to their chests.

"I'm sick of being that person, Ryder."

"What do you want, love?"

"You."

"Be more specific," he told her with a hint of steel in his voice. "I want you. Badly. But I'll give you whatever you say you want. If that's me taking you hard all night long, that's what you'll get. If you need sweet kisses and caresses, great, no problem. If all you can handle for now is me holding you, you got it. I can't read your mind, though. You need to tell me."

She bit her lip, and at that moment she looked like a nervous teenager on her first date.

"I want all of that . . . but I'm not sure . . . maybe just cuddles tonight? Baby steps? Is that okay?"

Ryder nodded immediately. "Of course that's okay. We can sleep out here if you want," he offered.

She immediately shook her head. "No. That couch sucks. I feel bad enough as it is that you've spent as many nights on it as you have. You've already seen my room. It's stupid to pretend you haven't. Besides, I need to tell you . . . well . . . everything. And I'd feel better doing it in my space. Where I'm comfortable."

Ryder squeezed her waist and kissed her forehead. "Go ahead. I'll be in shortly."

She looked up at him. "If you hate my space, don't tell me, okay?"

Ryder's brows drew down into a frown. "Why would I hate it?"

She shrugged a little self-consciously. "I don't know. It's just . . . it doesn't match the me I am now."

Her words were awkwardly phrased, but he knew what she meant. "From the glimpse I got, I'd say it matches you perfectly. Now, go. I'll be there in a few minutes." He punctuated his words with a squeeze, then took a step away from her.

She looked confused about his words, but did what he ordered, reaching out to pick up her glass of water before turning and padding to her room.

Ryder immediately went to the front door and checked the lock. Then he grabbed one of the chairs sitting next to a small table and tipped it against the door. It wouldn't keep anyone out, but it would make one hell of a racket if anyone tried to enter the apartment. Then he took the other chair and propped it against the guest-room door. As he'd told Felicity, Ryder was fairly certain no one could climb up the side of the building to get in through either of the bedroom windows, but he wasn't going to take any chances.

Last, he went into the guest bathroom in the hall and got ready for bed, just as he'd done every night since he'd been there.

As he stood in front of Felicity's bedroom door, he took a deep, calming breath. He felt as if he'd waited forever for this moment. At times he hadn't been sure he'd be able to break through Felicity's walls. But she was letting him in tonight. He'd make sure she didn't regret it.

He turned the knob and stepped into her space. He closed the door behind him, locking it for good measure. Then he spun around and stared at the woman he wanted more than he wanted his next breath.

She was sitting in the middle of her bed, looking unsure. Before he lost focus, Ryder let his gaze swing around the room.

He'd seen her room earlier when he'd searched the apartment, but purposely hadn't lingered, as much as he'd wanted to. Walking into her private space after being in the austere living area was like walking into the Garden of Eden after spending years in purgatory. The assault on his senses almost made him forget he was looking for any signs that Joseph Waters might still be in the apartment.

It smelled fresh and clean, as if she'd just done laundry. The scent of lilacs was, not surprisingly, stronger here than in the outer room. The riot of pastel colors around the area was calming. The quilt on the bed was thrown back, and Ryder wanted to run his hand over the obviously expensive pale-pink sheets on her bed to verify their softness. A softness he wanted under him as he held Felicity in his arms. It was quiet in her room as well; no sounds from the downtown square penetrated through the window high above the back alley. The only sense missing was that of taste, and Ryder knew that would be satisfied by Felicity herself. The taste of her lips against his, the perspiration of her skin as he ran his tongue over her body, and the ultimate pleasure of finding out what she tasted like as she came under his tongue.

He looked at the posters on the wall, the pictures on the dresser, the worn stuffed giraffe on the bed, the books on the floor. He took it all in, this time without having to worry whether or not Joseph Waters was lurking nearby. The difference between this room and the others in the apartment was shocking. While every other square inch was pristine, here in her room, chaos reigned.

Ryder smiled. He loved it. Every inch. *This* was the real Felicity. The mess here was exactly what he would've expected from someone as full of life as she was. He felt comfortable here. Relaxed.

His eyes came back to Felicity. She was biting her lip, and her brows were furrowed. Even as he watched, she chewed on her bottom lip uncertainly.

Not wanting her to stress for one more second about what he thought, Ryder quickly strode to the bed. He put a knee on the mattress, and she quickly scooted over. Without saying a word, he lay down and pulled her into his arms. He pulled up the sheet, which was just as soft and luxurious as it looked, and settled against the pillows.

At first, Felicity lay stiffly in his arms, her head resting on his shoulder, but as time passed, she slowly relaxed. Her arm tentatively moved across the black T-shirt over his belly to rest on his chest. She wiggled closer, getting comfortable. Then she finally sighed.

"Comfy?" he asked.

"Very."

"Good." He didn't say anything else, letting her take the lead on their conversation. He had a million questions, but as he'd told her earlier, he wouldn't push.

"I'm a slob," she said after a minute had passed.

He chuckled. "Naw. If you had more furniture in here, you'd be able to put all your books away."

Neither said anything else for a minute or so, then, as if she couldn't resist, Felicity asked, "So? You haven't said anything about my room. Don't you want to know why it's so different from the rest of my place?"

Ryder tightened the arm that was around her shoulders for a moment, then said, "I want to know anything you want to tell me. But you absolutely don't have to explain this room to me."

She lifted her head then. "I don't?"

"Nope."

"Why?"

"Because I can see the real you loud and clear when I look around this room."

She put her head back on his shoulder. "And who is the real me? I'm not sure I even know anymore," she said quietly, if not a little nervously.

"Underneath that badass exterior you try too hard to project is a hard-core science nerd. Who probably majored in math of some sort in college. Who loves a good sci-fi book. But along with that nerd is a woman who is a romantic at heart. From the flower posters on your wall to the soft pastel quilt on your bed. These sheets under us tell me that you're a woman who likes to be comfortable. And the pictures of the ones you love scattered around your space tells me that you'd do anything for a friend. Even leave if it meant keeping her and her children safe."

Ryder felt Felicity swallow several times as she tried to gain her composure. When she did finally talk, she blew him away with her strength.

"It was in college. My friend Colleen was dating Joseph. He was abusive—mentally and physically—but she refused to leave him. One night I called the cops when he was hurting her. When they arrived, Colleen denied anything was wrong. She refused to press charges, and since Joseph hadn't hit her anywhere the cops could see, they were helpless to do anything.

"He was really upset that I dared to interfere and started to make my life a living hell. He planted drugs in my apartment, which got me kicked out as well as expelled from school before I could graduate. I lost a job with an engineering firm I had lined up. The charges for dealing drugs were eventually dropped. But he killed Colleen, then he did his best to frame *me* for it.

"I was eventually cleared because Colleen was found beaten to a pulp with both her legs and arms broken. The coroner determined that whoever killed her had to have been strong enough to overpower her and then snap her bones. Joseph literally beat her to death, Ryder. With his bare hands." She shuddered and closed her eyes.

Ryder clenched his teeth to keep from swearing out loud. He didn't want to do or say anything that would make Felicity stop talking so he could get as much information as possible to his handler and make Joseph Waters pay for every single thing he'd done to the woman in his arms. *His* woman. He had no doubts about that whatsoever.

She continued her tale. "I moved back home with my adoptive mom. She took me in when I was seven, and at first, I was so scared she'd send me away. But from the very first day, she told me I was staying. When I came to her after Colleen was killed, she was so scared for me. She was the one who encouraged me to leave. Told me that Joseph wasn't going to stop coming after me. She even gave me what little savings she had to help me start a new life."

Felicity gestured to a picture across the room of a woman. "She was beautiful. Had long brown hair that I wished I had more than once instead of my blonde hair. Her eyes were so kind, it was the first thing I noticed about her when I first came to her house as a foster kid. She always had something nice to say about everyone . . . except Joseph. She hated him for what he was doing to me as much as I did. So I left with her encouragement. I called her on March third every year, the day she first brought me home. I used a burner phone so Joe couldn't track the call.

"After the first time he found me when I was living in San Antonio, I realized that I needed to get serious about hiding. I'd been using my real name and not being as careful as I should've been about using my mom's credit card. I used some of the money my mom gave me and bought myself a new identity. Megan Parkins was gone, and Felicity Jones was born. I had a Social Security number and a fake birth certificate, but I was scared to use them. Somehow using a different name and picture ID didn't seem too bad, but if I used that Social Security card, I'd feel like a criminal. So I lived off the radar. Paid cash for everything. Got jobs where I could get paid under the table. I started to work out more, because I was bored, and anything else cost money, but also because I think a part of me thought if I changed what I looked like on the outside, it would make me stronger on the inside. That being stronger would make me feel less vulnerable.

"I saved a lot of money. The more I saved, the less I wanted to spend. It felt like as long as I had the cash hidden in my stuff, the better off I was. I lived off cheap food and even cheaper crappy apartments. I eventually made my way up here to Castle Rock and met Cole when we literally ran into each other while jogging. I liked it here, and liked Cole. I took a chance and used the money I'd saved up to open Rock Hard Gym with him, and you know the rest."

"Tell me about your trip to Chicago earlier this year," Ryder said softly.

She turned over, putting her back to him, and Ryder immediately curled up behind her. He wrapped an arm around her waist and pulled her back into him. He propped his head on his other arm and leaned into her, nuzzling her hair. His larger body surrounded her, giving her his warmth as she continued her story.

"Every couple of days, I checked the Chicago news. Maybe in the hopes of reading something about Joseph getting arrested or something. But I saw an article about a fire in my old neighborhood. There was a picture of a burned-out shell of a house with a car half-burned sitting in the garage."

Her breath hitched with a sob, and Ryder tightened his arm, showing her his support the only way he could at that moment.

"It was my mom's house. They found her in her bedroom. Dead. The police suspected foul play, and I *knew* in my gut Joseph had murdered her."

Ryder could hear her sniffing and knew she was crying. His heart broke for her, and his hatred for the man who'd done this to her continued to grow.

"I had to go home for her funeral. I *had* to. I drove all the way out there and sat in the back of the church during the service. She had so many friends. So many, Ryder. The church was full. I even went to the graveside ceremony. I pretended to be there for someone else, sitting on a bench in front of a stranger's grave, but I never would've forgiven myself if I missed my mom's funeral. I killed her, Ryder. I might not've lit the match, but as surely as I'm lying here, I killed her."

Ryder turned her then. She stared up at him with her blue eyes swimming in tears. They fell out of the corners of her eyes and dripped into her hair next to her ears. She clutched his biceps as she lay under him staring into his eyes, her misery and self-loathing easy to see in the low light coming from the bathroom.

"No, love. You didn't kill her."

"I did. And I can't let it happen again. He'll kill Grace. Or her babies. Or you. I just can't—"

Ryder cut her off. "I hope he tries," he bit out.

That surprised Felicity. She blinked. "What?"

"I hope that fucker tries to kill me. I want to be face-to-face with him when I slit his throat. Listen to me, Felicity. You did *not* kill your mom. That motherfucker did."

"But if I hadn't stayed away for so long, he—"

"No," he interrupted again, not wanting to hear whatever bullshit she was thinking. "If you hadn't stayed away for so long, he would've killed *you*. You did everything right."

"But my mom is dead. I never got to see her again after I left. I miss her, Ryder. I miss her so much." Her tears started leaking as if a faucet had been turned on behind her eyes.

"I'm so sorry. Tell me about her. Everything. Every memory you've got. I want to hear them all."

She blinked up at him. "You want to hear about my mom?"

"Yeah, love. I want to know everything about her. How she smelled, and what your favorite memories of her are. What your life was like when she first brought you home. What she did for a living. What her favorite foods were. You haven't talked to anyone about her in years. Telling me about her will help you grieve, and remember her."

And she did. For an hour Felicity talked about her mother. Told Ryder every little thing about the woman who'd taken her in at an age most kids were past all hope of ever getting adopted. She cried. A lot. But she also laughed at some of the sillier stories she shared. When she was done, she looked up at Ryder and said, "Thank you."

They'd changed positions a few times in the last hour, and currently he was propped up on an elbow, holding his head in his hand next to her. He ran his free hand over her head and leaned forward and kissed her forehead. Then he turned to lie on his back and pulled her back into his side. "You're welcome. She sounds like an amazing woman."

"She was."

"He's going to pay for what he's done," Ryder said, knowing his voice was too harsh but not able to tone it down. "He's going to pay, and then we'll go back to Chicago and you can properly pay your respects to your mom. No hiding at the cemetery this time."

Felicity nodded against his shoulder. Ryder knew about grief. He'd grieved when his own mother was sick and when she'd died, but it wasn't the same. Felicity hadn't gotten to say goodbye. Hadn't seen her mom or felt her arms around her for the last decade. Joseph would pay for that and more.

"I'd like that."

Surprisingly, he felt the tension leave her body. As he'd hoped, talking about her mom had released some of the stress she'd bottled up since she'd been to Chicago.

"Has he done anything else?" he asked softly.

She nodded against his shoulder once more. "I got a note in the mail a couple of weeks ago. About the same time you came to town."

"Do you still have it? We might be able to get DNA or something off it."

She shook her head against him. "I threw it away."

Ryder forced his body to stay relaxed. "Anything else?"

"A newspaper clipping of Colleen's death. And of course the picture in my apartment tonight. And your slashed tires."

Ryder's thumb brushed back and forth on the warm skin at the small of Felicity's back. She hadn't protested when he'd slipped his hand under her T-shirt. In fact, when he'd begun stroking her, she arched into his touch and seemed to melt farther into his side.

He nodded. "Believe it or not, this is a good thing."

"It is?" Her words were almost slurred.

With the emotional turmoil she'd been through in the last couple of hours, Ryder wasn't surprised she was losing the battle to stay awake. "Yeah, love. The more he tries to mess with you, the better my chance of finding him and killing him are."

The last part slipped out. He hadn't meant to admit to her, again, that he was going to kill Joseph, but she didn't tense in the slightest.

"Good," she mumbled.

"Yeah, good," Ryder agreed. He said nothing else, letting Felicity finally sleep.

He stayed awake for a long time, simply holding her in his arms. She snored slightly, and even drooled a little on his shoulder, and he loved every second of it. *This* was the Felicity he wanted. The one who let all her shields down around him. Her leg shifted and hitched over one of his, and Ryder closed his eyes.

Yeah. He liked this. *Loved* it.

In her bed. Surrounded by everything that made Felicity who she was.

Joseph was a dead man walking. It was only a matter of time.

Chapter Eleven

A week later, Felicity wasn't sure she'd done the right thing by telling Ryder everything. She'd woken up the morning after she'd spilled her guts and had thought things would be awkward between them, but they hadn't been. When her alarm went off at its usual time, letting her know to get up so she could get her workout in, he'd simply kissed her on the forehead and slipped out of bed.

When she'd wandered out of her room after getting changed into workout clothes, he'd met her in the kitchen, looking as hot as ever, with a can of V8 juice, her usual morning beverage, and told her he'd meet the locksmith to take care of changing her lock and Cole would meet her downstairs for their usual workout.

Just when Felicity thought Ryder was going to ignore the intimacy they'd shared, he'd grabbed her hand when she turned to walk out of the kitchen and pulled her back into him. He'd kissed the hell out of her, and then had gently pushed her toward the door, saying, "Better not be late. Cole'll kick your ass even harder if you are."

The smile he'd bestowed upon her had carried her through the butt kicking Cole had given her in the gym.

She hadn't met the locksmith, but now had a brand-new shiny lock on her apartment door and a permanent shadow. If it wasn't Ryder or

Cole, it was one of the Anderson triplets. She wanted to be pissed, but couldn't. She felt safer with them watching her every move. Safer, but not completely secure. Especially when Grace had called that morning and told her that the cops had turned up at Ace Security to question Logan about a tip they'd received about a report of excessive force used against a client's ex-husband.

She knew it had been Joseph. Of course it was. It was how he operated. When she'd told Ryder, his jaw had tightened, but he hadn't blown up. Hadn't lost his shit. He'd merely shrugged and said, "Logan will handle it. From what I understand, my brothers are pretty close with the cops around here. If he needs backup, I'll call my handler and have him step in."

"Just like that?" Felicity had asked.

"Just like that," he'd returned.

That had been seven days ago. Now she was standing in her apartment with Ryder. She'd showered after her workout, and he'd made them a breakfast of omelets and bacon. She'd thought telling Ryder everything would make him stop obsessing about what he didn't know about her past and move their relationship along like any normal couple, but now it seemed like all he thought about was protecting her. And she didn't want that. She was ready for more. More than ready. But wasn't sure where Ryder stood.

"How about a break from things around here?" Ryder asked.

She tilted her head at him. "What kind of break?"

"Bailey is going to head down to Colorado Springs for another appointment with the tattoo artist that is doing the new ink on her back. Want to go?"

Felicity couldn't help the excitement that tore through her. "Yes," she said immediately. She loved Bailey. They'd bonded when the other woman had been stalked by her ex-gang-member boyfriend, and Felicity knew she'd found a kindred spirit. Felicity had given Bailey the name of the tattoo artist down in Colorado Springs who was transforming a horrible tattoo on Bailey's back into a beautiful work of art. "Is Joel going too?" she asked.

"No. Alexis and Blake are going to take him and two of his friends on a hike up to the top of Castle Rock today."

Felicity's brows raised. "All the way up there?"

Ryder chuckled. "Yup. They figured it'll tire them out, and after they get back and stuff the kids with pizza, they'll crash."

"They're probably right," Felicity agreed.

"And I feel like I should probably warn you . . . I'd like to talk to my buddies while we're down there," Ryder said, changing the subject slightly.

Felicity smiled. "I'll finally get to meet these elusive 'friends' you've been talking to on the phone?"

His lips quirked up, but didn't quite make it into a smile. "Yeah, love, you'll meet them. I feel like I should warn you, though, they're going to have some information about Joseph you may or may not want to hear."

She tilted her head as her smile died. "What are you saying?"

"I'm actually asking. Do you want to be in our conversation about him, or would you rather we discuss the situation when you're busy with Bailey at the tattoo shop?"

"You're asking?"

"Yeah. If it's too much and you can't handle any more right now, I'll make sure we have our talk before you get to the pool hall. If you want in on it, I'll hold them off until you get there."

"You'd do that?"

Ryder grabbed one of her hands and pulled her into him. She let out an *oof* when she crashed into his chest. "Fuck, yeah. This is your life we're talking about. I have no right to keep you out of it. But if you don't want to, or can't deal with it, I'll make sure you don't have to."

She liked that. A lot. "I want to be there," she told him.

"Then you will be."

Felicity looked up into Ryder's hazel eyes. They were looking at her with an intensity she hadn't seen in a long time. She and Ryder had slept in each other's arms for the last week, but for some reason, this seemed more intimate to her. One of his large warm hands had snuck under the hem of her shirt and was lying on her lower back. The other rested between her shoulder blades, holding her to him.

He brushed his thumb across the sensitive skin of her lower back, and his hazel eyes were fixed on hers.

"What?" she asked softly. "Why are you looking at me like that?"

"I've been around the world doing my thing. I saw women and children in some of the worst situations you could ever imagine. Some were completely broken, mere shells of who I imagine they used to be. Others were scared shitless. Still others were pissed way the hell off. I never knew how someone was going to react around me, or if I was with a team, us. But I've never really thought about how they *felt* about what happened to them. I only saw them for a short time, then passed them off to someone else to deal with the aftermath of their situation."

Felicity tilted her head, not sure what he was getting at.

"I always thought what I did was the hard part. Physically getting the women out of their situations, being shot at, shooting at others. Killing. But now I realize I've been wrong. Way wrong. What I did was in a lot of ways the easy part. Yeah, it was dangerous, but the situations the women were in were *always* dangerous. But now I realize that it's the continuing on after the rescue that's the hard part. You've shown me that."

"Ryder, I—"

He didn't let her finish her thought. He interrupted her with a kiss. It was short, but intense. Then he pulled back. "I admire the fuck out of you, Felicity. You don't deserve what he's doing to you.

All you did was try to help a friend. But with no experience, you've managed to keep ahead of him for a decade. That's amazing. You *will* be free of him."

"I hope so," she whispered. "But I'm not sure I know how to live a normal life."

"I'm used to getting a call every couple of weeks and running off to wherever I'm sent to track down and kill the dregs of humanity." Ryder shrugged a little self-consciously. "If you'll help me, I'll help you. We'll try to live a normal life together."

That sounded amazing to her. "Okay."

"Okay." Then he leaned down and kissed her again.

As they kissed, he picked her up and placed her on the counter. She spread her legs, inviting him to get closer to her. She felt feminine and desired as his hands caressed her sides and thighs as they kissed.

Way before she was ready, he pulled back reluctantly. "I need to call Nathan. He's waiting for me to let him know if we're going with him and Bailey down to the Springs."

Felicity looked up at him and licked her lips. She could still taste him on her and loved the desire she saw in his eyes as his gaze flicked from her lips to her eyes, then down her body.

"Maybe we should stay here instead," she suggested, at the same time pulling up his shirt to caress his bare chest. She also tightened her thighs around him, trying to hold him in place. His hard erection pressed against her, making a jolt of desire shoot through her body. "I know we need to find Joseph, but this . . . you feel good."

He pressed himself harder against the crotch of her jeans and spread his fingers across her belly while his thumb pressed hard against her clit.

She inhaled at his aggressive touch and arched her back. Ryder used his free hand to press against her chest until she had no choice but to lie back on the cool granite countertop. He slid his hand around to her back and helped her hold the position, her back arched, head back, legs spread, open to him.

"Ryder," she moaned as his thumb continued its assault on her body. She gripped his biceps, her fingers curled, her nails lightly digging into his muscles as they flexed with his movements.

"You have no idea how hard it's been for me to sleep next to you every night and not touch you like this," Ryder informed her.

"I . . . I wasn't sure you wanted me anymore."

"Not want you? Fuck, love, I've jacked off in the shower every morning just so I could walk upright."

She didn't answer with words, but simply arched her back a fraction of an inch more even as her feet inched upward and she hooked her ankles together at his ass.

Ryder tried to control the lust coursing through him. He wanted to rip off all Felicity's clothes and take her right there on the counter. Her tits were begging for his mouth, and feeling her feet press his hips harder against her core was driving him crazy.

"Tell me what you want," he ordered. He wasn't the kind of man to take anything that wasn't freely given. Not only that, but over the last week, he'd learned that a feisty Felicity was much more exciting to him than the scared and uncertain woman she'd been when he'd first met her.

He'd wanted her then, but his desire for her had grown exponentially as he got more and more pissed off at Joseph and what he'd done to her.

"I want to come," Felicity ground out. She lifted her head, and Ryder immediately moved his hand to support her neck. Her blue eyes were stormy. Her pupils huge with lust. She pressed her hips upward into his thumb. "I need it."

Without breaking eye contact with her, Ryder increased the speed of his thumb over her clit. He pressed his erection into the scalding heat between her legs, mimicking the act of making love as he caressed her.

To her credit, Felicity didn't look away from him. She held his gaze even as her fingernails dug into his arms. Her thighs tightened against him as she writhed under his touch between her legs.

For several moments they stared at each other as he brought her closer and closer to the edge, ignoring his own mounting lust. He knew she was on the verge of orgasm even before her eyes closed and her head dropped back as the muscles in her legs began to shake.

Ryder looked down her body just in time to see her stomach tighten with her impending orgasm. She clenched his hips with her thighs, dug her heels into his ass, and groaned as she exploded.

He'd never seen anything more beautiful in his life. She was fully dressed, wearing jeans and a T-shirt, which had hiked up above her stomach, and he wanted her more than he'd ever wanted another woman. As she continued to tremble under him, Ryder kept the pressure on her clit, pressing and rubbing even as he thrust against her as if he was actually inside her body.

Then it was his turn to close his eyes and groan as the mere thought of making love to her in the near future, on this very counter, and feeling her hot wet body around his cock, sent him over the edge.

When he opened his eyes and peered down at Felicity, he wasn't sure what he was going to see. Regret. Embarrassment. Awkwardness. None of those emotions would've surprised him. But what he saw in her gaze floored him.

Satisfaction. Contentment. A serenity he hadn't seen on her face since he'd met her.

"You okay?" he whispered as he finally moved his hand from between her legs. Even before she answered, he pulled her upright and clasped his hands at the small of her back, holding her to him. In return, she laced her own arms around his shoulders. He felt her fingers playing with the hair at his nape.

"I'm more than okay. Thank you."

Ryder knew he was grinning like a loon, but said, "It was my pleasure, love."

At his words, she shifted against him, obviously noting that he was no longer hard. "Was it?"

He wasn't even embarrassed. "Oh yeah. I can't even begin to tell you how amazing that was. How amazing *you* are."

Felicity unhooked her ankles and let her legs drop. Ryder stood back and helped her jump off the counter. He needed to change as much as she did, but when she took a step away from him to head to her room to change, he grabbed hold of her hand and brought it up to his lips. He kissed the palm and let his lips rest there for a prolonged moment before looking into her eyes and saying, "I like this side of you, love."

"What side?"

"The side that isn't afraid to ask for what she wants and needs. Now that I've seen her, I'm not going to let you hide her away from me again."

Felicity raised the hand he'd kissed and palmed his cheek before saying, "It's a good thing. Because she's a greedy bitch, and she's going to want to see, sooner rather than later, what you're packing down there." She gestured to his crotch with her head.

Ryder laughed as she grinned saucily at him and walked away, her hips swaying more sexily than he'd ever seen before.

Yeah, he liked this Felicity Jones. A fuck of a lot.

Chapter Twelve

Felicity sat next to Bailey in the tattoo parlor as the artist worked on the ink on her back. The crude tattoo that Bailey's ex-boyfriend had put on her was gone, and in its place a masterpiece was slowly emerging. There were three huge mountains and a river at their base. Mist was rising from the water, and the tattoo artist was currently working on shading in a beautiful sunset behind and around the mountain peaks. There were several birds embedded into the design, the same birds that Grace and Logan had on their own bodies. Felicity had one of the same bird designs put on her arm as Bailey was being worked on.

"How you doing?" Felicity asked her friend.

"I'm good. Surprisingly, the shading doesn't seem to hurt as much as the outlines of the mountains did."

"It's going to be so amazing when it's done, Bail," Felicity told her friend. "Seriously."

Bailey picked up her head and propped her chin on her hands as she pierced Felicity with a look. "Thank you. Now tell me what's going on with you and Ryder. I tried to get Nathan to talk to me on the way down, but he claims it's none of his business."

Felicity leaned back in the chair, picked at the bandage covering the new tattoo on her arm, and shrugged. "In a nutshell, a man who I've been trying to avoid has found me. He's pissed at something I did a decade ago. I was really scared at first, but now I think I'm just angry at the whole situation."

Bailey blinked. "What? Are you serious? Why didn't you tell all of us this before?"

"Because it wasn't an issue," Felicity said. "It wasn't until I drove home for my mom's funeral earlier this year that the guy found me. He followed me back to Castle Rock, or had one of his flunkies do it. He bided his time, and now he's been . . . I'm not sure of what word to use for what he's been doing."

"Stalking?" Bailey suggested a little aggressively.

Felicity shook her head. "No. Taunting. We both know he's in town and that he could simply kill me at any point. But he gets off on scaring women. Scaring me. So he's doing little shit to annoy me and try to break me."

Bailey's eyebrows drew down in concern. "But he won't, right?"

Felicity shook her head. "I can't deny I was freaked out at first. I wanted to run again. But Cole wouldn't give me the money I put into the gym to start it up. Then Ryder came into town." She shrugged once more. "Now I'm just pissed."

"And you and Ryder?"

Felicity pressed her lips together. "I like him."

"And?"

"I think he likes me back."

Bailey laughed then. "I don't think there's any 'think' about it. Nathan didn't have details, but he did tell me that Ryder has been sleeping at the gym with you for almost the last month."

"He's protecting me."

"Is that all?"

"Well, up until this morning, yeah."

"What happened this morning?" Bailey asked immediately, not missing the opening.

It had been a long time since Felicity had talked to a girlfriend about anything related to boys. It felt good. "He . . . we . . . well, let's just say I'm hoping that tonight we'll do more than just fall asleep in each other's arms."

Bailey held up a hand, and Felicity fist-bumped it as they both grinned.

"Do you remember what you told me about the Anderson brothers a while ago?" Bailey asked.

Felicity scrunched up her nose and shook her head.

"You said that you were sorry there weren't any Anderson brothers left for you." Bailey paused dramatically before continuing. "Looks like there *is* one more Anderson brother for you, after all."

Felicity just stared at Bailey for a second before her lips twitched. Then she smiled. Then she was laughing. She laughed until tears were streaming from her eyes. Bailey joined her, and the tattoo artist had to stop and hold the needle up and out of the way since her canvas was moving too much with her giggles.

When they'd finally calmed down enough for the tattooist to continue, Felicity said, "I had forgotten all about that. But what are the odds?"

Bailey stretched out a hand to her friend. Felicity grabbed it.

"I'm not sure I'm the best person to give advice. Grace is probably much better at it than I am, and you've known her longer, but if Ryder is anything like his brothers, you have *nothing* to worry about. I don't know your story or anything about the man who is taunting you, but you'll get through it. I have no doubt. You're strong and insightful, and Ryder looks at you like Nathan looks at me. When I'm having a bad day, struggling with my crappy past decisions, all it takes is waking up with Nathan's arms around me to make me realize how lucky I am. One thing I've learned is that I can't change my past. All I can do is look forward to my future. And for the first time in a really long time, I can say that I honestly do look forward to it. As long as Nathan is by my side, I can handle anything life throws at me . . . even a hormonal teenage brother who is determined to be a 'real man' like Nathan and his brothers are."

"Thanks," Felicity whispered. "I needed to hear that."

Bailey squeezed her hand, then winced as the tattooist's needle struck a sensitive spot on her back. "What are we doing after I'm done here?" she asked, obviously wanting to concentrate on something other than the tattoo on her back.

"Ryder said he wanted to take me to meet some of his friends here in Colorado Springs. You and Nathan are invited, but I wasn't sure what your plans were for the rest of the day."

"How do you feel about that? Are you okay with meeting his friends?"

Felicity knew what Bailey was asking, and she loved her all the more for it. The truth was, she had no problems with meeting Ryder's friends. He'd told her stories about the men over the last week, and she felt as if she already knew them. "I'm okay," she told Bailey. "If you want to come, that's cool, but if you want to get home and have some alone time with Nathan before you have to pick up your brother, I wouldn't blame you."

Bailey grinned, but gestured to her back with her eyes. "Not sure I'll be able to do much with this on my back."

"I'm sure you can be creative," Felicity fired back, feeling snarky.

Bailey stared at her for a moment before smothering a laugh, not wanting to make the tattoo artist have to pause again because she was laughing. "True. God, it's good to see you like this again."

"Like what?" Felicity asked.

"Like *you*. Outspoken. Full of comebacks. Your eyes not full of worry and fear. I swear to God you were one of the only reasons I didn't bolt back when I was sure Donovan was going to find me. You were so strong. I've hated seeing you so unsure and scared lately. So it's good to have you back."

"It's good to *be* back," Felicity said honestly. And it was. She felt one hundred percent stronger with Ryder at her side. She knew without a doubt that with Ryder next to her, she was safe, but she also knew Joseph better than anyone. Ryder couldn't be with her every second of every day. Joseph would wait until the perfect moment to strike and was going to get to her, eventually. But she was done cowering in fear. She didn't know what he had planned, but nothing she did would speed it up. He'd act in his own time, and no one else's. Her new attitude felt liberating.

"If it's truly okay with you, I think I'll take you up on your suggestion and take Nathan back to our house and have my wicked way with him," Bailey said with a grin, as if she really was thinking about all the ways she could make love to her man without being on her back.

The two friends smiled at each other. The tattoo artist sat back and patted Bailey's arm. "That's it for today. I think one more session to even out the shading and add in the little details you want, and we'll be done. Wanna see it?"

Bailey nodded eagerly. Felicity got up and went to stand behind her.

She heard her friend's breath catch as she saw the additional work that had been done on her back. "I can hardly believe it," she said in a whisper. "I can't tell the other tattoo was there at all."

"And *I* can't believe some asshole put that shit on you in the first place. Fucker."

With wide eyes, both Bailey and Felicity looked over at Alicia, the incredibly talented tattoo artist who had been working on her art for the last three sessions. She hadn't ever had one comment about what she was covering up, except to say she'd easily be able to make it disappear.

"What?" the woman asked a little belligerently. "If you must know, I was so upset after that first session that I got shitfaced drunk. My girlfriend had to talk me off the ledge. I wanted to hotfoot it up to Denver and find anyone who ever called themselves an Inca Boy and kill the motherfuckers myself. Oh, and Bailey, I'll cover up whatever other ink you want for free too. Us women have to stick together."

"Oh . . . uh . . . thanks."

"See you next time," Alicia said, waving off Bailey's gratitude. Then she spun around and went up to the front of the store, most likely to get her next appointment.

Felicity's wide eyes met Bailey's. Alicia hadn't ever really said much about the tattoo she'd been tasked with covering up, and Felicity hadn't thought she had much of an opinion about it. Guess she'd been wrong.

"Everything go all right?" Ryder asked after Felicity had said her good-byes to Bailey and Nathan at the tattoo shop. She and Ryder were on their way to a pool hall/bar called The Pit. Apparently it was where he and his friends hung out whenever they weren't out on a job. Each of the six men had "regular" jobs as well as being hired mercenaries and used the pool hall as a place to relax and even to have meetings about upcoming and previous jobs they'd done.

"Yeah," she said, answering Ryder's question. "Bailey's tattoo is amazing. Alicia is a true artist."

"You get a new one too?" Ryder asked, gesturing to the small bandage on her forearm.

Felicity nodded. She fingered the bandage. "A bird like Grace and Logan have. I know it's their thing, but I talked to Grace a while ago, and she said she wouldn't mind if I got one too."

"I can see that," Ryder said immediately. "You guys are as close as sisters."

"We are," Felicity agreed. "I can't imagine not being able to see her every day."

As if he could read her mind, Ryder said, "You won't have to. We're gonna make it so you can put even more roots down in Castle Rock so you never have to leave."

She smiled weakly at him. "I hope so."

Ryder didn't try to placate her. He simply rested one of his big hands on her leg and squeezed. He left his hand there until they pulled into the parking lot of a hole-in-the-wall building.

An old wooden sign hung crookedly on the side of the building proclaiming that they'd arrived at The Pit. A picture of a set of three pool balls was next to the lettering. There was only one window in the front of the building, and it looked as if it had never been cleaned.

She stared at the ramshackle building in dismay and turned to Ryder when he began to talk.

"It looks like a piece of shit, but that keeps the yuppies and college kids away," he said softly. "It's not as bad on the inside as it looks from out here."

"God, I hope not," Felicity said before she could stop herself. Then she slapped a hand over her mouth and mumbled, "Sorry, that was rude."

Ryder merely smiled. He climbed out and walked around to her side of his sports car. He held out his hand. "Nathan had the same reaction, and by the time we left to get the two of you, he was a convert. Come on, love. You can see for yourself."

She took his proffered hand and couldn't help but marvel at his strength as he pulled her upward out of her seat and into his side as easily as if she weighed no more than a child. He closed the door and beeped the locks as he wound his arm around her waist and pulled her into his side.

Felicity snuggled in close, loving being near him. She'd missed him today. Which was crazy because they'd only been apart a couple of hours. But since they'd been together practically twenty-four/seven over the last couple of weeks, she'd gotten used to him being around. Close by.

Ryder held open the surprisingly thick door for her and gestured for her to enter the dimly lit bar ahead of him. She walked in and stopped, letting her vision adjust from the bright Colorado sunshine to the darkness of the interior of the building. Ryder had been right, it wasn't a complete dive inside.

It was surprisingly big. There was a large open room with tables and chairs sprinkled sporadically around the area. Felicity could see a door leading into a back room that was filled with row after row of pool tables. At this time in the afternoon, there weren't a lot of people there, but she could still hear the clink of pool balls hitting each other emanating from that back room. A large bar ran along the right side of the room, and she noticed a huge bear of a man standing behind it, smiling at them. Before she could decide if she wanted to risk smiling back, Ryder squeezed her waist.

"Come on," Ryder said into her ear. "I want to introduce you to Dave before you meet the rest of the guys."

Felicity shivered at the feel of Ryder's breath on her ear. For a split second she wanted to tell him that she didn't want to meet his friends, after all. That she didn't care about Joseph. She'd been looking over her shoulder for so long, she'd gotten used to the threat Joseph posed. She wanted to think about something else. About Ryder. Wanted to tell him that she wanted to go straight home. To her bed. With him. But she took a deep breath and forced herself to walk calmly next to Ryder as he steered her to the bar.

Ryder grinned down at her, as if knowing exactly what she was thinking. She decided he had to be able to read minds when he leaned down and whispered, "Don't worry, as much as I like my friends, I'm not about to spend all day shooting the shit with them when I'd rather have you all to myself back at your place."

Goose bumps rose on her arms at his words, but she concentrated on putting one foot in front of the other so she didn't fall flat on her face. Tripping over her own feet wasn't exactly the first impression she wanted to give his friends.

Ryder steered her over to the large bar, and once again she was struck by the openly friendly look on the bartender's face as they neared. He was tall, probably a few inches over six feet. His hair was cut fairly short on his head, but he had a short beard that covered the bottom half of his face. There were speckles of gray interspersed with the black. His lips were large, his nose looked like it had been broken a few times, and she could see a long scar trailing down the side of his neck, disappearing into the neckline of the tight black T-shirt he wore. He was dark skinned, either from his heritage or simply from being in the sun, Felicity couldn't tell. His arms were covered in dark tattoos, every single one black, with not one splash of color among them.

All in all, he was an imposing man, one she would definitely not want to meet in a dark alley. He looked like he could be a hired goon for someone like Joseph Waters . . . which didn't make her feel too comfortable to meet him.

"It's about time you brought your woman down here to meet us," the large man boomed.

Ryder didn't comment on the other man's words, but instead simply said, "Dave, I'd like you to meet Felicity Jones. Felicity, Dave. The best bartender Colorado Springs has . . . bar none . . . pun intended."

Felicity bravely stuck out her hand. If Ryder wasn't concerned about her meeting his friend, then she needed to stop thinking about the large man hauling her over the bar and slitting her throat. It wasn't nice, and she trusted Ryder implicitly. "It's nice to meet you."

The other man grabbed hold of her proffered hand, engulfing it with both of his huge hands. "You're all the guys have been able to talk about," he gushed. "And you're as beautiful as Ace said you were. Welcome to The Pit. Anything you want to drink is on the house . . .

unless you're a lush, then I'll have to cut you off at some point, but I doubt you are because Ace wouldn't be with someone who would drink excessively. I—"

"You wanna give my girl her hand back, Dave?" Ryder interrupted.

The bartender looked confused for a moment, then dropped her hand he'd been shaking nonstop as he'd been talking. "Sorry, sorry." He chuckled. "I have a tendency to ramble sometimes. Ignore me."

Felicity grinned. Her earlier fears that Dave could be a hit man had disappeared from almost the moment he began speaking. He had a low, rumbly voice, and he was large, really large, but he acted more like a big kid than a rough-and-tough bartender. She nodded to his arms. "I like your ink."

Dave beamed and held out an arm. "Thanks! Got my first one the day I turned eighteen and haven't looked back since. Every time I get a new one, the artist tries to talk me into throwing some color on there, but I like the black. Don't need no red, blue, or yellow messing up what it's taken me years to accomplish."

"The guys in the back?" Ryder asked as if he was used to Dave's random comments. He put his arm back around Felicity.

"Yup. They've been waiting for you to get here."

"Great." He looked down at Felicity. "What do you want to drink, love?"

"Just water . . . if that's okay."

Ryder kissed her temple, then pulled back to look at her. "Of course it is. Why wouldn't it be?"

Felicity shrugged. "We're in a bar. Water's not exactly standard fare."

"Fuck standard fare. You want to drink Kool-Aid, I'm sure Dave would find a way to make that happen."

"Damn straight," Dave piped up from behind the bar. "Don't have any sugar powder right now, but I can make sure to have it next time if you want it."

Felicity smiled at him. "Thanks, but just water is great."

"You want it in a glass to make it look like it's alcohol?"

Felicity tilted her head in question. "Why would I?"

The bartender shrugged. "Sometimes it keeps others from being nosy and asking why you aren't drinking. There are a few recovering alcoholics who like to shoot pool that do that. It lets them blend in and play pool in peace."

"I'm good. A regular glass is fine. Thanks."

Dave shook his head. "Ladies in this bar don't get water in a glass unless they specifically request it." He reached under the bar and came up with a bottle of cold water, still dripping from the ice in whatever cooler he pulled it out of. "It's much harder to slip something into a capped water bottle than an open glass." He broke the seal on the plastic bottle, but kept the cap on, before handing it across the bar to Felicity.

"I hadn't thought of that. Thanks."

"You're welcome. Ace?"

"Whatever's on tap is fine."

Within seconds, Dave set a pint on the scarred bar for Ryder.

"Later, Dave."

"Later. It was great to meet you, Felicity. Don't be a stranger," Dave called as Ryder steered them toward the back room with all the pool tables.

She waved with her free hand, then looked up to Ryder as she heard him chuckle. "What?"

"He likes you."

"Cool. I like him too."

They entered the large room in the back, and Ryder immediately turned to the right. There were a few tables set up around the room around the pool tables. There were a few groups playing pool, but it was the table with six men sitting around it that immediately held Felicity's attention.

She suddenly wasn't sure she wanted to meet Ryder's friends. She could tell with one glance the men at the table weren't your average Joes. As she and Ryder walked toward the table, they all stood. Felicity gulped and stopped in her tracks.

"What's wrong?" Ryder asked, looking all around them for whatever had alarmed her.

"I think I changed my mind," she said softly. "Maybe I'll go talk to Dave while you have your meeting. You can catch me up on the way back up to Castle Rock."

Ryder looked from her to his friends, then back down at her. He smiled. "They're harmless," he soothed.

"Harmless my ass," Felicity muttered under her breath.

But of course Ryder heard her. His smile grew wider. He moved until he was standing in front of her and blocking her view of his friends. He took her head in both his hands and tilted her face up to his own. "What happened to my badass, not-scared-of-anything Felicity?"

"I'd be stupid not to be scared of a group of men who look like your friends."

Ryder moved and grabbed the hand that wasn't holding her bottle of water. He held it up between them and fingered her pinkie. Then he looked into her eyes and said, "You'll have them wrapped around your little finger even before you open your mouth."

Felicity shook her head and bit her lip.

"You will. And you know why?"

"Why?" she whispered, loving the feel of his calloused fingers against her own.

"Because you're with me."

"And that's all it takes? Do they like all your female friends?"

"I've never brought another woman here before, love. You're the first."

She gaped up at him.

"But that's not the only reason they'll bend over backward to do whatever it takes to put you at ease." He didn't give her a chance to ask why. "Every single man at that table abhors violence against women. They'd sooner hurt a puppy than do anything to make you feel uncomfortable or out of place. Trust me, Felicity."

She swallowed visibly, then nodded.

"But, with that being said, if you feel as if the conversation gets too intense, or you don't want to hear anything more about Joseph, all you need to do is let me know. Then you can go and sit with Dave until we're done. He'll make sure you're safe."

And that made Felicity's back straighten. She wanted to know what they knew. *Needed* to know. These were Ryder's friends. She was safe here. "I'm good. Let's go see what they have to say."

Ryder didn't pull away immediately. He continued to stare down into her eyes.

"What?" Felicity whispered.

"When I made the decision to meet my half brothers, I knew my life was going to change, but I had no idea how much. I feel like I've waited my whole life for you. That everything I've done, the person I became in order to do my job as a mercenary was so I could be right here, right now, to protect you."

"Ryder," Felicity protested.

"I'm standing here, about to meet with a group of men I've known for years, trust with my life, who I haven't seen in a while. And all I want to do is throw you over my shoulder and take you back to the gym and lock ourselves in your room and bury myself inside your body so far that neither of us will be able to remember a second we weren't together."

Felicity felt her body weep for the man baring his soul in front of her. "Yes," she whispered, not able to get any other words past the lump in her throat.

"Tonight," Ryder said firmly.

"Yes," Felicity repeated.

He didn't move for a long moment, but simply stood in front of her as if memorizing every feature on her face. "No matter what we find out when we go home, you're going to be mine tonight. In every way."

He wasn't asking, but Felicity answered anyway. "Yes," she said for the third time. She didn't like the "no matter what we find" thing, but she knew that being away from the gym meant Joseph could leave another nasty surprise for her. But fuck him. For once in her life she was going to take what she wanted and damn the consequences.

Joseph Waters wasn't going to win. No way.

Chapter Thirteen

Ryder stopped short in front of the table and gave a general chin lift to his buddies. He pulled Felicity to his side and wrapped an arm around her waist. He tugged her into him, and she stumbled, turning sideways to keep from falling, not that he would've let her. Her front was plastered to his side now, and he could feel her quick breaths on the skin of his neck.

"Felicity, I'd like you to meet my friends." He nodded at each man as he introduced them. "Gray, Meat, Arrow, Black, Ball, and Ro."

Each of the men in question smiled at Felicity and gave her a small chin lift.

"Hi," Felicity said softly. "It's good to meet you all." Then she looked up at Ryder. "Please tell me those aren't their real names."

He chuckled. "No, love. But it's what we call each other."

She scrunched up her nose and looked at Meat. "I don't care what you and Ryder call each other, but I can*not* call you Meat. I just can't."

Meat snorted. "You can call me by my real name, Hunter."

She pantomimed wiping her brow. "Whew."

Ryder smiled. As the group sat back down, he introduced his friends using their given names this time. "You can call them whatever you're most comfortable with, love. Gray is Grayson. You know Meat is Hunter. Arrow is Archer, Black is Lowell, Ball is Kannon, and Ro is Ronan."

He watched as Felicity thought about it for a moment, then nodded. "Okay, I can manage Gray, Arrow, Black, and Ro. But it's gonna have to be Hunter and Kannon for you two, sorry."

It was obvious his friends thought Felicity was hilarious by the grins he rarely saw on all of their faces.

Gray leaned across the table and speared Felicity with his gaze. "It's good to finally meet you. Ace has been telling us about you since the night he met you."

Her surprised gaze turned to Ryder. "He has?"

"Yup," Meat said. "First call I had with him, he told me he'd met his future wife."

Even as Felicity blushed, Ryder warned, "Enough."

Arrow shrugged. "You have to understand, Felicity, we aren't easily impressed. We've seen and done too much. So for you to have made such an immediate impact on Ace, we knew you were special."

"I said, enough," Ryder growled. "Fuck, you keep this up, she'll be running screaming from here wondering what in the fuck she's gotten herself into."

The guys all laughed, and Ryder ground his teeth together. His friends were going to ruin his relationship before it could even start. Just as he was about to stand up and haul Felicity out of there, regardless of the fact they hadn't talked about her situation yet, he felt a slight pressure on his thigh. He looked down and saw Felicity's hand resting there.

He glanced up at her face and saw she was smiling.

Relieved, he covered her hand with his own.

"Not that I'm not enjoying your amusement at my expense . . . but can we please get the topic of Felicity's asshole stalker out of the way before we continue talking about my love life?"

The men around them sobered at the reminder of why they were there.

Ro leaned his elbows on the table. "Joseph Waters. Thirty years old. Grew up in Chicago. Got his business degree from Northwestern. Six feet tall. Never been married, although he's dated a lot, and more than one girlfriend has disappeared."

Ball took up the narrative. "We haven't been able to track down his parents yet. We think they must have different last names."

Felicity spoke up then. "His dad is some sort of bigwig in Chicago. I don't know his name, but my old roommate told me that he had a lot of power."

"Joseph has been a person of interest in two disappearances, but both times he was cleared by someone in the Chicago PD, and the cases still haven't been solved," Black noted.

"He's on the payroll of a company called Tyson Enterprise in Chicago, but I haven't been able to find exactly what it is that he does there," Arrow added.

Right then, Ryder's phone rang. He pulled it from his pocket and looked down. He held it up and said, "Rex." Then he clicked it on and placed it in the middle of the table.

"Hey, Rex. This is Ace. The rest of the guys are here. And Felicity too."

"Hello, Felicity," a melodious and deep voice from the phone said. "I'm sorry to make your acquaintance this way, but it's good to meet you."

"Same," she replied.

"Did you find out anything more about Joseph Waters?" Ace asked.

"Joseph Waters," Rex began in a tone that was decisively colder than a moment ago, "is the son of Garrick Watson. The man claims to be a Mob boss, but he's really just a big fucking bully."

"Why haven't we heard of him?" Ro asked.

"Because he mostly keeps to himself in Chicago. Hasn't tried to branch out, and sticks to intimidation of the local businesses and running guns and drugs. He's worked with a couple of local biker gangs, but thus far hasn't dipped his toes into anything that would put him on my list."

There was silence around the table, and Felicity leaned into Ryder and said quietly, "I don't understand. What list?"

Rex answered her question. "We'll never get all the illegal drugs or guns off the street. Intimidation isn't good, but it's not as bad as human trafficking. Or kidnapping. Or stalking. Or pimping. Women and children are what my mercenaries are concerned about, Felicity. Taking down the assholes who seek to abuse and exploit the fairer sex. If men want to shoot each other over some stupid dispute over territory, that's their issue. But I cannot overlook violence against children. And using a woman for their own pleasure without her consent is weak and disgusting."

Ryder could see the confusion in Felicity's eyes. He tried to clarify. "Mountain Mercenaries only takes jobs involving women and kids, love."

"But, men are abused too. Look at your own father."

Ryder pressed his lips together and fought to figure out how to respond to her in a way she'd understand. Black came to his rescue.

"It's not that we don't care about men being hurt and abused, Felicity. For example, if we get sent in for a hostage recovery and there happens to be men there as well as women and kids, we'll liberate them too. But, Rex has made it clear what his operation concentrates on. He's gotten a reputation, and many times he's the first person who is contacted when a situation arises. The government, the wealthy, the politically motivated, they all contact Rex when we're needed. But there are plenty of other mercenary groups that aren't as picky and will hire themselves out no matter what the job, but not us."

"As I said," Rex continued as if he hadn't been interrupted, "I keep my eye on Garrick Watson, but he hasn't given me any reason to care one way or another what he does in his corner of Chicago."

"Until now," Ryder said succinctly.

"Until now," Rex agreed. "The man has no use for women. He runs his operation with his brothers. None of them are married. He doesn't sell women, isn't involved in trafficking, and even though he's a mean son of a bitch, and ruthless, he doesn't use children or families as leverage when extorting money from local businesses. When he was twenty, he *was* married for a short time. His wife had a son, but unfortunately, died in childbirth."

"Joseph," Ryder said.

"Yes. Joseph Waters. He was given his mother's maiden name as an added layer of protection. Garrick knows that many of his enemies wouldn't hesitate to use the boy against him. Joseph was raised in the family. Was taught the ways of their local empire, but somewhere along the line, he went off the rails. Garrick is not happy with his son. More than once he's had to bail him out of trouble, both figuratively and literally. Rumor on the streets is he's ready to wash his hands of his son, once and for all. He's brought too much negative attention to Garrick's operation and doesn't seem to grasp the basic tenet of the entire operation."

"And what's that?" Felicity asked quietly.

"Discretion," Rex said. "I've only talked to Garrick once, in regard to a mission I was considering taking on. There was a rumored shipment of women from the Philippines that was supposed to arrive via truck in his area. I contacted him and strongly suggested that he might want to make sure it was diverted. I managed to convince him that if his goal was to be discreet, that wasn't the way to do it, as I would make it my goal in life to bring down everything he'd worked so hard to build up."

"Holy shit," Felicity breathed. "What happened?"

"He gave me the particulars of that shipment and where my men could intercept it. We haven't talked since, and I've left him alone. He knows where I stand on the subject of the abuse of women and children and hasn't attempted to cross the line. As I said, he doesn't want any attention brought to his little operation. He's a big fish in his small pond of Chicago and has no ambition to expand . . . or get on my bad side."

"So . . . Joseph Waters?" Ryder asked. "He's in Castle Rock and gunning for Felicity."

"Yeah. I'll be having a word with his father," Rex said in a deadly tone.

"That's not good enough," Ryder said hotly. He knew Felicity was looking at him with wide eyes, but he continued. "Talking to Daddy isn't going to make his son back off. He's obsessed. Dangerous."

"I'll excuse your tone this time, because I know you're worried about your woman, but be careful, Ace," Rex warned.

Ryder struggled to keep his temper in check. In all the years he'd been working for Mountain Mercenaries, he'd never spoken to his handler with the kind of disrespect he was showing right now. He took a deep breath. "My apologies, Rex."

Not acknowledging his words, Rex simply said, "Do what you've been doing. Stay close to Felicity. Stay alert. Garrick isn't going to be happy that he's on my radar again. He'll rein in his son."

"And if he doesn't?" Ryder asked.

"Then Garrick will find out what having me up in his business means. I'll ruin him. He won't have a penny to his name, and he'll be run out of Chicago faster than you can snap your fingers."

"Can he do that?" Felicity mouthed to Ryder.

He nodded. "You'll let me know if you find out any updated information?" Ryder asked his handler.

"Of course. Felicity?" Rex asked.

"I'm here," she said.

"I'm sorry for what you've been through over the last decade. No woman should feel so threatened that she has to leave everything she knows. I hate that you've been on your own for so long, but you aren't anymore. Ace is a good man. He'll keep you safe."

"I know he'll do everything he can," she said quietly, not taking her gaze from the man at her side.

"I'll be in touch," Rex said, then the line went silent.

Ryder reached out and grabbed his phone, clicked it off, and stuck it back in his pocket.

"Now . . . how can we help you?" Gray asked Ryder. "What do you need from us?"

"Information," he said immediately. "I've got Felicity covered. My brothers and her friend Cole are watching over her when I can't. So far he's only done little annoying shit. But I have a feeling he's going to be pissed after talking with Daddy and will also likely get impatient that he's not seeing the reaction from Felicity that he wants."

"And what's that?" Ro asked.

"Fear."

Ball turned to Felicity. "You aren't scared?"

"I'm terrified," she returned immediately. "But I'm more pissed. I like Castle Rock. Love my friends, my godsons, my business. And I'm sick of running. So I'm gonna fight. If that bastard thinks I'm going to run again, he's wrong."

"You know, I'm cooler than Ace," Meat said suggestively. "You could come over to my place and—"

Black shut up the other man with a smack to the back of his head. "Shut the fuck up, Meat."

Felicity giggled.

Ryder sat back and watched his woman relax around his friends. He liked it. A lot.

His friends were all large men. Muscular. Fully capable of killing another human with their bare hands. But they were treating Felicity as if she was a little sister. For the most part, keeping their language clean, putting her at ease. He would miss them when he moved up to Castle Rock, but he knew without a doubt he and Felicity would be making many trips down to the Springs to hang out at The Pit and to catch up. He might be quitting the mercenary job, but if any of these men needed him, he'd be there for them in a heartbeat.

"You ready to go home?" Ryder asked Felicity during a lull in the conversation.

"You don't want to play a game of pool?" she asked. "Hunter challenged you, you know."

"I have better things to be doing up in Castle Rock than hanging out with my friends and beating their asses at pool." Ryder watched as her pupils dilated at his words. He ignored the good-natured ribbing that floated around him. It was as if he and Felicity were the only two people in the world at the moment. He held his hand out to her, his palm up, eyebrows raised in challenge.

"Sorry, guys," she told his friends without looking away from him. She put her hand in his. "I'm going to take Ryder home and tuck him into bed."

His friends hooted and hollered with laughter, and even Ryder had to smile.

He glanced at his friends as he stood, hauling Felicity up next to him, then bending and tucking his shoulder into her belly. He threw her over his shoulder and chuckled as she gasped in surprise, then burst out laughing.

"You know how to get ahold of us," Gray told him. "Let us know how we can help."

"Will do," Ryder reassured him. Then he turned and headed for the exit.

He was still smiling as Felicity called out a goodbye to Dave as he strode without pausing toward the front door of the bar.

"Come back anytime," Dave called out.

Ryder didn't stop until he was at his 370Z. He flexed his shoulder and brought Felicity down until she was standing in front of him with her back to the passenger-side door. She had a huge smile on her face, which was flushed from hanging upside down over him. As much as he wanted to throw her in the car and hustle her up to her apartment, he needed to make sure she wasn't upset over anything that she'd just heard first.

"You okay?"

The smile stayed on her face as she said, "Yeah, Ryder. I'm good."

"Even knowing what me and my friends do?"

Her smile slowly died, and a look of seriousness spread across her face. He'd never seen her look so serious before. "Ryder, I already knew the kind of man you were before I stepped foot in that pool hall. But in case I didn't, your friends and that Rex guy made it more than clear— you're a hero. I don't know how many people you've saved, but I know every one of them would throw themselves at your feet in thanks if they could."

"I'm no hero, love. I've killed a lot of people."

She waved her hand in the air as if his words were a pesky fly. "Assholes who deserved to die."

"It truly doesn't bother you?"

She shook her head. "No. If it comes to it, I want you to shoot Joseph between the eyes and make sure he's dead. I don't trust that if arrested, he'll stay in jail. Not with his connections, and apparently his father's as well. I can't tell you how many times I wish I had a gun so I could kill him myself."

Ryder's eyebrows shot up at her words. "That's not you, love. You don't like to kill the mice that make their way into the gym every now and then. I've seen the humane traps you've set out for them."

"The mice never did anything to me. They're just doing what they're destined to do. But Joseph is a horrible human being. He deserves to die. Seriously, Ryder. All I want is to live my life in peace, and I don't think he'll ever let me do it as long as he's alive. Promise me if you get the chance, you'll kill him. But only if you won't get in trouble for it. I'd hate for *you* to end up in jail for getting rid of that asshole. I don't think conjugal visits would be as satisfying as what we're hopefully going to be doing tonight."

Ryder choked back a laugh. Figured his Felicity could go from talking about him killing someone to them making love in the space of a breath. "If at any time you need to change the outcome of the night, all you have to do is say so," he felt compelled to say, even though if she did, he'd end up with the worst case of blue balls a man had ever felt.

Felicity stood up on her tiptoes and pulled his head down to hers. She brushed her lips over his once, lightly, and her warm breath feathered over his lips. "Nothing could make me *not* want you buried deep inside me tonight."

He was kissing her deeply as the last word was leaving her lips. His tongue swept in and out of her mouth, mimicking what he would be doing with his cock as soon as he got her on her back on her bed.

It was her hand on his rock-hard dick that brought him back to where they were and what they were doing. He reached down and grabbed her wrist, pulling it off his crotch and holding it firmly at the small of her back.

She wiggled against him, rubbing her erect nipples against his T-shirt. "Ryder," she complained. "I want you."

"And you'll get me. But it won't be in the parking lot of The Pit. Behave," he told her sternly, knowing the tenderness in his gaze belied his words.

She leaned up and kissed his chin. Then the crease of his jaw. "Take me home," she said quietly between kisses. "Make love to me."

Without a word, Ryder reached for the handle of the car door. He pressed her into the seat and jogged around the back of the vehicle to his side. He sat and looked over at the woman who would soon be his in every sense of the word.

Felicity was sitting with her seat belt on, with one leg hitched up on the seat. If she'd been wearing a skirt, he could push up the hem and stroke her . . . He cut off his thoughts.

They had about an hour drive, and he needed to be able to think about more than sinking into her hot, wet body as he did it. Ryder started the engine and smiled over at Felicity. "Talk to me."

"About what?" she asked, running her fingers up and down the seam of her jeans suggestively.

"About anything other than how many times you're going to come for me tonight," he said tightly.

She laughed then. A deep chuckle that held no fear. No worry. It was a sound he wanted to hear for the rest of his life. As she began to talk about babies Nate and Ace and how glad Grace was that they were sleeping through the night, Ryder smiled.

He should be worried about Joseph and what might be waiting for them when they got back to Castle Rock, but he couldn't. Tonight he'd make Felicity Jones his in every way. Nothing could ruin his good mood.

Chapter Fourteen

He'd been wrong. Joseph Waters *could* ruin his good mood. Ryder had pulled around the back of the gym and parked next to Felicity's PT Cruiser. The white envelope under her windshield wiper shone like a beacon.

He managed to get out of his car and to the envelope before Felicity. He gingerly picked it up using a corner of his shirt so as not to disturb any trace evidence or fingerprints that might be on it, and peeked inside.

His heart stopped beating for a moment, before starting up again twice as fast as before.

The drive up from Colorado Springs had been intimate and pleasurable. Felicity had been relaxed and flirty. They'd talked about nothing deep for the entire trip. No talk of killing anyone. No talk of Joseph Waters or his father. She'd told him more stories about her mom, and he'd reciprocated. It was . . . normal. And he'd liked it.

But now he was looking into an envelope at the contents he knew, *knew*, would upset Felicity. Possibly even make her revert back to the scared, ready-to-bolt headspace she'd been in when he'd first met her.

"What is it?" Her voice didn't waver, but the lightness that had been in it for the last couple of hours was gone.

"You don't need to see this," Ryder told her, closing the envelope and pulling out his phone. He needed to call the cops. Continuing to report Joseph's crazy wouldn't make him stop, but when Ryder killed him, it would assist in making sure it was a clear case of self-defense.

Felicity put a hand on his arm. Her hand was warm on his skin, and he raised his head to look her in the eyes.

"Every time I've received one of his 'gifts,' I've been alone. I didn't have anyone to lean on. I'm not super thrilled to see what he's done this time, but it's not like we didn't expect it. I know you're upset, but maybe I can figure out what he's planning by seeing whatever he left. He loves to taunt me." She shrugged. "It's what he does."

Ryder ground his teeth together and tried to come up with a reason she shouldn't see what was in the envelope. She didn't give him a chance.

"Please, Ryder. Whatever's in there isn't going to change our plans for the night. I'm not letting him get to me anymore. We'll deal with this shit, then go upstairs and climb in my bed, just like we've done every night in the last week. Except this time, I'm going to get to do all the things I've dreamed about doing to you since the moment I saw you."

Without a word, Ryder palmed the back of her head and brought her face to his. He kissed her as if he needed her to breathe. And it felt like he did. He'd never wanted a woman as badly as he wanted Felicity Jones.

He drew back way before he was ready and sighed. He brought her into his side, prepared for any kind of reaction she might have, and held the envelope open so she could see what was inside.

It was a stack of pictures. Only the one on top could be seen, but it was enough. It was a photo, taken with a high-quality zoom lens, of Joel and two other boys walking along a path. The date stamp on the photo was from today.

Felicity inhaled deeply, and her lips pressed together hard enough for Ryder to see them turn white with the pressure. But she simply looked up and said, "Hand me your phone, and I'll call the police to report it. It'll be better coming from me. It's my car the envelope was left on."

Kissing the side of her temple, Ryder handed over his phone. Inwardly he sighed in relief. Felicity was holding it together. Oh, he had no doubt she'd have a reaction later, but for now, she wasn't freaking. Wasn't bolting for her car to ride out of town. It was enough.

Joseph Waters watched from his rented sedan a couple of parking lots over. He trained his binoculars on Megan's, gleefully anticipating the look of horror and fear on her face when she realized what he'd left her. Having the fucking mercenary there with her was annoying, but it might make things more interesting. If he could fuck with someone close to Megan at the same time he fucked with her, all the better.

Joseph huffed out a laugh when he saw Ryder use the edge of his shirt to pick up the gift. As if he was stupid enough to leave his DNA or fingerprints behind. That was an amateur move. Megan would know the pictures were from him. The grin on his face grew when he saw how pissed off the mercenary was when he looked inside the envelope.

But his grin faded when he watched Megan's reaction. Or nonreaction, as it were. Clenching his fingers around the binoculars, Joseph could hardly believe it when she didn't cry. Didn't look around in fear, wondering if he was watching.

She merely put out her hand and raised the phone Ryder gave her to her ear.

Bitch. Fucking bitch.

You don't think I'll do it, do you?

Dropping the binoculars, Joseph gripped the steering wheel with all his strength. His mind raced with all the things he wanted to do to Megan. To show her exactly how it felt when someone fucked with your life . . . just as she'd done to him all those years ago.

Taking a deep breath to calm himself, Joseph's mind whirled with the possibilities. He'd play with her for another week or so, then he'd make his move. He just needed to wait for the perfect time to strike.

He knew exactly what he was going to do too.

He had arrangements to make.

Megan would rue the day she dared interfere with his relationship with . . . what's-her-name . . . back in college.

Starting up the engine, Joseph sedately pulled out of the parking lot so as not to draw any attention to himself. He was much more calm now that his plan was coming to fruition.

"One more week, Megan. And you'll belong to me. Mind, body, and soul. And I guarantee you won't enjoy it. Not one second."

His evil chuckle reverberated around the interior of the car as he drove away from downtown Castle Rock.

Two hours later, Ryder and Felicity were finally locked up safe and sound in her apartment. The cops had arrived quickly, and Ryder had a feeling the fact he was related to the Andersons had something to do with their speedy arrival. But he didn't care. He had no problem using whatever connections possible if it meant getting results.

Thankfully, the detectives had listened to Felicity explain who she suspected had left the envelope with the pictures and why, and had taken the threat seriously. They'd encouraged her to file a protective order against Joseph. She hadn't balked when the detectives said they wanted to take the envelope and pictures with them.

He watched as Felicity dropped her keys into the basket on the little table on the kitchen counter and headed straight for a cabinet. She took down a glass and went to the water dispenser. She filled it and immediately chugged down half of the water. She took a deep breath, then finished the rest. Then she refilled her glass before turning to him.

"You want some water?"

Ryder felt his lips quirk, but managed to suppress the grin that wanted to come out. He'd been extremely worried about her lack of a response to the pictures Joseph had sent, in fact still was, but seeing her maintain her nightly ritual calmed him somewhat. He shook his head. "I'm good."

Felicity shrugged and turned to open another cabinet to the shelves that held her food. "You hungry? I could whip something up before we head to bed."

Ryder stalked toward her and wrapped an arm around her waist, pulling her back into him. She immediately melted into his embrace. Ryder used his free hand to pull the glass from her hand and safely set it on the counter before turning her to face him.

"I don't want anything to eat. I want to know what you're thinking."

Felicity sighed and clasped her hands together at the small of his back. She gave him some of her body weight and looked up at him. "I'm okay."

Ryder shook his head. "No, love. I want to know how you are. Seeing all those pictures of Grace, her kids, Joel and his friends, and my brothers couldn't have been easy."

Her lips quirked upward in a small smile. "It wasn't. I'm pissed and scared out of my mind. I couldn't deal with it if he hurts someone else because of me. But I'm trying not to freak. You're here. Your brothers are aware of the danger, and I have no doubt Logan will sit on Grace and his boys until Joseph is found. It sucks, but frankly, I'm not surprised. He's done shit like this to me before. Followed me around, put pictures of me in envelopes and left them for me to find. He likes freaking me out, and trust me, in the past, I was totally freaked."

"But you're not now?"

She didn't answer right away, thinking about his question. Finally, she said, "I'm upset, yes. I don't like the fact he followed Alexis and Blake and took pictures of them and Joel and his friends. I am definitely not happy he got close enough to Grace and her babies to take those pictures either. But you called everyone and told them what happened so they'll be hyper alert. I have to believe that they'll guard their loved ones with their lives."

Her eyes dropped, and she stared at the top button of his shirt as she continued. "My mom didn't have anyone to watch over her. Maybe if she had a man who loved her as much as Logan loves Grace, or Blake loves Alexis, or even Nathan loves Bailey, she wouldn't have died."

Ryder's heart was breaking for the woman in his arms. He moved a hand under her chin and encouraged her to look up at him once more. When he had her eyes, he palmed the side of her head gently. "Men like Joseph are cowards. They get off on scaring those they think are weaker than them. When they find out their targets aren't in fact scared, they usually back off."

"Joseph isn't going to back off," Felicity said immediately.

"I know. That's why me and my brothers aren't going to let down our guard. Not only that, but now the police are involved. And my friends down in the Springs. I'm going to be at your side until he makes a mistake, love."

"I know." She took a deep breath and closed her eyes. "Can we be done talking about Joseph now?"

"Absolutely." He'd give her whatever she wanted. "What do you want to talk about instead?"

She smiled then. A seductive smile that he felt in his dick. Her arms moved from behind him to his stomach. "How about if we don't talk at all?" She slowly pulled the shirt from where it had been tucked into his jeans and began to unbutton it. Her fingertips brushed against his belly and chest as she moved upward. When she had it all the way open, she laid her palms flat against his chest and seductively ran them up and down.

"You might not be hungry," she purred, "but I'm suddenly ravenous."

Ryder moved his hands down to her ass and palmed the shapely globes. "You are, huh?"

"Uh-huh," she replied. "Starving." Her thumbs found his nipples and flicked over them with a rough touch.

Ryder felt both his nipples and his cock turn rock hard at her touch.

He squeezed her butt cheeks once more, then moved his hands to the back of her thighs. "Up," he ordered.

Felicity had leaned into him and was running her nose up and down the edge of his jaw, and pulled back at his order. "What?"

"Jump up," Ryder said again, pressing against her legs to let her know what he meant.

A gleam appeared in her eye, and she curled one leg around his outer thigh before giving a little hop.

Ryder boosted her up and moved his hands to support her ass as she curled her legs around his waist. He was on the move before she opened her mouth.

"In a hurry?" she whispered, leaning into him and wrapping her arms around his neck. Her tongue lazily swirled around his earlobe, and Ryder hitched in a breath when she took the piece of fleshy skin into her mouth and nipped on it before she sucked.

Without a word he strode into her bedroom, straight to the welcoming mattress. The quilt was still thrown back from when they'd gotten out of the bed earlier that morning. Without warning, he dropped her on her back.

She squeaked out a small noise in surprise, but Ryder didn't give her a chance to speak. He was immediately on top of her. His mouth meeting hers, devouring her. He'd wanted her from the first moment he saw her. Had spent many an hour awake and hard as she trustingly slept in his arms. He'd thought after the nasty surprise Joseph had left for her, she might retreat back into the protective shell he'd painstakingly chipped through over the last weeks.

But he should've known better. His Felicity was tougher than that. Once she decided she was done being scared of the man she'd been running from most of her adult life, that was it.

Still without a word, and not taking his mouth from hers, Ryder pulled back just enough to reach down and unbutton and unzip his pants. Getting the hint, Felicity did the same.

They undressed themselves, keeping their mouths fused together as much as possible, only breaking apart when she drew her shirt over her head. Everywhere Ryder's bare skin touched Felicity's, he felt little electric sparks.

He'd been tortured once. His captors had used water and a car battery to try to force him to tell them what they wanted to know. The zaps of electricity had been painful, and even after he'd been rescued, he swore he could feel the jolts of the current running through his body at random times.

He felt those jolts now, but instead of being painful, they were erotic as hell. He pulled his mouth away from Felicity's with reluctance and flattened his body over hers. He wrapped his feet around her ankles. He could feel her nipples brushing against the hair on his chest, tickling him even as they tempted him. They were touching from their toes to their fingertips and everywhere in between. He hadn't had more than cursory glances of her body, but it didn't matter.

She lay panting under him, her ocean-blue eyes huge in her face. The moisture from their kisses shone on her lips, and he could smell her arousal wafting up from between their bodies.

"I want you," Ryder said softly.

She grinned and pushed her hips up as much as she could, which wasn't much. "I can feel."

"I want *all* of you," Ryder clarified, ignoring her attempt at levity. "I want the right to lie next to you every night. I want to stand by your side as you show that asshole he hasn't broken you. When I take you, enter your body, you're letting me claim *all* of you. You're giving me the right to tell men who ogle that fine ass of yours to fuck off and to bring you home and take you until we're both limp."

The lust had faded a bit from her eyes, but it had been replaced by something else. Yearning.

"This isn't just sex for me, love. Not even close. Not ever with you. Will you let me in? Give me all of you?"

She didn't respond right away, which didn't concern Ryder in the least. He could practically see the wheels turning in her brain. He wanted her to think about his words. Wanted her to take this as seriously as he was.

"Only if you give me those same rights back," she said finally. "I'm not a delicate flower, no matter what you might've seen when you first met me."

"Done. And not once did I ever think you were a delicate fucking flower, love. I saw you. Saw that iron core inside you. It's what drew me to you in the first place."

"Good. Now . . . are we done with this touchy-feely conversation yet? I need you."

Ryder didn't answer her with words. He let go of her hands and eased down her body until he was lying flat on the bed, his hands on her thighs, pressing her legs open.

She didn't resist in the least, dropping her knees and moaning.

Ryder stared down at her pussy for the first time. Reverently, he ran his fingers over the blonde hair between her legs. It was so fine and light, it was almost white. "Fuck, you are so beautiful," he breathed.

"It's just hair," Felicity breathed.

"No, love, it's *your* hair," he returned, then leaned down and got to work showing her how much he loved her natural color. He didn't ease into his attentions, however. No, he couldn't hold back the lust he'd been controlling for weeks. Not with her scent in his nostrils and her pink lips spread open in welcome.

Ryder attacked her as if he was a man starving. The first taste of her on his tongue only stoked the fire he had for her. Shifting up to his knees so he was kneeling over her and could get at her better, he pulled her hips up onto his legs.

He heard himself grunting as he licked up her slit over and over, but couldn't stop. The more he tasted her, the more he wanted of her. He opened his eyes and looked up her body even as he closed his lips over her clit and used his tongue as a vibrator over the little nub. Felicity's arms were thrown over her head, and her back was arched as he brought her closer and closer to the edge.

Her eyes were closed as she shivered and shook in his arms. He'd never felt as powerful as he did right at that moment. He'd had women before, but hadn't ever wanted one with this intensity. He always took the time to make sure whoever was in his bed was satisfied, but he'd never felt the bone-deep need to make sure she was completely delirious with pleasure. His dick had never been harder. All his attention was focused on the woman in his arms and under his tongue.

He moved back down between her puffy lips and licked upward once more, collecting the fresh juices leaking from her body on his tongue.

"Ryder," she moaned.

He took one hand from her ass then and pressed his index finger inside her. She tightened around his finger, as if trying to keep him out, but he didn't stop until his knuckle was touching flush against her body.

Ryder watched as he eased his finger out and couldn't resist bringing it up to his mouth and sucking all her cream off. He caught her gaze then. Her pupils were so large in her eyes that they almost obscured the blue irises.

"Fucking perfect," he murmured before dropping his gaze back between her legs. Without warning, he shoved two fingers in her tight sheath, groaning at the feel of her body clenching against him.

"It's . . . fuck . . ." Felicity swore as he pulled his fingers out, then roughly pressed them back inside her. "It's been a while for me," she rushed out. But she didn't pull away from him, instead pressing her hips up as he withdrew his fingers once more.

"How long?" Ryder asked, knowing he was being a dick, but feeling as if he was watching the entire scene from high above the bed rather than actually participating. He'd wanted her from the second he'd seen her, and having her was more than he ever dreamed it could be.

"Uh . . . ," she breathed. "I don't know."

"How long?" Ryder demanded again, turning his hand as he thrust inside her once more so that his thumb brushed against her clit once he'd pushed his fingers inside as far as he could go.

Her hips jerked up, and he roughly thumbed her bundle of nerves as he waited for her answer.

"Years. Maybe six?" she gasped.

Satisfaction tore through Ryder. He should've felt guilty, it hadn't been that long for him, but he couldn't deny that he was glad she hadn't been with someone after she'd moved to Colorado.

"You get yourself off?" he bit out.

"Yeah."

"How?"

They were practically grunting their words, but Ryder didn't care.

"My clit."

"Vibrator?"

"On my clit," she gasped as he pressed harder on the body part in question. "Can't . . . ," she panted, then hurried the rest of her answer, "get off with just penetration."

It was good information to have. Ryder wasn't so conceited to think that his dick would somehow have magic powers as soon as he got it inside her. If she needed direct stimulation on her clit to get off, that's what he'd give her.

He eased his fingers out of her body and immediately reached for his dick. He used her natural lubrication to make his motions smoother. His thumb never stopped its ministrations as he pleasured himself. When he was on the verge of exploding, he reluctantly tore his hand away from his body.

He leaned over and grabbed the condom he'd dropped next to the pillow when he'd undressed himself. He'd torn it out of his wallet before throwing both it, and his pants, over the side of the bed. He quickly rolled the rubber down his sheath. He wanted to be ready to fuck Felicity as soon as *she* was ready. After she'd come for him.

Ryder wanted to spend all night petting and caressing Felicity, but knew he didn't have nearly the control to do so and not come himself, so he firmed his jaw and got to work. He held her ass in the air and devoured her once more. Licking, nibbling, and learning exactly what his woman liked. When he felt her begin to shake once more, he covered her clit with his mouth and sucked, hard. She jerked in his grasp, and he felt her fingers dig into his arms, but he didn't stop.

Her hips tried to flex away from him, but then immediately pressed upward once more. Looking down, he caught her gaze. His jaw worked as he added his tongue into his sucking action, and still he refused to let her drop her gaze.

"Oh my God, Ryder. That feels . . . fuck, it hurts, but it's so good," she gasped.

He didn't let up, and squeezed her ass hard as he continued.

As if he was inside her head, he knew the moment she was on the edge. Every muscle in her body tensed, and she pushed harder up into his mouth. Her lips opened and she gasped for air.

Ryder had her almost bent double now, her ass in the air supported by his hands, her body weight on her upper back and shoulders. Her eyes were closed, and she drew herself up into a half sit-up. With one more hard suck, she careened over the edge.

Her thighs shook, her belly rippled, and her mouth opened in a silent scream.

Ryder didn't give her a chance to come down before dropping her ass and scooting up, pressing her still-shaking thighs wide as he did, congratulating himself for having the foresight to put on the condom earlier, because he honestly didn't think he'd be able to stop and do it at the moment.

Looking down, seeing her legs spread open, the pink of her inner lips coated with the come from her orgasm, Ryder didn't even think. He notched the head of his cock between her legs and pressed inside.

She jerked at his movements, but didn't pull away. Instead, she thrust her hips up at the same time he pushed inside. Ryder threw his head back and reached down and grabbed the base of his dick just in time to keep himself from coming.

Her body was still shaking and clenching with her orgasm. He forced his cock between her tight muscles until he couldn't get any farther inside her. Bracing his hands on the mattress at her shoulders, Ryder loomed over the woman he loved with his entire being.

"Mine," he growled, not capable of saying anything else.

"Mine," she returned fiercely, lifting her knees to grip his waist, and digging her fingernails into the sensitive skin at his sides.

Ryder had planned to be gentle once he got inside her. To show her how much he cared about her. But at her actions, and her fierce claiming of him, he lost the control he'd been holding on to by a thread.

Closing his eyes and throwing his head back, Ryder pounded into her, sliding easily in the wetness between her legs. The sound of their lovemaking was loud in the small room. Noises that he might've been embarrassed about once upon a time, with another woman, but with Felicity, they were perfect.

His balls slapped against her ass with every downward thrust, and the wet sucking noise of her body trying to keep him inside her every time he pulled back only ratcheted up his lust and desire for her.

Ryder felt sweat bead on his forehead as he desperately tried to hold back his orgasm. He wanted their first time to last forever, but unfortunately, he knew it was only a matter of seconds before he lost it.

Grinding his teeth together, he glanced down at Felicity. She was smiling up at him, watching him closely. The satisfaction and possessiveness in her gaze did him in. He thrust inside her twice more, and on the third thrust, planted himself inside her as far as he could get and erupted.

Ryder felt the warmth from his come fill the condom around his cock, and he wished for a moment that he was filling her up instead. It was crazy, he'd never felt that way before, but he wanted to coat her with his essence. Claim her. Mark her.

Cognizant of the fact she hadn't come once he'd entered her, Ryder kept himself planted inside her body, but leaned up. He snaked a hand between their slick bodies and zeroed in on her clit.

"Oh," she exclaimed as he began to roughly manipulate the bundle of nerves once more. "Ryder, I . . . I already came."

"I know. Do it again. I want to feel it this time. From start to finish. On my cock this time."

She was obviously still ramped up from her earlier orgasm, because it didn't take long before he felt her inner muscles clamp down on his slowly softening dick. It felt amazing. He felt his cock twitch and start to come back to life. He increased the speed of his thumb and was rewarded with her orgasm. He felt it ripple up his erection, now at full mast once more, until she was once again shaking uncontrollably.

Ryder reached down and held on to the end of the condom as he pulled out of her body, all the while strumming her clit with the other hand. He ripped off the used prophylactic and gently pushed two fingers inside her still-spasming body. He then scooted farther up on the mattress and stroked himself as she came down from her second orgasm.

Ryder wasn't sure he could actually come a second time, no matter how hard he was, but smelling their arousal and feeling her jolt under him every couple of seconds was making the stroking of his dick all that much more pleasurable.

Then he felt his hand being pushed away and looked down. Felicity's eyes were on his hard cock, and her hands were wrapped around it, giving him the hand job of the century.

It was his turn to moan. "Fuck, Felicity . . . God, your hands feel so good."

"Mmm," she murmured. "*You* feel good."

A spurt of precome escaped the hole at the tip of his dick at her words.

She giggled, then got serious. One hand reached below him to caress his balls as the other sped up on the length of him.

As if she could read his mind, she knew exactly when to speed up her movements and how much pressure to apply.

When he was on the verge of exploding, he tried to warn her. "Love, I'm close. Let me pull back."

She didn't respond verbally, but her grip tightened, and she brought up her knees to clench against his sides. She was still lying on her back, and Ryder felt like a letch hovering over her as she jacked him off, but he couldn't have stopped her at that point if a gun was pointed at his head.

He tried to keep his eyes open and on hers as she forced him over the edge, but at the last minute, he threw his head back and groaned, long and loud. Ryder fell forward and caught himself with a hand next to her shoulders and shuddered as spurt after spurt erupted from his cock and landed on her naked body under him. He felt drained and exhausted. It had been a long time since he'd come more than once in one night, and never so close together.

He stayed propped above her for a long moment, memorizing the sight of her. She was beautiful. Absolutely beautiful. Finally, his eyes came up to hers. They were twinkling with humor, thank God. She wasn't disgusted by what he'd done.

"Mine," he said softly.

"Yours," she affirmed. "But you're mine now too."

"Fuck yeah. Yours," he agreed.

Then Felicity said, "You think we have the energy to make it to the shower?"

And just like that, Ryder was rejuvenated. Thoughts of Felicity slick and wet and glistening from the water cascading over her shoulders was enough to make his dick twitch once more.

Jerking in surprise, as she'd been gently holding his flaccid cock, Felicity gaped as he grew semihard in her hand. "Seriously?" she asked, one eyebrow arching.

Ryder merely laughed and rolled off her. Groaning at the loss of her hand on him, he told himself that he had the rest of his life with her. He didn't need to fuck her to exhaustion their first night. He'd save that for their second. He stood up next to the bed, completely unworried about his nakedness, and held out his hand. "Come on, we'll shower, then get some sleep."

She put her hand in his, letting him pull her upward. "You think you can sleep like that?" she gestured toward his almost fully erect cock.

Ryder felt himself blush, but merely shrugged as he towed her toward the bathroom. "Yeah, love, I can sleep like this. Have been for the last few weeks."

As he waited for the water in the shower to get hot, Ryder grinned down at Felicity. Things might not be completely safe for her yet, but they would be. He couldn't live without her now. He'd been serious earlier when he'd warned her that if they made love, he wouldn't be able to let her go. She was his now. Just as he was hers.

Chapter Fifteen

Felicity stood at the back of her PT Cruiser with her hands on her hips.

"Are you going over to . . . What's wrong?" Ryder asked, coming up beside her.

So yeah, on the relationship front, the last week had been amazing. Ryder had made love with her every night . . . and a couple of mornings as well. She'd never been with a lover as attentive as he was . . . or as inventive.

Not only that, but he was considerate, affectionate, and respectful. Oh, he was also bossy, over-the-top security conscious, and possessive to boot, but she could overlook all his negatives because the good things about the man way outshone the bad.

Like the way he always got her a glass of water right before they went to sleep, no matter how exhausted he was after they made love.

Like the way he always grabbed her stuffed giraffe and gave it to her when he was done worshiping her body and they were ready to sleep.

Like the way he called to make sure Cole was waiting for her in the workout room downstairs before he let her go down into the gym by herself.

Like the way he cradled baby Nate or Ace and murmured sweet nothings to them to get them to stop crying.

Like the way he called Rex every day to see if the man had gotten any more information about Joseph.

Like the way each morning when they found another annoying, creepy stalker gift from Joseph, he got all "I'm gonna kill that motherfucker."

This morning was no exception.

The back of her beautiful PT Cruiser was covered in bumper stickers. Not only on the bumper, but on the back window and tailgate as well. Not cute ones either. They were extremely offensive. Nazi party slogans, the KKK logo, anti-lesbian and anti-gay pictures, and to top it off . . . political stickers.

"Fuck," Ryder ground out, reaching out and putting his arm in front of Felicity and forcing her to take a couple of steps away from the vehicle. Then he sighed. "Are you still going over to Grace's today?" he asked, finishing his thought from earlier.

The morning had been going so well, Felicity thought. She worked out with Cole, and Ryder had an omelet waiting when she arrived back upstairs in her apartment. They'd had a leisurely breakfast and afterward had taken a shower together. Ryder had bent her over, ordered her to masturbate while he fucked her with an intensity that had her coming almost immediately. She liked when he was tender and loving with her, but she absolutely adored it when he lost all control and simply took what he wanted and needed from her.

While they got dressed after their shower, they'd discussed the upcoming day's plans. She was going to visit with Grace that morning before coming back to the gym and getting some paperwork done. After Joseph was caught, hopefully soon, she and Cole had decided to have another black-light night, as it had been a while since they'd had one. Everyone seemed to enjoy them, and it was an easy way to spotlight the gym and sign up new members.

Ryder was headed to Blake's house. Surprisingly, the two had become fairly close. After the drama with their dad had been handled, both men were able to put it behind them and appreciate each other.

Felicity wished women were able to do that . . . put aside their differences once and for all after hashing them out.

They made plans to meet up back at the gym later that day. Ryder would give Cole a break from "hovering over" her, as Felicity put it. She hated always needing someone around her, but even she wasn't dumb enough to refuse the bodyguard. Joseph was out there just waiting to make his move.

"Yeah," she said, answering his question. "Since I'm babysitting later this week, Grace wanted to go over the thousand and one notes she's made for each baby." It was said in jest, but Ryder didn't even crack a smile at the reference to Grace's obsessive need to make notes about her children's supposed quirks and needs.

"Is Logan going to be there?"

"I don't think so. But Bailey is. Alexis was planning on being there too, but I think she had to bail. Something about a real-time training session with that hacker guy she's been working with."

"I'll stay until you're ready to go then."

Felicity wanted to protest. Wanted to tell him she didn't need a babysitter, but then she thought back to all the shit Joseph had been doing recently. The missing-person signs he'd posted all over downtown Castle Rock with her picture and description on them. She thought Ryder was going to lose his shit when he saw them. She'd never seen him look so furious. She'd come face-to-face with the mercenary that morning. Seeing the anger on his face made her realize that she never wanted to be on the receiving end of that amount of testosterone. But it also made her feel safe. He would kill for her. Weirdly, it comforted her.

Other things were annoying, but not as blatantly threatening as that "missing" poster had been. Dead flowers on the sidewalk outside the gym, the police showing up several times because of reports of a disturbance, more pictures of her going about her days, a cookie delivery with each sweet decorated with a number . . . when put in the right order, it turned out to be Ryder's cell phone number, and they'd even discovered a rattlesnake in the men's locker room at the gym one day.

Felicity sighed. "But you were going to go over and visit with Blake," she protested.

"He'll understand," Ryder told her. "You're way more important than anything else I might have planned."

"We can't spend every second together," Felicity argued.

"Why not?"

"Why not?" she echoed. "Because."

Ryder smirked. "That's not an answer, love."

"Because we'll get sick of each other. Because most people have jobs they go to every day. It gives them time away from the person they're dating."

"I won't get sick of you, no way. And we both have jobs . . . they're just not nine-to-five jobs. We're lucky in that we can make our own schedules."

"You have a job?" Felicity asked, her eyebrows shooting up in surprise. "I thought you quit working for Rex."

"I did. One of the things I was going to talk to Blake about when I saw him next was becoming a part of Ace Security."

Felicity stared at Ryder for a moment before smiling huge and throwing herself at him.

He went back on a foot, but curled his arms around her, steadying them both. "I take it that meets with your approval?" he asked dryly.

"Oh my God, yes!" she said. She leaned up and kissed him, keeping her arms around him. "I didn't even think about that, but it's perfect. And they're okay with you joining them?"

"They came to *me* with the offer," Ryder told her. "I was going to discuss more details with Blake today, then see what you thought before I officially accepted."

Felicity tilted her head to the side in confusion. "You were going to talk to *me* about it before accepting the job? Why?"

"Seriously?" he asked with one brow arched.

"Uh . . . yeah?"

"I'm the newcomer here, Felicity. You're already settled in. Grace is your best friend. This is your territory. I didn't want you to feel as if I pushed my way into your family circle if you didn't want me there."

It was Felicity's turn to ask, "Seriously?"

His lips twitched, but he managed to keep the smile from his face. "Yeah."

"For God's sake, I'm not eighteen and a jealous teenager. Logan, Blake, and Nathan are your *family*. I would never say that I didn't want you working with your brothers, no matter what was going on with us. Besides . . . from what I've seen . . . you're good. They could totally use you on their team. Shit, with your connections, you could really help Ace Security get to the next level . . . whatever that is. I don't know how it all works. But they'd be lucky, really lucky, to have you join them. And not just because you're related."

"I have an appointment with a real estate agent next week," Ryder told her. "Come with me?"

Felicity stared up at him. "Of course. I'm going to miss you in my apartment, though."

"No, you won't."

"Ryder, yes, I will. You've been living there with me for like, a month. I'm used to you hogging the covers, leaving the toilet seat up, and making a mess anytime you cook." She smiled to make sure he knew she was teasing. She really didn't give a shit about those things, but was trying not to get all morose at the thought of him moving out. "But you do get me my water every night, so that kinda negates the other stuff."

"You won't miss me because I want you to move in with me," Ryder said, ignoring her teasing. "We'll find a house we both like, hopefully not too far from downtown so we can be close to the Ace Security office and the gym."

She gaped up at him. He'd mentioned something about her helping him find a house, but she'd thought it was an offhand comment. Or something he wanted her to do later . . . much later. Her eyes filled with tears she refused to shed. She wasn't a crier. She was tough and badass, dammit. "Really?" she croaked.

"Really," he confirmed.

Felicity smiled then and buried her face into his neck. "Yes. Fuck yes."

Ryder leaned over a little and clasped his arms around her, lifting her feet off the ground and walking toward his sports car.

Felicity giggled, but kept her head buried in the warm skin of his neck and went limp, letting her legs dangle and knock against his as he walked. She didn't care where he was taking her. When he stopped, she picked up her head. He put her back on her feet, and she realized they were standing next to his car.

"You really want me to move in with you? It seems like a big step considering the amount of time we've known each other," she felt compelled to warn him.

"Love, I knew the second I saw you that I wanted you to be mine. I warned you before I took you for the first time that if you let me inside your body, that was it for me. So this doesn't really seem like that big of a step. You're mine. I'm yours. I'm moving to Castle Rock because you're here. Thus, it seems like a natural thing to move in together."

She beamed.

"And to give you fair warning, I'm going to ask you to marry me. Soon. And you'll take my name. I know Bailey doesn't believe in marriage, and Nathan took her last name, but you're mine, and I want no doubts who you belong to."

"Holy shit," Felicity said, but didn't elaborate on her shock, simply stared at him with her mouth open.

Ryder was the one to smile this time. "I fucking love surprising you."

Then he kissed her. Hard. Deep. It was a claiming. In the parking lot behind Rock Hard Gym, Felicity's defaced car feet away.

And she didn't give a shit. Even with the threat of Joseph looming, Felicity was happier than she'd ever been in her life. She never dreamed this could be her life. A thought struck her, and she pulled back.

Ryder was reluctant to let her go, but finally allowed it.

She caught his gaze, and they stood there, arms around each other for a long moment before Felicity said, "I love you."

"Good."

She frowned. "Good? That's all you have to say to my declaration of love?"

He smirked. "Yup."

Felicity struggled to step out of his arms, but he refused to let her go. "If you think I'm going to marry a man who can't admit that he loves me, you're insane. I don't care how much you spout shit like 'You're mine.' Ownership isn't love, and I can't live my life without hearing it. Did you know I never had anyone tell me they loved me until I was eight years old? It sucks, and I won't do it again. You hear me, Ryder? You might be hotter than any actor I've ever seen and a big bad mercenary, but I need the words."

She glared up at the man she loved with all her heart, but she'd been honest. If he thought he was too manly to tell her that he loved her back, she wouldn't be able to be with him. It sucked, but she *needed* the words.

"What have I been calling you since practically the first time we met?" he asked.

Felicity was confused. What in the world was he talking about? Here she was opening her heart to him, and he was asking weird questions. "I don't know. Let me go, Ryder. I need to get to Grace's."

"Listen to me," he ordered. "The first time we met, you were arguing with Cole and insisting he give you the seed money you invested into the gym. Grace, Logan, and I all crowded into the room, and you started to have a panic attack. I helped you through it. What did I call you?"

Felicity stopped struggling and looked up at Ryder in confusion. "I don't remember."

"Fair enough. But think, Felicity. What nickname do I have for you?"

Her eyes widened as she realized what he meant. "But . . . you call everyone that."

He snorted a laugh. "I certainly do *not*. Only you, love, only you."

The pesky tears were back in Felicity's eyes. "Oh."

"Yeah. Oh. I've loved you from that first meeting. You were scared out of your mind and desperate to leave, and you were glorious. You weren't backing down, no matter that you were surrounded by five men. But it wasn't just that. It was something about you. It was as if I recognized you as mine at first glance. I knew bone deep that you would make my life better simply by being in it."

"Ryder."

"In case that wasn't clear. I love you, Felicity Jones, or Megan Parkins, or whatever you want to call yourself. You're mine, and I know that's a little cavemanish, but I'm yours too. You own me. Heart, body, and soul. You could stomp my heart into pieces if you ever left me. I want to spend the rest of my life with you by my side."

Felicity nearly melted at his feet. She'd been feeling vulnerable, thinking she was the only one sharing her feelings, but it was obvious now how wrong she'd been. "Was that a proposal?"

"Fuck no," Ryder said immediately. "You'll know when I ask you to marry me."

He always knew what to say to prevent her from falling apart in a mushy mess at his feet. She appreciated it. She wanted to be tough Felicity Jones, not a weak, crying mess. "You're awfully confident. Maybe I'll ask *you* to marry *me*."

"Do so and I'll put you over my knee and paddle your ass."

Felicity blinked, then giggled. "What? Why?" she asked when she had controlled her laughter.

"Because I'm the man. And the man does the asking."

Felicity rolled her eyes. "Whatever."

He put his hand on her cheek then. "Humor me, love. I'll be the first to admit that women have all the same rights as men, but let me do this."

"Fine," she told him in a huff, not really upset in the least, but it was fun to egg Ryder on. "But it better be one kick-ass proposal."

He grinned. "Challenge accepted. Now that we've covered the fact that we love each other and that you're moving in with me, can we please get out of this fucking parking lot where we're sitting ducks for Joseph-fucking-Waters and get you to Grace's where you can ooh and ah over my nephews?"

"You'll call the cops and report the newest harassment?"

"Of course. I'll also get in touch with the security company and see if there is any video of Joseph putting the fucking stickers on your car. Although, as much as I hate to admit it, I'm guessing he was probably smart enough to stay to the shadows and never show his face. Oh, and I'll arrange for that shit to be removed from your car while I'm at it."

"Awesome. Thank you. Then, yes, I'm ready to go to Grace's so I can ooh and ah over my godsons. Lead on, oh supreme ruler of our household."

He merely shook his head. The hand that had been on her cheek moved up and over her hair before clasping the back of her neck. He leaned in and said softly, "I love you. From the bottom of your feet to the top of your beautiful black hair."

"My mom used to say that to me," she whispered.

"I know. You told me."

"And you remembered," she said in awe.

"I remember every single thing," he said, then kissed her lightly on the lips. "Now get in so we can go."

She smiled as she pulled away and climbed into the passenger side of his car. Joseph Waters might be a sadistic asshole, but ultimately he'd led her to Ryder. He'd hate knowing that, and she hoped like hell she had the chance to tell him.

Joseph watched the 370Z pull out of the parking lot from the driver's seat of his piece-of-shit rental and clenched his fists. He'd hoped to see Megan pitch a fit at seeing her beloved car covered in the offensive stickers, but instead it seemed as if he'd just witnessed some sort of lover's tryst.

She wasn't acting like he wanted her to.

She was supposed to be scared.

Supposed to be freaked out.

Supposed to be packing and leaving town.

It wasn't his ultimate plan, but he would've taken advantage of it and snatched her before she left the state.

But she was ruining things.

They were ruining things.

That damn Ryder Sinclair was giving her false courage. Convincing her he wasn't going to get his hands on her. As if.

His father had called earlier and had been beyond furious.

"You need to forget about her and get home."

"No. She needs to pay for interfering."

"Listen to me, son. This has gone on way too long. I thought you'd given up this asinine obsession. I got a call from Rex from Mountain Mercenaries. He's not happy. And if Rex isn't happy, I'm not happy. He's given me one chance to make this right. Come home. Today."

You need to speed this up or Father is going to get involved.

Nodding to himself, Joseph started the engine and pulled away from the downtown area. He had some more work to do before he could end this. It would mean not being able to leave Megan with any gifts for the next couple of days, but hopefully she'd let down her guard while he was gone. And when he got back, the game would be back on.

Chapter Sixteen

Felicity stomped her foot like a fifth grader. "Ryder, you *have* to go."

"No, I don't."

"Dammit. Yes, you do."

"I'm not leaving you and the twins here by yourselves."

"We're *fine*," Felicity insisted. "Nothing's happened in days."

"That doesn't mean that Joseph is gone," Ryder said.

"I know that, but I'm not an idiot. I'm not going to step foot outside of this apartment while you're gone. The babies are asleep in their cribs. It's been a long day and I'm exhausted. I'm going to sit right here on the couch and watch TV until you get back."

Ryder leaned in, caging her body between his and the counter behind her. "I don't like this."

She laughed a humorless laugh. "Neither do I. But Blake texted that he needs you, and now he won't answer his phone, and I can't get Alexis to answer hers either. Logan and Grace are up in Denver at that play, and Nathan and Bailey haven't heard anything. You can't ignore this."

She looked up at Ryder. He was stressed. It was clear as day on his face. It was obvious he didn't want to leave her alone in the apartment, but it was just as obvious he wanted to get to his brother.

They'd been watching television and relaxing when he'd received the text. It had been short and sweet.

I need you. My house. ASAP.

That's all it said.

It could be a trick. But what if it wasn't?

"I don't trust Joseph. This feels like a setup."

"Me neither," Felicity said. "But what choice do you have? And the text came from Blake's phone. Let's say it wasn't him and Joseph was fucking with you. He had to have gotten Blake's cell somehow. What if he's in the house and has both him and Alexis hostage right now? You can't risk it."

"I can't risk *you*," Ryder returned immediately. "I can wait until Nathan gets there and calls me to tell me what's up. What if Joseph decides to burn the gym down with you inside?"

"At the first smell of smoke, I'll grab the babies and get out."

"And if he's waiting for you?"

"Then I'll fight him," Felicity insisted. "But that's not his style. You know that as well as I do. He isn't going to kill me that easily."

Ryder's jaw worked in frustration. They'd talked about this exact thing the other night. Joseph wouldn't just come right out and shoot her. He'd take her somewhere and torture her first. Which would suck. Huge elephant balls. But it would give Ryder, his brothers, and even the Mountain Mercenaries time to find her. Felicity wasn't exactly looking forward to being tortured, but knowing her man and his friends would be coming for her would make things easier.

"Go check on your brother," Felicity insisted. "I'll be right here waiting for you to get back. It's late, I won't go out, no one is in the gym downstairs. I'll check more houses online and see if I can find one we both like. Tomorrow we can call the real estate agent and make an appointment to go see the ones on our list so far."

"Don't open the door to anyone. No one, love, I mean it," Ryder ordered.

"I won't."

His jaw flexed as he ground his teeth together. "And at the first sign of trouble, you text me, and I'll come back."

"I will."

He sighed. "I don't like this. But I need to check on Blake."

"Go, Ryder. So you can hurry up and come back and we can go to bed."

"Okay."

"Okay," she echoed.

But neither moved. Finally, Felicity stood on her tiptoes and kissed Ryder lightly, then moved her lips to his ear and whispered, "I still owe you that blow job from last night. I didn't mean to fall asleep, but when you ate me to those two orgasms, I couldn't stay awake. If you're up to it, I'll make good on my debt when you get home."

She could feel him smiling.

But when he took her head in his hands and tilted her eyes up to his, the smile was gone. "You don't owe me anything, love. I'll take whatever you want to give, but you will never owe me a fucking thing."

"Okay."

"With that said, as long as my brother is okay, when I get back, I want you on your knees in front of me taking my cock."

She shivered at the carnality of his words and the image that immediately sprang to her mind, of her naked at his feet, Ryder fucking her face as she looked up at his beautiful body. "Deal."

"I love you."

"And I love you," she returned.

Ryder kissed her on the forehead, then let go, turning to grab a glass out of the cupboard. They had been out all day, and Felicity hadn't had nearly as much water as she usually did. He filled it with water from the dispenser and handed it to her.

She smiled at him and took a large swallow. "What is it with you and my water ritual?" she asked.

"I like caring for you. You started drinking water every night to keep you healthy, and I want to make sure you live a nice long life." He shrugged. "So, you want it, and it keeps you around longer, so I'll make sure you have a big glass of water every night for the rest of our life."

She smiled and chugged the entire glass. She handed it back to him with a smile.

"More?"

"Yes, please. I want to stay hydrated for what's to come later on tonight."

He filled the glass once more and handed it to her. She took a sip, then pushed at his belly. "Go. See what Blake wants. I'm gonna check on the babies, then check out houses until you get home."

He nodded, kissed her on the forehead once more, then turned and left.

Felicity locked the door after him and then went to check on Nate and Ace. They were sleeping soundly. She stood at the door to the guest room, watching them sleep for a long moment. Logan and Grace had gone up to Denver for the evening to see a performance of *Cats* and hadn't hesitated to leave the twins with Felicity and Ryder. It made her feel good to know, even with the shit going on with Joseph, that they trusted her to take care of their children. And she would.

Felicity would guard those two little humans with her life. Nothing would happen to them on her watch. Nothing. She'd gladly go with Joseph before letting Nate and Ace get sucked into his drama.

Satisfied the babies were sleeping soundly, Felicity went back into the living area. She made sure the baby monitor was turned on high and grabbed her water on her way to the couch. She sipped at the water, her thirst slackened from the glass she'd chugged earlier. Feeling mellow and a tad sleepy, she held the glass in her lap and settled against the cushions to finish the forensic show she and Ryder had been watching before he'd received the text from his brother. When it was over, she'd pull out her computer and look at houses.

Ryder couldn't shake the feeling of dread that had settled on his shoulders like a death shroud ever since he'd received the text from his brother. Something was wrong. But he didn't know what.

He pulled into Blake's driveway and climbed out, striding up to the front door of the house with large steps. At first he thought it was weird that his brother lived in the house he'd grown up in, where he'd been so horribly abused by his mother, but the more he got to know Blake, and Alexis, the more he realized that it was cathartic for him. That living there and creating new, good memories helped Blake get over the hurts of his past.

Besides, he and Alexis had done so many upgrades to the house, apparently it was hard to even recognize it as the same place. An addition on the back, updated landscaping, completely new kitchen and bathrooms. Grace told him it was like a moth turning into a butterfly.

Ryder pulled out a pistol and knocked on the door before stepping to the side so as not to make himself a target for Joseph or anyone else who might be aiming at him through the door. The bad feeling he had might be because his brother was in trouble. He wasn't going to take any chances.

He tensed when he heard the locks on the door unlatching, and then it was cracked open.

"Who's there?"

It was Blake.

Ryder lowered the gun, but didn't put it away. "It's me, Ryder. What's up?"

"Hang on," Blake ordered, then shut the door. It opened immediately after he removed the chain. "Hey, Ryder."

Ryder waited impatiently for his brother to tell him why he'd summoned him, but when the other man just stared at him as if he was waiting for Ryder to explain why *he* was there, Ryder swore. Long and inventively.

He reached for his phone and dialed Felicity's number. It rang four times, then went to voice mail. He swore again.

"What the fuck?" Blake asked. "Ryder?"

Ryder looked up at his half brother and saw the man was on alert. "You text me about twenty minutes ago?"

"No." Blake's answer was short and to the point.

"You sure? Maybe Alexis did?"

"I'm sure. We've been . . . er . . . busy for the last half hour or so. We just came downstairs to make something to eat when I heard your knock on the door. Neither of us sent you a text."

"Fuck," Ryder swore. "I need to get back to Felicity, but can I see your phone first?"

Blake immediately turned and disappeared inside his house. Ryder stepped into the entryway, but went no farther. This wasn't a social call. He needed to get back to the gym. Now. But first he needed to check his brother's phone.

Blake came back to the door with Alexis following behind him. She was almost a foot shorter than Blake, but Ryder knew how tough she was. Remembered all she'd been through, and seeing for himself how happy she and his brother were made him have hope that whatever Joseph had planned for him and Felicity would end the same way.

"Here it is," Blake said, holding out his phone to Ryder.

He took it and quickly pulled up the text history. The last text Blake had sent to him had been two days ago when they'd had a short conversation about the paperwork to add him to the Ace Security business.

Ryder clicked on his name on Blake's phone and sent himself a test message. Within seconds his phone dinged with an incoming text. Ryder compared that one to the one he'd received earlier. Both said they were from his brother, and both had the same phone number.

Shaking his head, he turned the screen and showed Blake and Alexis what had brought him over to their house.

Alexis reached for the phone, then hesitated. "Can I see it?" she belatedly asked.

Ryder handed it over impatiently. He needed to get back to the other side of the city. To Felicity. He felt it in his gut.

Alexis clicked a few buttons, then as if realizing that Ryder was on the verge of bolting, handed it back. "If I had more time, I could probably track down the sender. At least what cell towers the message came from. But honestly, if someone knows what they're doing, it wouldn't be hard to use a burner phone and manipulate the number."

Ryder shook his head. He knew that, but hadn't even considered it in his worry for his brother.

"Go," Blake ordered. "I'm right behind you."

"*We're* right behind you," Alexis countered. "I'll call the cops and have them meet us there."

Ryder didn't stay to listen to his brother argue with his woman. He didn't exactly want Alexis in the middle of whatever was happening back at the gym, but he didn't really want her staying at the house by herself either. If this was the beginning of whatever Joseph had planned, he wouldn't put it past the man to hurt all of Felicity's friends, knowing it would ultimately hurt her.

He hadn't hesitated to use her mother to get to her, so it was an obvious conclusion that he would use her friends in much the same way. Felicity knew it, and that was why she'd wanted to run in the first place, but for some reason Ryder hadn't been thinking that way tonight when he'd gotten the text that was supposedly from Blake. He shook his head in regret. He was an idiot, and Rex would've kicked his ass if he'd done something as stupid as that on one of his missions.

Ryder raced back to the gym. Blake's house wasn't far, but it was way too far for *his* peace of mind. He calculated that he probably hadn't been gone more than thirty minutes, but all it would take was a minute or two for Joseph to snatch Felicity.

He didn't bother pulling into the parking lot at the back of the gym. Ryder parked right in front of Rock Hard Gym. He was relieved when everything seemed exactly like it had been when he'd left earlier, but the hair on the back of his neck was still standing straight up.

He was unlocking the front door of the gym when Blake pulled up behind his car. Cole had given Ryder a key to the gym with a smirk and a smack on the back the other week. Had told him that he owed him the world after he'd convinced Felicity to stick around. It had made Ryder feel good that he'd been so easily welcomed by Felicity's friend, but now he was even more thankful because it meant he didn't need to wait for Cole to arrive to unlock the door.

He'd tried to call Felicity once more on his way back to her, but once again the phone just rang and eventually went to voice mail.

His heart in his throat, Ryder ran through the deserted reception area to the hallway at the back of the space. He took the stairs two at a time and burst into the hallway at the top. He fumbled with the key for an uncomfortable amount of time before he finally got the door to Felicity's apartment open. He ran in and stopped short at the sight that greeted him.

Everything looked normal.

Felicity was on the couch. Sleeping.

He gulped. He hoped she was sleeping.

Ryder strode over to her, and, as if watching someone else's hand move toward her throat, he checked for a pulse.

It was there. Slow and steady.

He let out a breath. *Thank fuck.*

He heard Blake and Alexis enter the apartment, but he ignored them. Reaching a hand down, he shook Felicity's shoulder lightly. "Wake up, love."

She didn't even flinch.

Ryder frowned. He knew Felicity was tired from their day, but she'd always been somewhat of a light sleeper. She'd spent the last decade on the run—of course she was.

He shook her again, harder. "Felicity," he said, louder this time.

She slept on, oblivious to everything going on around her.

"Stay here," Blake ordered.

Ryder looked up to see he'd been talking to Alexis. He had a gun out and was creeping down the hallway to the bedrooms. Ryder put his hand back on Felicity's throat, her pulse reassuring him that she really was just sleeping soundly and not dead.

Blake returned after less than a minute carrying baby Ace.

Ryder frowned. "Where's Nate?"

Blake stopped in his tracks. "Nate?"

"Yeah. Felicity was babysitting both kids while Grace and Logan went up to Denver to that show she's been wanting to see."

"He wasn't there," Blake said softly.

And there it was.

Ryder's stomach flipped, and he pressed his lips together to keep from throwing up.

He looked back down to Felicity and frowned.

"The cops are on their way," Blake said.

But Ryder wasn't hearing him. His eyes were roving around the room, looking for whatever had been used to knock Felicity out. Because she was definitely out. There was no way she would've slept through Joseph coming into the apartment and kidnapping Nate otherwise.

Ryder knew he hadn't been gone that long. Maybe Joseph had conned his way into the apartment somehow and used chloroform to disable Felicity. He mentally shook his head. No, she wouldn't have opened the door to anyone.

His eyes landed on the pictures he'd encouraged Felicity to display out here in the living area. She'd put up a few pictures of Grace and her. Grace with the babies. A group picture of Alexis, Bailey, Grace, and herself. Every single picture was lying facedown on the shelves they'd been sitting on.

Then he noticed something he hadn't seen before. Her giraffe. Her beloved stuffed giraffe was lying in the middle of the floor, its head ripped from its body. Ryder couldn't take his eyes away from it for a long moment.

"He's been in here," Ryder whispered.

"How did he drug her?" Blake asked, coming up next to the sofa. He'd passed Ace off to Alexis, who was now standing at the door to the apartment waiting on the police officers to show up. "Could he have gassed the place? Put a hose through the air-conditioning duct or through a window somehow?"

"Ace is fine," Ryder said through clenched teeth, indicating the now-awake baby babbling in Alexis's arms.

"Could he have drugged something then? I mean, you're fine. What did she eat that you didn't?"

Ryder's eyes went to the glass on the coffee table. The empty glass. The one he'd filled with water for her. Twice. "Fuck. The water. It's her ritual. She drinks a full glass every night. *Every* night. It's her thing."

"And you don't?" Blake asked, eyeing the water dispenser.

Ryder shook his head. "No."

"How'd he know?"

Ryder shook his head once more, even as his eyes swept the room once more. He didn't know what he was looking for. "I have no idea. Cameras? Watching through the windows? I have no fucking idea."

The brothers looked at each other for a long second before Blake said, "We need to call Logan. Tell him about his son."

Ryder took a deep breath and looked down at Felicity. Not only had he failed her, but he'd failed his brother and sister-in-law too. He felt the hate well up inside him. He'd hated before, but not like this. Never like this.

It was one thing to rescue a woman who'd been held captive as a sex slave and find she'd been reduced to a shell of who she'd likely been before. It was one thing to break into a room where a woman was being held captive by an ex-lover who held a knife to her throat. It was one thing to pick up a child who was so scared, every muscle in her body stiffened at his touch, even if it was gentle.

It was another thing altogether to drug his woman, kidnap his nephew, and expect him to take it lightly. A switch had been flicked inside Ryder, and he wasn't sure he'd ever be the same again. Hate welled up inside him, so thick and viscous it made breathing difficult. Joseph Waters was a dead man. Ryder would make sure his death was slow and painful. He'd bring him to a place the mercenaries had in the mountains and extract his revenge from his flesh inch by fucking inch. The man would wish he'd never even heard Felicity's name by the time he was done.

Felicity.

Ryder looked down at the woman he loved. Her eyes were closed, but she was alive. He sat on the couch and pulled her into his arms. He should be doing something right now. Talking to Logan. Trying to call Rex. Going to meet the police officers. Something.

But all he could do was bury his face into Felicity's hair and thank God she was alive and safe. As the feelings of hate warred with the feelings of relief that she was in his arms, Ryder mentally planned.

Joseph would be contacting Felicity; he was sure of it. He'd just have to be ready when he did.

Chapter Seventeen

Felicity heard low voices all around her. She was extremely groggy but forced her eyes open. She didn't recognize where she was. The room was lit by light coming in from a half-opened door nearby, and she saw Ryder standing at the foot of the bed she was lying on, talking with Blake.

"Ryder?" she said, although it came out more as a croak than an actual word.

Within seconds, he was at her side. "Hey."

"Where are we?"

He didn't answer for a second, but then said, "The hospital."

Felicity crinkled her brow. *The hospital?* She couldn't remember anything. "Are you all right?"

His lips quirked, but he didn't laugh. "I'm fine. We're here because of you. Do you remember what happened last night?"

She immediately shook her head, but asked, "Joseph?"

The anger and frustration was easy to see in Ryder's hazel eyes as he nodded. "Do you remember me getting a text from Blake?"

Felicity frowned, but then nodded. "Yeah. You were worried about him." She saw Blake shift next to her, but didn't take her eyes off Ryder.

"Well, it was a setup, just like I thought in the first place. I shouldn't have left you alone."

"Did he rape me?" Felicity asked, not really wanting to hear the answer, but scared not to at the same time.

"No." Ryder's answer was swift and succinct.

"Then what?"

"He drugged you. With ketamine and Rohypnol. In your water."

Felicity let that sink in. No wonder she didn't remember what happened. "Why? Just to prove that he could?"

Ryder ran a hand through his hair, and he looked away from her for the first time. Felicity had been confused and nervous when she'd woken up, but it was nothing compared to how she was feeling now. A pit formed in her belly, and she felt her hands begin to shake. "What happened?" she asked in a whisper.

Ryder looked back at her then, and she felt Blake's hand press into her calf. Felicity steeled herself.

"Nate is gone."

Felicity blinked. "What?"

"Nate. Joseph drugged you, then entered your apartment and took Nate. We know it was him because the external cameras showed him clearly. Fucker even made a point to look up, straight into the lens, and smirk as he was leaving."

"But you found him, right?"

Ryder merely shook his head.

Felicity stared at him for a moment, then her gaze swung to Blake. "Joseph has called, though, hasn't he? To tell you how much money he wants?"

She felt Ryder's finger on her chin as he gently forced her to look at him. "Joseph hasn't called, love. Nate's been gone for twenty hours. We don't know where he is and have no leads."

Felicity blinked. Then promptly began to hyperventilate. This was her worst fear come to life. Someone else she loved had been hurt because of her. Grace and Logan had to be devastated. God, the twins had been put under her care, and she'd failed them. Utterly. Tears sprang to her eyes, and there was no way she could hold them back. Not hiding them or even trying to wipe them away, Felicity looked up at Ryder helplessly.

"Breathe," he said firmly. "Slow down your breathing or you're going to hurt yourself."

She tried, but it was impossible. There wasn't enough air in the room. She was suffocating.

Ryder took hold of her head and brought his face inches from hers. "Breathe with me. Watch me. That's it. In . . . hold it . . . out. Good. Again."

Felicity did as Ryder ordered, mimicking his breathing and eventually slowing down her own breaths long enough to get a steady stream of oxygen into her lungs. She was aware of Ryder brushing her tears away with his thumbs, but she hardly felt it through her grief.

"Grace must hate me."

"She doesn't hate you," Blake said from the foot of the bed. "Not at all."

"I need to go to her." Felicity didn't know if her best friend would even want to see her, but she had to be there for her.

"As soon as the doctor arrives and checks you out, we'll head over to their house," Ryder told her.

Felicity nodded. She slumped back against the pillow and closed her eyes. She felt Ryder's hand grasp hers and felt stronger simply because he was there with her. He didn't try to tell her everything would be all right. He simply held her hand.

Sometime between when she learned about Nate being kidnapped and the doctor coming in to release her, Felicity's grief changed to anger. Joseph had no right to drug her. No right to come into her apartment uninvited. And definitely no right to steal a helpless baby. Enough was enough. He'd terrorized her for years. Killed Colleen. Killed her mom. And hurt who knew how many people in his life. She was done.

"I'm done," she said, wiping the tears from her face.

"What?" Ryder asked.

"I'm done hiding from him. I'm done making him feel like he has the upper hand." She reached out and grabbed Ryder's forearm where it rested on the bed next to her. "I'll do whatever it takes to bring him down. Be bait. Drive to Chicago and march right up to his father's house. I don't care."

"We're going to find him and get Nate back," Ryder told her.

"Damn straight we are," Felicity said firmly.

At her words, Ryder's lips twitched.

"It's not funny," she fumed.

"I know it's not. Believe me. But I'm so fucking happy that you aren't crying anymore. I'd much rather you be angry than broken."

"I'm furious," she informed Ryder.

"Me too, Felicity. Me too."

She opened her mouth to respond, but the doctor interrupted by entering the room.

Within an hour, Felicity had been released, and Blake left to go back to Logan's house. Nathan was already there with Alexis, Bailey, and her brother, Joel.

Now she and Ryder were on their way to the police station. Logan hadn't wanted to leave Grace's side, so he asked Ryder to talk to the officer in his place. Since Felicity didn't want to be anywhere but at Ryder's side, and she was too chicken to go and see Grace yet, she was going with him to the station.

"How do you feel?" Ryder asked.

Felicity looked over at him. They were in the reception area at the police station, waiting for the detective. "I'm okay."

When Ryder didn't respond, but ground his teeth together hard enough to make his jaw flex, Felicity put a hand on his arm. "I'm *okay*," she repeated.

"He put enough ketamine and Rohypnol in your water to kill you," Ryder bit out.

"But he didn't," she said, then added, "Look at me."

Ryder's eyes met hers, and she almost flinched at the pain and anger swirling in the dark depths. She'd seen glimpses of the mercenary behind his eyes in the past, but at the moment, Ryder looked like he would kill anyone who even looked at her wrong. "He didn't," she whispered.

"I handed that glass to you," Ryder said softly, the anger in his eyes only dimming a smidge. "I served up that poisoned water on a silver platter."

"Don't," Felicity ordered. "Don't let him get to you."

"Too late," he said, barking out a laugh. But it wasn't a happy sound. It was self-deprecating and filled with so much derision that Felicity nearly choked on the tears in her throat.

She got off the chair and kneeled on the floor in front of Ryder. She reached up and cradled his face in her hands, as he'd done so often to her. "You're going to kill him," she said softly so no one in the station could overhear her. "You're going to find Nate and bring him home to Grace and Logan. Don't let your anger get in the way of that."

For the first time since she'd woken up, Felicity saw an emotion in her man's face other than absolute fury. "He could've killed you."

"But he didn't. That was his mistake." She took a chance saying that, but it was what she'd been thinking ever since she realized what had happened. "He could've killed me and been done with it. And then taken Nate just to be a dick. But he wants to taunt me with the fact he took the baby. He's going to contact me, soon. I know it, and so do you. I need you to be clearheaded enough to be my backup. If you're too blinded by rage, you can't do that effectively. You hear me?"

Ryder had closed his eyes halfway through her little speech, but at her question, they opened, and he tilted his head into one of her hands.

"I hear you, love," he said softly. "You can trust me."

Felicity sagged in relief. It was the first time he'd used the endearment since she'd woken up. She'd half been afraid she'd lost him. But her Ryder was back.

"Good. And you know what else?"

"What?"

"I still owe you that blow job." She said it to try to lighten the moment. She wasn't exactly in the mood for sex, and it was obvious he wasn't either, but her words worked. His lips quirked up in what would have to pass for a smile.

"That you do."

They looked at each other for quite a while until a voice asked, "Felicity Jones and Ryder Sinclair?"

Felicity turned and saw the detective standing in the door of the waiting area. She struggled to get up, but Ryder was there helping her stand before she could get her feet under her. They walked hand in hand into the back area of the Castle Rock Police Station.

After they'd gotten settled into the chairs in front of Detective Chris Baker, he told them why he'd called them down. "Just to be sure there was no connection between your godson's kidnapping and what happened a year or so ago, we called the state penitentiary and checked on Grace's parents. They were interviewed and didn't admit to knowing anything about the abduction of their grandson."

Felicity gasped. She hadn't even thought about the Masons being involved. Of course, it wouldn't surprise her, they were truly awful people. And they'd probably love to see their daughter's child in danger. "Do they somehow know Joseph?"

Detective Baker looked uncomfortable for the first time. He fiddled with a pen on the desk in front of him and refused to meet their eyes before saying, "After speaking with both of them, we don't think they're involved at all. Margaret didn't have any reaction whatsoever to Joseph's name, and when she learned about her grandson's disappearance, she seemed genuinely surprised. Then she laughed. Said her daughter deserved it. Walter didn't seem to have much of a reaction at all. He's not having an easy time of it in prison. The other inmates don't think much of him."

"She laughed?" Felicity asked in an incredulous tone.

"Yes, ma'am."

"That *bitch*," she bit out. "I knew she was heartless, but God, that's her flesh and blood."

Ryder put his hand on her leg and squeezed. "She didn't care about her daughter in the least, why would she care about her grandson?"

"I don't know, but still. That's just . . . I don't know what that is."

Ryder squeezed her leg once more, then turned back to the detective. "Have you told my brother or Grace this?"

He shook his head. "No. I was going to tell them when they came into the station today."

Felicity looked up at Ryder in concern. If Logan had heard what Margaret Mason had said about his son, he would've lost it. Neither he nor Grace needed that bitch's negativity right now. She was very glad they had come to the station to talk with the detective instead of Logan and Grace.

The detective spoke again. "So, with the Masons ruled out, we're still checking video surveillance in the downtown area to see if we can't find more evidence. We have some interviews lined up and . . ."

Felicity tuned out the detective and turned her gaze to Ryder. They both knew what the cops would find. Nothing. Yesterday they'd learned that the gym's cleaning lady, Mrs. Hanley, had been found murdered in her home. They'd had no idea she was missing because the gym was still being cleaned on a regular basis. By who, they had no concrete evidence of, but had a pretty good guess. They figured the woman's death was most likely how Joseph had gained access to the gym in the first place.

No, the cops wouldn't learn anything new by watching surveillance tapes of Joseph stealing little Nate out of her apartment and the gym.

They already knew who had done it. All they had to do now was wait for the asshole to contact her and finish his decadelong stalking, once and for all.

As if he had come to the same conclusion, Ryder suddenly stood. "Thank you for letting us know," he said abruptly.

"Uh, you're welcome," the detective stammered. He shook Ryder's hand, and the next thing Felicity knew, her man was leading her out of the stuffy police station.

The drive back to Logan and Grace's house was done in silence. Ryder took her hand once more when they arrived. Felicity needed that connection. She was trying to be tough and brave, but it was difficult.

"Has Rex said anything?" Felicity asked Ryder before they made it to the front door.

He shook his head. "No."

"But he's trying, right?"

Ryder turned to her then. He put his hands on her shoulders and looked down at her. She was again struck by the intensity of his gaze. On the outside he was calm and collected, but all it took was one look into his eyes, and the lethal killer was revealed.

"They're all doing everything they can to find Nate, love. Rex has been calling in favors, and the guys have reached out to their contacts as well. We're going to find him."

Felicity bit her lip. "Joseph is going to want me to meet with him. He's going to throw it in my face that he knows where the baby is and I don't."

"You're not going with that fucker. No way. I can't lose you, Felicity."

She looked up at him, her eyes filling with tears. "Even if it means your nephew dies?"

Ryder closed his eyes then, the frustration and helplessness clear to read on his expression before he shuttered it. But as soon as they closed, his eyes opened again, and Felicity gasped at what she saw there.

"It won't come to that. I won't let it. Felicity, you need to know that *you* are my first concern. Will always be from here on out. You come before everyone. I love you, Felicity. More than I ever thought I could love anyone in my entire life. I'd move heaven and earth to make sure you have enough to eat, a roof over your head, whatever material things your heart desires, and that you're safe."

"Ryder—" she began, but he interrupted her.

"That being said, I'm trying to stay confident that Rex will find Nate. If not him, then my team. If not them, Alexis will uncover something in her searches. She's got that computer-guru guy helping her. Joseph is smart, but not *that* smart. He made a mistake. I feel it in my gut."

"So you don't think he killed Nate?" Felicity asked. It was her greatest fear.

Ryder immediately shook his head. "No. It's just like you said. He wants to taunt us with the fact that he knows where the boy is and we don't."

"What's taking him so long to contact me?"

"I don't know. But he will. And soon."

"I hope so."

"Believe it. We're going to end this."

And with that, Felicity tipped forward and laid her forehead on Ryder's chest. His arms came around her, and they stood like that for a few long minutes. Absorbing each other's love.

They were interrupted when Nathan opened the front door. He, Bailey, and Joel had been camped out at Logan's house as well. Logan had wanted Blake and Alexis there too, saying they'd be safer if the families were all together, but they'd refused. Alexis was frantically using her computer skills to see what she could find about Joseph and said she'd be more effective at her own house or at Ace Security's offices.

"Logan just got a call. Number showed was yours, Ryder. It's him. He wants to talk to Felicity."

She stiffened and felt Ryder do the same.

"My number?" Ryder asked as he immediately turned to his brother.

Even though he was completely focused on what Nathan was saying, Felicity's stomach clenched when Ryder reached out and grabbed her hand, intertwining his fingers with hers, showing her that he was still thinking about her even as drama swirled around them.

She held on tight as they entered the house.

"Yeah. We figure he's still using whatever contraption he's got to manipulate where the call is originating from."

Ryder nodded and headed for Logan, who was standing at his dining room table. They'd made it their headquarters for the moment. The table was piled high with papers, empty coffee cups, and three laptops.

Grace was standing next to the table with Ace in her arms. As if the baby knew something was wrong, his eyes constantly scanned his surroundings. Felicity didn't know much about babies, much less twins, but she imagined the little guy was searching for his brother. They'd been together in the womb and every day of their lives. It had to be a bit weird for Nate not to be by his side now.

Felicity's best friend looked exhausted. She had dark circles under her eyes, and it didn't look like she had showered that morning either. Her brown hair hung lank and dull around her face, and her eyes had lost the sparkle they'd had since her parents had been put in jail.

Logan didn't look much better. He had stress lines around his eyes that hadn't been there a couple of days ago. His body was tense, and he startled at the smallest sound. He also couldn't seem to be more than a body length away from his wife and child, as if keeping them in his line of sight would somehow keep them disappearing in a puff of smoke, like his son had.

Nathan went straight to Bailey's side. Felicity wasn't sure where Joel was, probably upstairs playing a video game.

Logan handed his phone over to Ryder without a word.

Ryder turned to Felicity and put the phone against his chest so Joseph wouldn't hear his words.

"You remember what we talked about, right?" he asked in a soft voice.

Felicity nodded and dutifully recited the plan. "Don't antagonize him. Listen and agree to whatever he wants. Try to get him to prove that he's got Nate."

"Good," Ryder nodded. Then he pulled her to him and kissed her forehead. He turned her so her back was to his chest, and he wrapped his arms around her, keeping the phone in his hands so it was in front of both of them.

The position was intimate, and she felt surrounded by Ryder. It gave her the courage she didn't exactly have at the moment. She felt Ryder take a deep breath against her back, and she did the same. She couldn't screw this up. Nate's life was at stake.

Ryder clicked on the speaker button, and Felicity immediately said, "Hello?"

"Megan. It's so good to hear your voice after all this time," Joseph drawled.

Felicity closed her eyes. She couldn't stop the trembles that moved through her. It had been a decade since she'd heard Joseph's voice, but she knew she'd never forget it. "Where's Nate?"

"Tsk, tsk, tsk," Joseph scolded. "Not even a few social niceties?"

"Where is he? I want to hear him."

"You're not in charge here," Joseph bit out, all amusement in his tone gone. "I am. And if you ever want to see that brat again, you'll temper your tone, be a bit more polite, and do exactly what I say. It's the least you can do since I've got something you want. You, and only you, will meet me at Clear Creek Canyon Park." He chuckled then, an evil sound that made Felicity's skin crawl. "I think the Andersons know exactly the spot I'm talking about, as it's where little Alexis spent a bit of time buried up to her neck. But I mean it, Megan, only you. You meet me there and I'll take you to the brat."

"How do I know you're telling the truth?" Felicity asked. "That Nate is even alive?"

"You're just going to have to trust me now, aren't you?"

"Trust you?" Felicity asked, the disbelief easy to hear in her tone. She struggled to hold back her words, remembering that she wasn't supposed to antagonize Joseph, but she couldn't hold back anymore. "You've done nothing but make my life hell for the last ten years. Why would I trust you now?"

"Because!" Joseph yelled. "I'm a man! Bitches lie, not real men. All women know how to do is fucking lie. You open your mouth and lies come spewing out. You have no integrity, and you're all fucking weak. You'll show up in three hours, or that precious baby will never know his parents. He'll grow up never knowing his real name or that he's got a twin out there somewhere."

Obviously hearing Felicity's gasp, he said, "That's right, Megan. I've got him stashed somewhere safe, and you'll never see him again if you don't follow my directions to the letter. Show up by yourself, bitch, or poor little Grace will never see her baby again."

And with that, Joseph hung up.

There was silence in the room for a second before Grace sobbed.

Logan took his wife in his arms, doing what he could to console her, but kept his eyes on Ryder and Felicity.

Ryder clicked on the icon on the phone to shut it off and dropped his arms. Felicity shivered with the loss of his body heat, but he immediately turned her to face him.

"You aren't going up there by yourself," he said.

"Damn straight I'm not," Felicity returned.

He blinked, and Felicity knew she'd surprised him. "I don't want to be anywhere near Joseph Waters," she told him. "He's batshit crazy, killed my mom, doesn't give a shit about any woman, and wouldn't hesitate to hurt me. I don't trust him as far as I can throw him. So yeah, I'm not going to go up to the middle of the Colorado wilderness and meet with the man who I've been running from for the last decade by myself. I know he said I should come alone, but he seriously can't really think I'll actually do it."

"But, he said he wouldn't tell you where Nate was if you weren't alone," Grace gasped from next to them.

Ryder answered her before Felicity could. "He's not going to tell her where your son is even if she *does* show up by herself. He's going to need to be convinced."

"And how are you going to do that?" Bailey asked. She'd been quiet up until now, but the question was a good one.

Felicity looked up at the man she loved with all her heart. She hated that she'd brought Joseph Waters into her best friend's life, but if anyone could help end the reign of terror he'd held over her for all her adult life, and get her godson back in the process, it was Ryder.

"My friend Black is one hell of an interrogator. He won't have any problem getting info from a coward like Joseph Waters. That asshole has had everything handed to him on a silver platter. It's one of the reasons why he's acting like a spoiled little kid when it comes to Felicity. The stunts he's pulled over the last week have been more annoying than truly threatening. But he's stepped over the line by taking Nate. Rex is pissed. And the head of the Mountain Mercenaries isn't a man you want on your bad side."

Ryder turned to Grace then. "We're going to find Nate," he told her with absolute conviction.

"I'm going with you guys," Logan said.

"Me too," Nathan piped up.

Ryder nodded. "We'll pick Blake up on our way north as well."

Felicity looked from Ryder to the Anderson brothers. The vibe in the room was intense, but she had no doubt that with the four men at her back, Joseph Waters would soon not be a problem anymore.

"We'll talk about strategy on the way up there," Logan said. "We only have three hours. We need to get going."

Ryder nodded. Then he walked over to Grace, stopped in front of her, and brought a hand up to the infant in her arms. He leaned over to speak into Ace's ear. "I'll find your brother, Ace. I swear on it."

As if the infant could understand his uncle's words, he waved his little arms in the air and cooed.

Felicity let the tears fall then. Ryder had so many facets to his personality, and she was in love with every single one. The considerate side that always treated her with respect. The romantic side that could make love to her for hours without a thought to his own satisfaction. The lusty side that took her how he wanted in whatever position he wanted. The hard side that she knew wouldn't hesitate to use deadly force if it meant keeping her safe. And finally, the tender side that took the time to reassure a little baby that he'd bring his twin back safe and sound. He'd make a wonderful father. An amazing husband. She wanted him. All of him.

Her tears dried as her resolve strengthened. Joseph wouldn't take Ryder away from her. No way. "Come on," she said, her voice husky. "Let's go end this once and for all."

Chapter Eighteen

Ryder's 370Z bounced on the dirt road. They'd turned off Route 6 onto the sad semblance of a road. He could feel the rocks scraping the underside of his sports car, but he didn't even flinch. He could replace the car. All his focus was on the upcoming confrontation.

His brothers were following right behind him in Logan's truck. He didn't know how Blake felt about being back where Alexis had almost died, but he honestly couldn't even think about that right now.

Obviously Joseph had done his research on the Andersons and had picked the location on purpose, to try to throw them off emotionally, but it wouldn't work. Ryder knew his brothers well enough by now to know all their thoughts were on what might happen in the next few minutes.

Nate's life depended on them doing everything right.

Ryder stopped at the end of the road and motioned for Felicity to climb over the console and get out on his side. He wasn't going to chance that Joseph would change his mind and decide to immediately shoot his woman. He didn't think that was his plan, but he wasn't willing to risk her life on it either.

He and Felicity figured that Joseph wanted to take her away somewhere private where he could torture her at his leisure. *That* was never going to happen.

Ryder knew his brothers were just as well armed as he was. He had a handgun in a holster at his back, one strapped to the holster at his side, and three knives hidden on his person as well. Felicity had wanted to carry a pistol, but he'd talked her out of it. He had the utmost confidence in himself, and his brothers, to be able to protect her. The last thing he wanted was for Joseph to somehow get ahold of any weapon Felicity might have. Besides, Ryder was the killer, not her. He'd do whatever it took to keep that from her conscience, no matter how confident she was that she could handle killing Joseph if it came down to it.

He gripped Felicity's hand tightly as he helped her climb out of the driver's side of his car. Ryder looked around for Joseph, but didn't see him. The hair on the back of his neck was standing on end again, letting him know the man was there, simply not showing himself yet.

Pulling Felicity into his side, making her less of a target, Ryder waited for his brothers to approach.

"He here?" Logan asked softly.

Ryder nodded. "Yeah, I can feel him lurking somewhere."

"Me too," Blake agreed.

Just then Joseph walked out of a break in the trees about twenty-five yards away.

"Women never could follow directions," he drawled as if he hadn't blackmailed the group into meeting him.

"Where's Nathan?" Felicity called out.

"Step away from them," Joseph ordered, walking closer.

Felicity went to do as ordered, but Ryder held on to her hand for a long moment. "Don't be a hero," he warned. "Don't believe anything he says."

She looked at him impatiently. "I won't. And trust *me*," she returned, "I'm not going to be stupid."

Ryder did the hardest thing he'd ever done in his life. He let go of Felicity's hand.

Felicity could feel her heart beating wildly in her chest. Letting go of Ryder's hand had been like hanging off a four-hundred-foot ledge and letting go of the only thing that was keeping her from plunging to her death.

She took four steps away from Ryder and his brothers, looking back to see them spread out in a line behind her. Tears threatened at seeing how thoroughly they had her back, but she blinked them back. She needed to be clearheaded and clear-eyed for whatever Joseph had up his sleeve. And she had no doubt he had something planned. The man was a sore loser and wouldn't have wanted them up here in the middle of nowhere without some sort of plan.

Felicity looked at the man who had been stalking and terrorizing her since she was twenty years old. In many ways he looked the same as he had back in college. He had the same air of superiority that he'd always worn like a cloak. His dark-brown, almost black, hair was cut close to his head. He had a bit more of a paunch than when he'd been younger, and there were more lines on his face.

His bright-blue eyes were just as piercing in intensity as they'd been back then, but she could also see a hint of uneasiness in the blue orbs. He'd probably expected Ryder to show up, maybe Logan too, but having all four Anderson brothers arrive, and looking as pissed off as they were, had rattled him.

"Well?" she asked. "I'm here. Now what?"

"You were supposed to be alone."

"Yeah, well, sorry, but I'm not that stupid. There's no way I was going to come and meet you by myself. I don't trust you, just as you don't trust me."

Joseph crossed his arms over his chest, as if settling in for a long conversation. "So, Megan, how does it feel to have someone butt into your life? Sucks, doesn't it?"

She grit her teeth. She hated how he said her old name. "My name is Felicity now."

He ignored her. "It took me a long time to find you, but I must say, the last six months have been quite entertaining. If I knew what lengths you'd go to stay under the radar, I might've let this little game continue a bit longer."

"What does that mean?" Felicity asked, hating that she was probably asking him exactly what he wanted her to, but, dammit, she had the right to know.

"It means if I'd known how desperate you were, how often you moved around, how you didn't make any friends, didn't use credit, didn't even have a real driver's license . . . I might've backed off and let you continue to live on the run. But, on the other hand, it was extremely gratifying to do the one thing I knew would make you come back to Chicago."

Felicity's hands clenched into fists. She refused to ask what he meant this time.

"Yeah, sweet little Megan. Your mom. I should've killed her years earlier. All this could've been done with way before now, but I was busy. It's not easy being the son of Garrick Watson. My dad kept me busy, but I was still able to build my own empire right under his nose."

Joseph laughed then, and Felicity's skin crawled.

"You might be interested to know that I did my best to get your mom to tell me where you were. She held on pretty well. Didn't beg for her life until near the end." He shrugged. "I would've played longer, but she jerked under my knife at the wrong moment, and I slipped. Cut her throat long before I was ready."

"You fucking bastard," Felicity ground out, and actually took a step toward Joseph before realizing what she was doing and halting herself. "She never did anything to you."

"On the contrary," he spit out. "She's a fucking woman. I have no use for *any* of you. If I had my way, you'd all be kept on your backs in the house. Not working. Not spouting your 'I'm as good as a man' shit. Because, news flash, you're not. No woman will *ever* be as good as a man."

"Cut the shit," Ryder barked out, obviously having reached the end of his rope. "Where's Nathan?"

At his words, Joseph suddenly moved, pulling out a handgun and pointing it at Ryder. "Shut the fuck up. I'm in charge here. I'm holding *all* the cards."

As if choreographed, all four brothers pulled their own guns and pointed them at Joseph at the same time.

"Back up, Felicity," Ryder ordered.

"No, don't, *Megan*," Joseph retorted. "Stay right where you are or you might end up with a bullet in your kneecap . . . to start with." Her stalker pulled out another handgun and pointed it at her this time.

Felicity froze. Her hands went up in capitulation. Her mind spun. She felt as though she was in the middle of the Wild West. She didn't particularly like having four guns pointed at her from behind . . . well, they weren't pointed at her, but she also wasn't convinced she was completely out of the line of fire either.

A bead of sweat rolled down the side of her face, but she ignored it. "I'm not moving," she said softly. "All I want is to make sure Nate is safe."

"Walk toward me," Joseph ordered, ignoring her words. "You come with me and I'll take you to the baby."

She didn't believe him for a second.

"Don't move, Felicity," Ryder growled from behind her, closer now. She didn't take her eyes off Joseph to check, but he sounded as if he'd moved a little to her left and closer.

"Stop moving," Joseph barked, obviously seeing Ryder's movements as well.

His gun swung from her right to her left. "You too, asshole. If you think I don't see you moving, you're just as stupid as Megan here."

Then he pointed both his guns right at her. Felicity looked down the barrels of the pistols into Joseph's blue eyes. He was furious.

"This didn't have to be so hard," he ground out. "All you had to do was follow one simple instruction. Come by yourself. But no, of course not. No bitch does what she's told. Not even your fucking roommate all those years ago. All I wanted was for her to do what I told her to, but she couldn't do it. She nagged, day in and day out. I couldn't fucking stand it. It's my right as the man to maintain discipline in my home. All I did was smack her around a little, and she wouldn't fucking stop crying. All night. Begging that she needed to see a doctor. Crying that her arm was broken. Fucking crybaby. I told her to shut up time and time again and warned her she'd regret it if she didn't. Finally, I had no choice but to shut her up myself. Fuck, the blessed sound of silence when she took that last breath and stopped sniveling was almost orgasmic."

Felicity listened with horror to Joseph describing Colleen's last moments.

"Joseph, can I—"

"No! You. Fucking. Can. Not!" he roared, then shot off a round.

The ground in front of her exploded in a cloud of dust, and Felicity felt debris hitting her legs. Luckily her jeans kept most of the damage to a minimum, but something hit her hard. She forced herself to stay upright, instinctively knowing if she crumpled to the ground, Ryder would shoot the man dead. And they'd lose the chance to find Nate.

Gritting her teeth, she remained upright, putting her weight on her right leg. As it was, she could hear growling coming from behind her. All four of the men were on the edge.

"Get your ass over here, right now!" Joseph yelled.

"I don't think so," a new voice boomed into the clearing.

Shocked, as Felicity hadn't heard anyone else arrive, she turned her head just enough to keep her eye on Joseph, not putting it past him to bum-rush her the second her head was turned, and saw a man she'd never seen before striding into the fray as if he hadn't a care in the world.

Ryder had never wanted to kill anyone as badly as he wanted to kill Joseph Waters. He'd thought he wanted him dead before. Now it was a certainty. The man had shot at his woman. Fucking shot at her. The only thing keeping him from filling the man with an entire clip of bullets was the knowledge that they'd never know where Nate was if he did. He had to keep the man alive and get him to Black. His friend and teammate would get the knowledge out of him, using whatever means necessary. Once they had Nate's location, Black would turn Joseph back over to him, and Ryder could have his vengeance. For him, Felicity, *and* Nate.

Just as his finger began to squeeze the trigger to take out Joseph's knee, he watched in disbelief as a man strode into the middle of the standoff as if he didn't even notice six guns pointed at each other.

"Garrick Watson," he said under his breath, letting his brothers know who the newcomer was.

Rex had sent a picture of the man after he'd been informed about the entire situation. He looked nothing like what someone might think a Mob boss should look like. He wasn't very tall—a couple of inches under six feet. His black hair was longish, swept forward over his forehead much like Justin fucking Bieber's. The style looked ridiculous on the older man. He was wearing a pair of skinny jeans and a white polo buttoned up all the way to his chin. A black suit jacket completed his ensemble.

Ryder might've called him feminine if it wasn't for the absolute lack of emotion on the man's face. It was a ruthless look that Ryder had seen on many an assassin's face. He was a man without scruples or tenderness. He'd read the file on Garrick Watson and intellectually knew the man wasn't exactly Mother Teresa, but even if he hadn't read the file on the stranger walking among them, he'd know with one glance he wasn't someone he wanted to be on the wrong side of.

And that, Ryder supposed, was how the man had gotten so powerful in Chicago. Lack of remorse, lack of compassion, and someone who had no difficulty getting rid of problems permanently, all combined to make him one scary motherfucker.

Knowing Garrick didn't teleport to the clearing, Ryder glanced behind him and saw a shiny sleek Lincoln Town Car parked behind their vehicles on the dirt road. Two muscular men stood in front of it, their arms crossed. Turning back to the scene in front of him, Ryder knew shit would get ugly real fast if something happened to Garrick, as his bodyguards wouldn't hesitate to shoot to kill, but for now, Joseph and his father were his concern.

Ryder's finger twitched on the trigger of his pistol. He so badly wanted to take out both Joseph and Garrick, but he held back, needing to see how the situation would play itself out.

As if seeing the same thing in the older man that he did, Felicity slowly began to limp her way backward toward him. Ryder kept his attention split between Joseph and his father, but sighed in relief when Felicity reached him. He shoved her behind him roughly and waited.

"Joseph, what did I tell you?" Garrick asked his son, taking the exact spot where Felicity had been, standing between the brothers and his son. He seemingly had no concerns about the four men with guns pointed at his back.

"Dad, what are you doing here?" Joseph whined.

"Cleaning up after you . . . again," Garrick bit out, his tone a little less congenial now.

Ryder glanced over at Logan for a split second. When he caught the other man's eyes, Ryder merely shrugged his shoulders, indicating he wasn't sure how this was going to play out and they should stay on their toes.

"There's nothing to clean up, Dad," Joseph said, the fake bravado easy to hear in his voice.

"The fuck there's not," Garrick returned. "Do you have any idea who you're messing with?"

"She needs to learn her lesson," Joseph tried again.

"Fuck her, she's not important," his dad said.

Ryder didn't like hearing anyone say that the woman he loved wasn't important, but he held his tongue.

"Mountain Mercenaries. Does the name ring any bells?" Garrick bellowed at his son. "Have you not heard one fucking thing I've said over the years about discretion?"

"You don't understand," Joseph tried again. "She butted into my life back then, and she needs to learn her place. Women don't matter. You've said it yourself. It's why you and my uncles aren't married. Because women are second-class citizens and not worthy of our attention."

"Then why are you *giving* her so much of your attention?" Garrick asked.

Ryder kept his gun trained on Joseph. At the moment, he was more of a threat than his father.

"She needs to pay," Joseph said again, stubbornly sticking to his point.

"If you don't put down your weapons and come with me right now, you will single-handedly ruin everything I've built over the last thirty years," Garrick said with a hint of steel in his voice. "Tell Mr. Anderson where you stashed his son, and this'll all be over. You'll come back to Chicago with me, we'll compensate him for any mental anguish you put him and his family through, and this'll be done."

"No!" Joseph exclaimed. "I won't."

Garrick took a step toward his son. "Where is the infant?" he asked in a low tone.

Joseph's eyes went from his father to Felicity.

Ryder put out a hand and made sure she was still covered. She was. She was standing stock-still behind him. Letting him protect her.

Trusting him. Even though the situation sucked, he felt a wave of love move through him.

"Look at me, son." When Joseph complied, Garrick continued. "We do not want the Mountain Mercenaries up our ass. Understand? Tell me where the infant is."

"No." Joseph sounded petulant, but absolutely unbending.

"I don't know where I went wrong with you," Garrick said with a shake of his head. "When you were born, I had such high hopes. You were inquisitive and smart. But by the time you were in the fifth grade, you were already showing signs of being a bully. You never understood that ruling people through respect and a little bit of fear is so much more effective than berating them constantly and using blackmail.

"I tried to teach you that there's a time and place for violence, but you seemed to thrive on it. When you were in high school and I had to pay off that judge to get you out of that assault charge, I thought you learned your lesson. But then you had to go and fuck it up again with that bitch in college, and I had to clean up that mess as well." Garrick shook his head and went on. "You're a disgrace. An embarrassment. I can't tell you how many of my men have come to me over the years to complain about you. To tell me all the ways you screwed up. At this point, I'm thinking I would've been better off without a son at all."

"I always did everything you told me to," Joseph protested. He clenched the pistol in his hand so hard, his knuckles were turning white. "But you were never satisfied. Never. You were the one who told me women were trash. That they were good for nothing but fucking. I watched you when I was still in elementary school with the whores you hired. You didn't let them get away with disrespecting you. I've only done what you taught me, Father. And this bitch disrespected me. And I'm not letting her get away with it."

Garrick took a step closer to his son. "I also taught you discretion. But you never learned that fucking lesson. You don't kill a bitch and dump her body to be found by the cops in your own neighborhood. You don't hit bitches where their screams can be heard by others. You brought this on yourself. I told you time and time again to let it go. That nothing she said about you would ever stick, but you wouldn't listen. Just like you never listen." Garrick shook his head and snorted in exasperation. "For once in your pathetic life, listen to what I'm saying. Tell me where the infant is."

"Fuck you," Joseph told his father, the hate easy to hear in his tone. "Go to hell."

"You'll be the only one going to hell today," Garrick responded. Then, without another word, he pulled a pistol out from under his suit coat and shot his son between the eyes.

Joseph fell backward, hitting the dirt with a thud. His sightless blue eyes stared up at the beautiful Colorado sky.

"No!" Logan screamed.

Ryder felt Felicity jerk behind him, but he didn't take his eyes off Garrick. The man had shot his son in cold blood without a moment's hesitation. There was no telling what else he might do.

The older man turned to face them, and all four brothers brought their pistols up and aimed them at the Mob boss.

Garrick held his arms open at his sides. One hand was open, the other still holding the pistol he'd used to kill his son, but his finger wasn't on the trigger. He first looked at Felicity. "I apologize on behalf of my son for the trouble you've had to endure for the last decade," he said in a formal tone. "I told him to stop. To leave you alone, and thought he had, but I was mistaken. You will be compensated for the trouble you've gone through, and you are free from any kind of retribution or attention from me or the rest of my family."

Ryder heard Felicity gasp behind him. He didn't know if it was in outrage or surprise, but he concentrated on the man's hand movements.

If his index finger even twitched toward the trigger of the pistol he was still holding, he'd blow him away.

Garrick then turned to Logan. The oldest Anderson brother had both hands gripping his pistol, and it was pointed right between Garrick's eyes. He didn't even flinch.

"I am going to do everything in my power to find your son and return him to you. My family and I have no beef with you and your brothers."

"You might not have a beef with us, but we now have one with you," Logan spat. "Your fucking son kidnapped my child."

Garrick merely shrugged. "Won't be the first time I'm hated, won't be the last. But honestly, *your* anger isn't what concerns me." Then he turned to Ryder and reholstered his pistol as if he didn't have a care in the world.

Thus far, the man hadn't shown any emotion, but his next words were almost pleading. He sounded more upset than when he'd been asking his son to put down his guns. "Ryder, please tell Rex that I apologize for my son. He was acting on his own. Rex knows I didn't approve of my son's activities. Make sure he knows that what he did was *not* sanctioned by me or my brothers."

"How did you know where we'd be?" Ryder asked.

Garrick shrugged. "Rex called me and informed me. I was already in Castle Rock to take my son in hand, but I was a little too late."

Ryder's head spun. He'd called his handler on the way up the mountain to let him know what was going down, but Rex hadn't mentioned anything about calling Joseph's father. *What the fuck?*

"So you'll tell him?" Garrick insisted.

"I'm not telling him shit until we have my nephew back," Ryder said calmly. "You want to keep the Mountain Mercenaries off your ass and out of your backyard, then you find Nathan Anderson and bring him home safely. *Then* I'll consider it."

Ryder knew he was pushing his luck, but the man in front of him wasn't stupid. He was ruthless and had just killed his own son. And he desperately wanted to keep Rex out of his business.

"Deal," he said, then nodded at Ryder. He ignored the other men and strode past them toward the sleek black Lincoln Town Car he'd arrived in. Two huge men, definitely bodyguards, stood next to the vehicle, their pistols now in their hands.

"We can't just let him walk out of here," Logan said, clearly agitated as Garrick walked back to his car. "We don't know where Nate is."

Blake put his hand on his brother's arm. "He doesn't know where he is."

"How do you know?" Logan spat, shaking off Blake's hand. "Maybe he was in on it the whole time. Maybe he's going to take my son in the place of his."

"I think he was being honest," Nathan added.

"Fuck," Logan swore. "Fuck, fuck *fuck*. I can't go home and tell Grace that Nate is still out there somewhere, and the only person who knew where he was is now dead. I just can't." He looked up at Ryder, pleading with his eyes for his half brother to do something . . . anything.

Ryder felt sick inside. The only leverage they had was Garrick's fear of Rex. He had no idea if the Chicago Mob boss really would look for little Nate, but he had to believe it. He'd get Rex to put pressure on him.

"I'm sorry, Logan. So sorry."

They all watched as the Town Car turned around and sped down the dirt road. As the car disappeared, sirens sounded in the distance. Ryder knew Logan had called Detective Baker, and he in turn had probably called the Denver SWAT team. The brothers turned to look at Joseph. He was lying where he fell. On his back in the dirt.

Felicity moved to Ryder's side, and he immediately raised his arm and settled it on her shoulders. He was pleased as he could be that Felicity was free to live her life where and how she wanted without ever having to worry about Joseph making it a living hell again. But at what price? He knew as if she'd said the words out loud that she'd prefer to have Joseph stalking her once more if only it would mean baby Nate was back at home with his parents and twin brother.

The quintet stood motionless and silent while they waited for the officers to arrive.

Tears fell down Logan's face soundlessly, and no one said a word, as they didn't know what *to* say.

Chapter Nineteen

It had taken quite a while to be allowed to leave the scene. Detective Baker wanted information about the kidnapping, and the Denver PD also had a ton of questions about Joseph and what had happened. Felicity didn't blame them. Dead bodies weren't exactly unheard of, but they also weren't everyday occurrences either.

The plan had been for Ryder to take Joseph out of the area before the police arrived at the rendezvous point. Ryder was going to take him down to Colorado Springs and to the rest of the Mountain Mercenaries. There, Joseph would've been interrogated, mostly by Black. The plan was that the brothers, and Felicity, were going to meet the officers and let them know that Joseph had run and that Ryder was hot on his trail.

But that had all gone to shit, and now they had to explain the dead body.

Logan, Blake, and Nathan let Ryder do the talking. They nodded in the appropriate places, and eventually the Denver PD detective allowed them all to go back to Castle Rock. He was made aware that baby Nate was still missing and reassured them that the CRPD would do whatever possible to find the baby, since he had been kidnapped in their jurisdiction.

Logan rode back home with Felicity and Ryder.

It was a mostly silent ride. Felicity had so many emotions, and adrenaline, whirling through her body, she almost felt sick. Relief. Terror. Disgust. Shock. And worry. Lots and lots of worry.

They pulled into Logan's driveway, and he said softly. "Please give me a moment alone with Grace so I can tell her."

"You want us to go?" Ryder asked.

"No," Logan answered immediately, and Felicity quietly sighed in relief. She didn't want to go anywhere. Wanted to be right by her best friend's side until her baby was back in her arms.

"Then we'll be right here until you need us," Ryder told his brother.

Logan got out of the sports car, his shoulders slumped, and headed for the front door. Felicity sat right where she was. "I've never seen him so defeated," Felicity said softly. "Even when Grace was missing for those couple of hours, he was more determined than scared. And he was so great with Blake when he was on Alexis's trail. But this . . . He doesn't think he's ever going to see his son again." Felicity turned awkwardly in her seat to face Ryder. "Do you think Joseph killed him?"

Ryder shook his head. "No. I think he did just what he taunted. Dumped him with someone with plans to go back and get him. I think he really did want to torture Logan with the knowledge that his child was being raised by someone else to be a part of Joseph's world."

Ryder brought a hand up to Felicity's face and slowly ran his thumb over the apple of her cheek. "It's over, love. You don't have to be afraid anymore."

A sob hitched through her chest, but she covered her eyes with a hand and did her best to control herself. If she started crying now, she wouldn't stop. It felt wrong to be so damn relieved when she knew how much pain Logan and Grace were in.

"God, I hate this," Ryder said softly.

Felicity nodded but didn't take her hand from her eyes.

A knock on Ryder's window made her look up. It was Blake. Ryder opened his door. "We can go in now," he said sadly.

Felicity opened her door and met Ryder at the front of the car. He grabbed her hand, and she did her best to control her tears once more. Even holding his hand felt different now that she never had to worry about Joseph tracking her down again.

They walked behind Blake into the house. The second they stepped inside, they could hear Grace crying as if her entire world had fallen apart . . . which she supposed it had.

They quietly stepped into the large living area and saw Grace and Logan sitting on the floor in the middle of the room. It looked like Grace had collapsed when her husband had told her the bad news about her baby.

Bailey was standing off to the side, holding Ace, and Joel had his arms around his sister, holding on for all he was worth.

The second they stepped into view, Grace's tearstained face turned to Felicity. "This is *your* fault. If it wasn't for you, I'd still have my baby!"

Felicity gasped and brought a hand up to her chest. It felt as if her best friend had just stabbed her with a knife, her words hurt that much. The tears she'd been holding back, barely, gushed out of her eyes. She took a step backward, wanting to flee. Wanting to be anywhere but there.

But Ryder wouldn't let go of her hand. Felicity reached down and tried to pry his fingers off hers, but he merely held on more firmly. "Oh my God, please, let me go," she begged. She couldn't handle this. It *was* her fault. If she'd fled when she'd planned, Nate would still be here. He'd be with his family.

"I'm sorry! I didn't mean it!"

Felicity looked up through her tears and saw Grace struggling to stand. She was staring at her and shaking her head.

"Leese. Please. I didn't mean it. It's not your fault. It's not."

This time when Felicity tugged at her hand, Ryder let go.

She stumbled a couple of steps toward Grace, and they fell into each other's arms. Both sobbed hysterically.

"I'm sorry, I'm so sorry," Felicity sobbed.

"No, *I'm* sorry," Grace returned, barely understandable through her gasps and tears. "I know it wasn't your fault. It was *his*. No one else's. You always told me not to apologize for stuff my parents did, so I'm telling you the same thing. Logan will find our son. I know it."

Felicity felt a hand at her elbow steering her and Grace to the couch, but she didn't lift her head from her best friend's shoulder. She held on as tightly as possible. They collapsed on the cushions, still holding on to each other and crying.

Before long, she felt someone at her back. It was Bailey. The other woman wrapped her arms around both Felicity and Grace. Felicity looked up and saw Alexis sitting behind Grace with her arms around her as well. The four of them huddled on the couch for at least half an hour. Talking quietly between bouts of tears.

Nathan put together a light dinner, but no one other than Joel really felt like eating.

When it was dark outside, Ryder came up beside her and leaned in. "Time for bed, love."

Felicity nodded. She hugged Grace and Bailey one more time, bid good night to the men, and followed behind Ryder, her hand held tightly in his. He led them upstairs to the room they'd been sleeping in since she got out of the hospital and shut the door quietly behind them. "Go on and get ready. I'll change and do my thing when you're done."

Felicity nodded and went into the small attached bathroom.

When he came back out, Ryder was wearing a pair of boxers and was pacing the room. He kissed her on the forehead on his way past her to the restroom.

Felicity put on a black tank top and took off her jeans. She climbed under the quilt and waited.

She didn't have long to wait. Ryder opened the bathroom door a minute later, stepped to the wall, and shut off the light, leaving the room in darkness. She heard him make his way around the bed and felt the mattress dip as he got in on the other side of her.

Then she was in his arms and could finally relax.

All day she'd been tense. She didn't have any doubt that Ryder would keep Joseph from taking her, but it had still been a very stressful situation. Then when Grace had blamed her for Nate being kidnapped, she'd felt her heart stop beating. It had been so like her sensitive best friend to immediately recant her statement and be genuinely remorseful for uttering it in the first place.

She melted into Ryder's arms. Burying her nose into the warm skin of his neck, she could feel the stubble of his beard against her cheek. Overwhelmed with sensations, the tears began to flow once more.

Ryder didn't once tell her to shush. He simply held her tighter and let her cry.

When she was finally all cried out, Felicity sniffed. Hard.

Chuckling, Ryder leaned over and grabbed a tissue from the table next to his side of the bed. He handed it over without a word.

Not feeling embarrassed in the least, although she supposed she probably should be, Felicity dried her eyes and blew her nose. She chucked the used tissue toward the table on her side and snuggled back into Ryder without checking to make sure she'd made her target.

"Fuck," Ryder said softly. "Am I glad to be here with you."

Felicity nodded. "Me too."

"I'm torn," he continued. "I'm devastated for Logan and Grace. Pissed way the hell off at Garrick and even Rex for sending him to the meet in the first place. But relieved as fuck that you're free."

Felicity could only nod again. *Yes.* She was feeling all that and more. Picking up her head, she whispered, "I love you."

"And I love you. So fucking much," Ryder said. "I want to fuck the shit out of you to celebrate you finally being able to go where you want and do what you want, but unfortunately, this isn't the time or place."

His words made her squirm, but she wasn't feeling the least bit ready to make love. "Do you think Garrick will find him?"

Ryder sighed. "I don't know. I just don't know. If he couldn't control his son when he was alive, I'm not sure he'll be able to figure out what Joseph had planned now that he's dead. I wish Black could've gotten his hands on him. We would've found out for sure if Nate was alive or dead."

Ryder paused, and after a couple of minutes said, "Don't take what Grace said to heart."

Knowing exactly what he was talking about, Felicity said quietly, "I'm trying not to. I mean, really, Nate being kidnapped *was* my fault. I was looking after them. Joseph was in town because of me. And he wanted to get at me by hurting those I love."

"Felicity," Ryder said gruffly, "don't."

"But be that as it may," she went on quickly, "I know that ultimately I did the right thing all those years ago in calling the cops on Joseph. He killed Colleen. He was an abusive asshole who liked to hurt women. You heard him. He didn't think we were equal by any stretch of the imagination. If it wasn't Nate, he would've hurt someone else. Joel, maybe. Or Bailey or Alexis. There's no telling what he would've done. I'm not sorry he's dead," she said fiercely. "Don't think I am. I only wish he would've died slower and more painfully."

"I think that's why Garrick did what he did. He knew if the Mountain Mercenaries got our hands on him, we would've learned everything about his operation there in Chicago. And Joseph *was* his son, even if he was a pain in his ass. So he killed him the most merciful way he could."

"Ryder?"

"Yeah, love?"

"I want to stay here until Nate comes home. But I know that you probably don't—"

"Don't finish that sentence," Ryder said harshly. "I go where you go. If you're here, so am I. I've slept next to you for the last month or so. Don't make me stop now. Not when you're free to be mine without any barriers whatsoever."

"Okay," Felicity said softly. "Ryder?"

He chuckled, relaxing now that she said he didn't have to leave her side. "What?"

"You're going to marry me, right?"

"Yes. But you're not allowed to propose to me. Remember?"

Felicity nodded. "I remember. But I only picked the name Jones because it was generic, and there are so many people with that last name, I figured it would be harder for Joseph to find me. I'm not attached to it. Frankly, I hate it."

"How do you feel about Sinclair as a last name?" Ryder asked, tightening his arms around her.

"I love it. Felicity Megan Sinclair."

"Beautiful," he murmured.

"So?"

"So what, love?"

"So are you going to propose?"

"Yeah. When we find Nate and things calm down. You'll get your proposal. Then we'll go and get married at the courthouse. No long, drawn-out waiting. Okay?"

"Sounds good to me. I've wasted enough of my life on the run as it is."

"Good."

"Good."

"Go to sleep, love. I don't know what tomorrow will bring. We need to track Joseph's movements from the time he took Nate until today. He disappeared after he took him, and that had to have been when he was stashing him somewhere. Rex and my teammates will find out everything they can. I'm thinking Logan and Grace will need to do some interviews and maybe some press conferences. The more attention we can bring to their missing son, the better. Detective Baker said he'd get an Amber Alert going as well. Grace is going to need you more than ever."

"Yeah." Felicity hugged Ryder harder. "I love you."

"Love you too. Now sleep."

Felicity didn't think she'd ever fall asleep, but she was out within ten minutes, the excitement of the day catching up with her.

She never knew that Ryder stayed awake for more than two hours, simply holding her. Never knew about the tears that leaked out of his eyes. Or about his whispered words, "Thank fuck you're safe."

Chapter Twenty

Thousands of miles away, in a rundown and dangerous part of San Antonio, Maria Gonzalez sat in a tiny, cramped bedroom inside a small apartment. Her bedroom door was usually locked from the outside, but after Maldad had left, he hadn't chained it closed behind him.

The man who had made her life a living hell hadn't ever told her his name, and Maria had begun to call him Maldad in her head after her first week in her prison apartment. *Evil.* It fit the man in every sense of the name.

He'd left a thousand dollars along with his "present" and told her to go home.

Home.

She wasn't sure how long it had been since she'd left her hometown of Fresnillo in the Zacatecas state of Mexico, but she estimated at least five years.

She'd been so stupid. Thought she knew everything there was to know about the world at eighteen. She was tired of looking after her younger brothers and sisters, not to mention her cousins, and had wanted more than working in the mines like her parents, aunts, and uncles did. When she'd read the advertisement in the paper for girls needed to move to the United States to work in a new and upcoming industry, she'd ignored her *mamá*'s warnings and had slipped out of their rundown house in the middle of the night.

At first everything seemed fine. She and four other women—girls—had met at a local bar. They'd been given new clothes and more money than they'd ever had in their entire lives. They'd gotten in a truck and been driven north.

But somewhere along the way, things had changed. The man who had been so nice to them in Fresnillo disappeared, and was replaced by a sullen older man who didn't speak more than two words to them.

When they got close to the border, they were ordered into small crates. Maria had been locked inside that small wooden box for hours. She thought she was going to die in there, but she hadn't. Looking back, she almost wished she had.

She was brought here to this apartment, where she met Maldad for the first time. She had no idea what had happened to the other girls who had traveled from Fresnillo with her, but she supposed it didn't matter. They were probably locked in a room, much like hers, forced to do the same things she'd been forced to do.

Maria had fought at first, but eventually had given in. Maldad owned her. He was free to do whatever he wanted to her, and it was his right to let anyone else he wanted do whatever they wanted with her.

And he had.

They had.

She'd been beaten and abused so horribly over the years, she was merely a shell of the idealistic young woman she'd once been.

But then a week ago, Maldad had arrived, unexpectedly. He'd unlocked her door, and instead of raping her, he'd shoved a bundle of blankets at her. He'd then thrown a US passport and a pile of money on the floor next to the dirty, stained mattress and said, "Go home, girl." He always called her "girl." All the men who visited her called her that. No one ever asked her name because they simply didn't care.

"Go home, girl," he'd said. "Take the baby and don't come back. Ever. Don't tell anyone where you got him or what happened here. If you do, I'll find you and kill you. Slowly and painfully."

He'd left as quickly as he'd arrived, not caring about the small infant he'd shoved at her any more than he cared about her.

Maria gazed down at the infant. He was adorable. His brown hair was long for how old she guessed he was. He was chubby, in the way only healthy babies could be. Maria's brothers and sisters had never looked as good as this child did. They were always hungry at home, never had enough to eat, and their dull eyes and protruding bellies showed it.

But they'd been loved.

Just as this child was.

Maria could see it from the expensive onesie the infant was wearing and from the glow of his perfect skin.

The first day, he'd smiled all the time and had no fear of her. Only a child who had never been hurt by others would be so free with his affection.

She'd been too afraid to leave her prison at first. She was scared it was a trap and if she set foot outside her room, Maldad would pop out of nowhere and hurt her for trying to escape. She'd tried to get away once before, a week after she'd been locked into her prison. A week after she'd been repeatedly raped by Maldad and his friends. They'd laughed when she'd cried and begged for them to let her go. To stop hurting her. The punishment for attempting to escape was a hundred times worse than what she'd endured the first week. She never made the mistake of trying to get away again. She learned her lesson the hard way all those years ago.

But after a while, the baby had gotten hungry. And dirty. And Maria didn't have anything to make a diaper out of except a torn T-shirt one of her visitors had left behind. So she'd carefully made her way out of her unlocked room into the kitchen. No one was lurking out there to beat her for stepping foot outside her prison. There wasn't any baby food, but she'd managed to mash up peas from a can in the pantry.

There was some evaporated milk, which she tried to dilute and give the child, but he wasn't having any of it.

Desperate, Maria had finally worked up the nerve to leave the apartment and walk down the street, with the baby in her arms. She wasn't going to leave him alone and chance one of Maldad's friends showing up and hurting him.

She bought some formula, a small box of diapers, and a box of cereal from a gas station.

The baby didn't exactly love the meal, but he was probably so hungry that he didn't have the energy to complain too loudly.

The way the baby's eyes constantly searched the room, and the way one of his little hands kept opening and closing, as if looking for something, or someone, unnerved her.

Wanting, no needing, information about the outside world that had been denied her for so long, Maria had been watching the Spanish channel on the small television for hours. She learned that she'd been living in the small apartment for three years. She'd gone from an innocent eighteen-year-old eager to escape the poverty of her homeland to a twenty-one-year-old who dreamed about the simple but safe life she used to lead.

With the infant fretting in her arms, Maria watched the news with fascination. So many things had changed in the last three years. But when a story came on about a missing child from Colorado, she froze. Maria stared at the television as a picture of the infant flashed on the screen. She tuned out the words from the reporter as more pictures were shown.

Pictures of his distraught parents.

Pictures of his uncles.

But it was the photo of his twin brother that caught her attention.

The missing child everyone was looking for was currently in her arms, crying. And he had a twin. His constantly moving eyes and his grasping hand made sense now. He was instinctually missing his brother and searching for him.

Maria looked down at the precious bundle. If *she* was this child's mother, she'd be frantic to get him back, just as she knew her own mother was for her. Even though she wasn't a child anymore, she knew deep in her bones that her *mamá* wouldn't give up trying to find out what had happened to her.

The money Maldad had thrown at her was sitting on the kitchen counter. Maria hadn't seen anyone in several days. It was the longest she'd ever gone without being raped or assaulted. Suddenly the urge to leave the apartment was overwhelming. Maybe it was a trick. Maybe the border agents would know at a glance the passport Maldad gave her was a fake. But wouldn't being caught at the border be better than staying here? Spending time in jail and being deported to where she wanted to go in the first place would be heaven compared to being raped every day and treated as if she was an object.

But the baby.

Maldad wanted her to take him with her over the border. Into Mexico. The man hadn't done one nice thing for her in three years. He certainly wouldn't start now. He had to have done something bad in order to have gotten the baby. If she took the child across the border, she'd be playing right into whatever horrible scheme Maldad had planned.

But on the other hand, the smiles and snuggles from the baby were the first friendly gestures she'd had since she'd been abducted. He was a helpless babe, and he needed her. Maria looked back up at the television. Even though an advertisement for some useless gadget was now being shown, all she could see was the frantic worry on the faces of the baby's parents as they'd pleaded with the public for any information about their kidnapped son.

Moving with a sense of urgency, and mentally berating herself for waiting so long to follow Maldad's orders, she ran into her former prison and scooped up the blanket she'd used for so long. Carefully swaddling the infant until he was in a cocoon of fleece, she continued to get ready to leave. The only shoes she had were an old pair of men's flip-flops. She'd worn them to the store, and they'd hurt her feet, but she didn't care. She needed to leave. Now.

Maria Gonzalez slipped out of the apartment much the same way she'd entered it all those years ago . . . silently and unnoticed by the drug dealers, prostitutes, and gang members who milled about.

Home.

She was going home.

Maria wasn't sure where she was or how to get to the border, but she had money in her pocket, a baby who was relying on her, and a renewed sense of urgency. She'd find the border crossing or die trying.

The tall Native American firefighter arrived at Station 7 later that day for his shift. He had the door open when he thought he heard something off to his right. He'd recently had a few experiences with his woman that made him extra cognizant of his surroundings. Turning his head, hoping not to see a coyote or another wild animal, he carefully looked into the bush with one hand on the doorknob and blinked at what he saw.

He cracked open the door and called out for his friends. Not waiting for them, he leaned down and picked up what he'd at first thought was simply a dirty blanket. But when he heard the faint cooing sound emanating from the material, he knew what he was looking at. Cradling the precious bundle in his arms, he read the note that was tucked into a fold on the baby's chest.

Missing baby. On televisión. Colorado. Nate. You take home.

The words were short and to the point, and the firefighter decided, because of the accent mark over the letter *o* in *televisión*, it was probably written by someone whose native language was Spanish.

"It's a baby," he told his fellow firefighters as he met them just inside the large station. "Maybe that infant who's been on the news out of Colorado. Call the cops. If it is him, his family needs to be notified as soon as possible that he's safe."

The fireman took one last look around the yard, as if he could find whoever had left the child. Seeing nothing, and somehow knowing searching would not only be futile but possibly dangerous to whoever had dropped off the child, the firefighter quietly shut the door.

He never saw the skinny young woman hiding in a row of bushes across the street, unwilling to leave before making sure baby Nate was safe. She'd made some poor decisions in her life, but this wasn't one of them. She climbed out of her hiding place and headed back to the fast-food restaurant she'd been dropped off at by the taxi she'd hailed near the apartment she'd been held captive in.

Her plan was to get another taxi and head south.

Home.

Detective Baker took a deep breath and rang the doorbell. The second he'd heard the news, he'd raced to the Anderson house. It wasn't often he got to deliver good news in a case like this one.

When he first heard the Anderson triplets were moving back to Castle Rock, he hadn't exactly been pleased. He remembered the brothers from when they were in high school. They hadn't exactly been troublemakers, but they definitely were on the radar of the local cops.

But they'd done more good than even Detective Baker probably knew since they'd returned. They almost single-handedly took down one of Denver's most notorious gangs, and they helped countless other people who needed their brand of security.

So when he'd heard that baby Nate had been found, safe and healthy, he'd been more than happy to take the drive out to Logan and Grace's house to give them the news personally.

The door opened, and the detective looked up into Logan's concerned face. It wasn't until right that moment that he realized the man might take his showing up in person the wrong way.

Glancing behind Logan, the detective saw the entire Anderson family was there. Blake and Alexis. Nathan and Bailey. Even Felicity and the Anderson's half brother, Ryder, were there. Logan's wife, Grace, stood at his side, their other baby, Ace, in her arms.

Not wanting to stress this family out more than they already were, Detective Baker smiled and announced, "We found him."

Epilogue

"Are you sure you don't mind sharing a wedding day with Blake and Alexis?" Ryder asked Felicity.

She smiled and shook her head. He'd asked her many times over the past few months, and every time she'd given him the same answer. "Absolutely not. He's your brother, and I love Alexis. Of course I don't mind."

Felicity marveled at the close relationship Ryder had with Blake, thinking it somewhat ironic considering their rocky start.

They'd even bought a house in the same neighborhood as Alexis and Blake. Felicity never spent another night in the apartment over the gym. She couldn't. It held too many bad memories. Not only of being stalked by Joseph, but the horror she felt knowing Nate had been kidnapped from there right under her nose. She'd stayed with Ryder in an apartment he'd rented on a short-term basis until they'd completed the purchase of their new home.

The proposal Ryder had teased her with came about a month after Nate was returned home. Ryder had taken her down to Colorado Springs to hang out with his friends and to shoot some pool at The Pit.

She'd had the time of her life. Ryder's friends were hilarious, and she'd had too much to drink. After she'd lost her tenth game of pool, and had laughed her head off at how bad she was, Ryder had handed her an envelope full of papers.

She'd opened it and been completely confused at what she'd found.

Inside were court papers officially changing her name from Felicity Jones to Felicity Megan Sinclair. Also included was a driver's license, a passport, and a Social Security card with her new name. Ryder had also included a bank statement, this one with both their names on it, and a contract for the house they'd decided they wanted to put a bid on.

She'd looked up in confusion and saw that he was on one knee.

In front of all his friends, and with no embarrassment on his face, he'd said, "Will you marry me?"

And what had she said? Yes? Nope, her drunk self had said, "But you already changed my name to yours."

He'd laughed and patiently explained. "I pulled some strings. After you were cleared by the Chicago PD for any involvement in Colleen's death, your mother's, and even of those bogus drug charges, I thought about what a pain it would be to try to get all new, legal identification documents. So I had the guys take care of it. They cut through the annoying red tape and got you new identification. Figured if we were going to get married, it would be more expedient to just change your name now, rather than after the wedding."

Laughing, she'd put her hands on her hips and said, "But I haven't said yes!"

"You will," had been his response. Then he asked again. "Will you marry me, love? Live with me? Make me the happiest man alive?"

There was no way she could've held out after that. She'd agreed, and now here they were. Ten minutes away from walking down the aisle.

They'd decided that since neither had any parents, they would walk down the aisle together. Arm in arm. Just like they wanted to be for the rest of their lives.

"We should've just eloped," Ryder murmured, running his hands down the silky-smooth material of her white gown. It wasn't a typical wedding dress, merely a silk sheath. No lace. No pouf. But Felicity loved it. The sleeves came down to her wrists, and it had a high neckline.

From the front it looked modest and demure, covering every inch of her skin. But the back of the dress dipped low. Very low.

Felicity felt sexy and very feminine. Ryder had seen her that morning in her dress for the first time when he'd accidentally walked in after she'd pulled it over her head. He'd ordered Grace and Bailey out and had proceeded to show her how much he liked it.

Felicity shrugged at his elopement comment. "Maybe. But I have to admit, I love that we're sharing this with your brother and Alexis. And that all your friends came up for it."

"Yeah, me too," he agreed. "I have something for you. It's not much, and I know you said it didn't matter, that you were an adult, but I did it anyway."

Felicity held out her hand as he handed her a festive bag with a ton of tissue paper sticking out the top. She peered in and pushed the wrapping to the side. When she saw what was inside, her eyes got huge. She pulled out her giraffe. The one Joseph had beheaded. With everything that had happened, she hadn't really had time to think about it. And being sad about a stuffed animal being destroyed felt stupid, all things considered.

She pulled it out and hugged it to her chest for a moment. "Thank you," she whispered.

Ryder kissed her forehead gently. "It's important to you; therefore, it's important to me."

"I have a present for you too," Felicity blurted, carefully placing her giraffe back into the bag.

"I got my present already today," Ryder said with a gleam of lust in his eyes. "I got to make love to my fiancée, and later I'll make love to my wife in the same day. You couldn't give me a better gift."

She smiled, remembering how he'd yanked up the skirt of her dress earlier and proceeded to blow her mind. The orgasm was the perfect way to make her relax before the ceremony.

"Wait here," she ordered.

He didn't look like he wanted to let her out of his sight, but he merely crossed his arms over his chest and smiled at her indulgently.

Felicity exited the small room in the back of the church and headed for where she'd stashed Ryder's surprise. She probably should have waited until after the ceremony, but she couldn't. This was too important.

Ryder paced the small room as he waited for Felicity to return with whatever present she'd gotten him. He was a little annoyed because they'd agreed not to exchange gifts before the ceremony. The giraffe he'd arranged to be mended didn't really count, in his eyes. He'd wanted to get her a diamond pendant or a tennis bracelet or something, but had refrained because they'd agreed on no gifts. He was mentally kicking himself, trying to decide if he could send someone to the store to pick up something he could give her after the ceremony when the door opened again.

He turned, expecting to see his soon-to-be wife enter. Ryder stood absolutely still and stared at the woman who walked through the door. Felicity had told him she had a surprise for him, but he'd never imagined this.

He stared at his fiancée as she entered behind the other woman, walked around her, and came to his side. "How . . ." Words failed him.

Luckily, Felicity understood him anyway. "I knew you wouldn't ever look for her, so I got Alexis to ask her hacker friend if he could find her." She gestured toward the woman standing next to them. "He did."

Grabbing hold of Felicity's hand as if he'd float away if he didn't, he stared at the beautiful stranger. He'd recognize her anywhere. She was an adult now; years had passed since he'd last seen her, but it was as if no time had passed.

Her black hair now brushed her shoulders and swung freely as she moved. She was slender and healthy. Tears sprang to Ryder's eyes. He wasn't normally a crier, but seeing Zariya in front of him . . . *smiling* at him, was more than he could take.

The last time he'd seen her was etched in his mind as if in glass. Scared out of her mind. Hurting. Bleeding. Flinching from him.

"Zariya," he choked out.

She held out her hand, and Ryder immediately took it in both of his. She smiled at him and didn't protest when he didn't let go. "It's so good to see you again," she said with a melodious accent.

Ryder just stared at her, wanting to know everything, but afraid to ask.

Felicity pressed up against Ryder's side. "Thank you for coming, Zariya. It's so good to talk to you in person."

Ryder's head came around at that. "You've been talking to her?"

Felicity looked up at him. "Well, of course." She looked back at the other woman. "I couldn't exactly spring you on her. So I called her up after I got her number. She's been living in South Carolina. Told her who I was. We've talked a lot, and she agreed to come and see you."

Suddenly needing to get the words out that he hadn't said all those years ago, Ryder said, "I'm so sorry, Zariya."

Zariya squeezed his hands, then finally let go. "Don't be sorry. You saved my life that day, Ryder."

"I . . . I don't understand."

"Felicity told me what you thought might've happened to me, and it probably would've if it hadn't been for a soldier. Not one of the ones who was with you that day, but a different one. My parents came and collected me and told me I was a failure. That my duty was to marry. They had another man, even older, ready to marry me. But first I had to be punished for humiliating them. I was tied to a stake, and everyone had rocks ready to throw at me, but a soldier happened upon me and snatched me up. He didn't even blink when my parents yelled at him.

He just took me back to the base and refused to let anyone near me. I was scared, really scared, but eventually I realized you had saved me from an awful fate."

"But I didn't . . . he . . . I . . ." Ryder shook his head in frustration.

"The man . . . he arranged for me to come to the United States. I was adopted. I've been living in South Carolina for the last nine years. I'm happy. And it's because of you, Ryder. I thought of you many times over the years. The memories of my time as a child in the village have faded, as has what happened to me, but I've never forgotten the soldier who took the time to smile at me. Bring me candy." A tear fell from her eye. "Who braided my hair."

Ryder couldn't take it anymore. He felt Felicity's touch at the small of his back, always there by his side, supporting him, as he held out his arms. "Please, I need to hug you."

Without a word, Zariya stepped into his arms. Ryder looked up at the ceiling as he did his best to keep the tears in his eyes from falling down his face. God. In a million years, he never would've expected this reunion would ever happen. Without letting go of the little girl turned woman in his arms, Ryder turned his head and looked at Felicity.

"I love you," he mouthed.

She smiled back and returned his words to him.

The wedding was small. The brothers had only invited close friends. Detective Baker and Detective Peterson from the Denver PD were in attendance, as were quite a few of Joel's classmates. Alexis's family was there, including her brother, Bradford, who'd gotten the time off from his new job as a cruise director for a large cruise line. He'd brought his partner, and the two men beamed at Alexis from their seats in the front row of the church.

All the men from Clayson's Auto Body shop, where Bailey worked, were there. Duke, Henry, Ozzie, Bert, and Clayson had showed up in their overalls. But they were quick to point out that they were their *good* overalls. Not stained with grease.

Brian and Betty Grant, Alexis's parents, hadn't stopped smiling since they'd arrived three days earlier. They'd insisted on paying for the rehearsal dinner and had generously paid for a honeymoon for not only their daughter and Blake, but for Ryder and Felicity too.

Francesca Scarpetti was standing at the back of the church, and as soon as the ceremony was over, she would be rushing back to her restaurant to make sure everything was running smoothly for the reception. It was being held at her Italian restaurant, Scarpetti's. When she'd heard about the double wedding, she'd insisted on it.

Bailey and Grace were standing to the left and acting as bridesmaids, and Logan and Nathan were on the other side as the groomsmen. Grace held Nate, and Logan held Ace. Both babies were sleeping soundly, as if the excitement of the moment didn't interest them in the slightest.

The wedding went off without a hitch, and Felicity only giggled once, when the pastor asked her, Felicity Sinclair, if she would take Ryder Sinclair to be her lawfully wedded husband. He'd definitely jumped the gun and caused confusion all around by officially giving her his name before they were married. But she couldn't argue that it made her life easier. She was pleased she wouldn't have to worry about changing her name . . . again . . . now that they were officially wed.

Later that night, as Felicity swayed back and forth on the makeshift dance floor at Scarpetti's in her husband's arms, she looked up at him and said, "I'm happy."

She felt his hands on her lower back, caressing her just above her ass with his fingers. She wished she could feel his fingers on her bare skin. Biting her lip, and wanting him . . . again, she looked up at him.

"I'm happy too, love. You're all I ever wanted in my life. All I'll ever want."

It was sweet. Very sweet. But Felicity didn't want sweet. She wanted passionate. The quickie they'd had on their way to the reception hadn't been nearly enough. Ryder had stopped by their house, carried her over the threshold, fucked her in their entryway, and had whisked her back out to his car and to Scarpetti's before she had a chance to think. She would've been embarrassed, but Blake and Alexis had arrived thirty minutes after them, and it was obvious her new husband had the same ideas as Ryder. Alexis had had a dreamy, yet satisfied, look on her face when she'd followed her husband into the restaurant.

Trying to take her mind off how badly she wanted Ryder, Felicity looked around the dimly lit space. She spied Zariya sitting at a corner booth, Ro at her side. They looked to be deep in conversation. She gestured to the duo with her head. "What do you think?" she asked her husband.

Ryder glanced over and saw who she was talking about. He looked down at her with a huge grin on his face and shrugged. "I can't lie. I'd be over the moon if that worked out. Seeing Zariya happy and with a man I like and respect would be like a miracle to me. But don't get your hopes up. Ro's a hard man to really get to know, and I can't see him settling down anytime soon."

"Hmm," Felicity agreed. "I just want her to be happy."

"She *is* happy," Ryder said. "Thank you again for tracking her down and flying her out here. Seeing her alive and well and healthy is a miracle."

Felicity smiled at him, then tilted her head to the side when Ryder dipped her and brought his lips to her ear. "Enough chitchat. Think we've been here long enough for Francesca not to give us the riot act if we leave?"

"We've cut the cake, danced our first dance, and the toasts have been given. I don't care if she bans us for life. I want to go home and fuck my husband," Felicity murmured, feeling goose bumps race down her arms at the feel of her husband's warm exhale against her neck at her bold words.

Without another word, Ryder took her hand and led her off the dance floor. He ignored the catcalls and good-natured ribbing from his friends and brothers.

Later that night, Ryder held his new wife in his arms and sighed. His life was so much better with Felicity by his side. His eyes roved over her hair. It was sticking up in all directions after their enthusiastic lovemaking. A week ago she'd been to a hairdresser and had gotten her hair dyed back to what she said was close to her natural color. It had been a little tough to get used to her blonde locks, but now he loved it. It was her, and it matched her new life. Lighter. Freer.

"Do you think you got enough new pictures for the house today, love?"

Felicity chuckled at his side. "Yeah, Ryder, I think the three thousand and forty-three pictures the photographer took should be enough."

He smiled. Felicity had filled their new house with photos. Since she didn't have to worry about having to pack up and run, or about anyone finding out who she really was, she'd gone whole hog in decorating. Every room in their house had pictures in it. On the walls. In frames on tables. Stuffed into every nook and cranny. Ryder couldn't look anywhere without seeing reminders of his wife's love for her friends.

One of his favorites was the one of her holding her acceptance letter to the University of Denver. He'd encouraged her to contact the university and see about transferring her credits and finishing her degree. Even though she wasn't planning on trying to get an engineering job, he was so proud of her for deciding to finish her degree. The grin on her face in the photo showed exactly how pleased she was with her decision as well. Joseph Waters might've tried to break his woman, but her strength and intelligence had won out in the end.

Felicity had even included pictures of both their mothers in her decorating frenzy. He loved seeing his mom's face, but he loved seeing the photos of Felicity and her mother even more. The women might not've been at their wedding today, but he still felt their love . . . and knew Felicity did too.

The other addition to their walls was the new signed agreement between Cole and her in regard to Rock Hard Gym. Apparently, Cole had seen his lawyer and had gotten Felicity's name added as soon as he heard about Ryder getting her name changed. He'd had it framed and had given it to her as a present. Cole had told her to put it on her wall so she'd never forget that he refused to let her leave all those months ago.

"I love you, Felicity Sinclair," Ryder whispered to his wife.

"I love you, Ryder Sinclair."

He felt his dick stir at her words, but didn't make a move to do anything about it. They had the rest of their lives together. He could give her an hour break.

As if she could read his mind, Felicity mumbled, "Give me a bit . . . then I'll be ready to go again."

He chuckled, knowing he wouldn't have the heart to wake her up later. She'd had an exciting few days. She deserved her sleep. Without responding verbally, Ryder leaned down, kissed Felicity's forehead, and held her tighter against his side.

He fell asleep almost as fast as his new wife did, content in the knowledge that his woman was safe . . . and finally legally his.

Nathan kissed Joel's forehead and stood up. He tiptoed to the doorway and paused to look back at the boy he considered his son. He closed the door and almost ran right into Bailey.

He pulled her into his arms and walked her backward down the hall toward their room. Smiling down at her, he said, "Something about weddings makes me super horny."

Bailey rolled her eyes up at him. "Everything makes you horny," she mock-complained.

He laughed and agreed. "True." Then he leaned down and picked her up, throwing her over his shoulder.

Careful not to screech too loud and wake up her brother, Bailey pretended to pound on his back as he carried her into their bedroom. He shut the door quietly and went to the bed. He leaned over, dropped Bailey on her back, and immediately climbed over her. They re-situated themselves until they were lying in the middle of the mattress.

Nathan got serious. "Are you sure you don't mind us not being married legally?"

She immediately shook her head. "We've been over this. You know I don't really believe in marriage. Besides, we've been living together, you took my name, we share a bank account. According to the state, we're married even though we don't have the signed paper."

"I just wanted to make sure today didn't make you sad in any way."

"Sad? No way. The ceremony was beautiful, and I'm happier than you know that Felicity and Alexis are satisfied and happy with their relationships. Are *you* okay with it?"

"Absolutely. I couldn't care less what anyone else thinks. You're mine. I'm yours. Joel is ours. I'm happy."

"What would you think about giving Joel a niece or nephew?"

Nathan's breath caught in his throat, and he placed a hand on her flat belly. "Are you . . . What are you saying?"

"I'm not pregnant," Bailey told him, putting her hand over his on her stomach. "But I wouldn't be opposed to it either. I've spent enough time with Nate and Ace to realize that I'd love to have your baby. I'd love for us to teach a child what true love is all about."

"Yes," Nathan said immediately. "I'm ready when you are."

"How about now?" Bailey asked, batting her eyes at the man hovering above her.

"Now's perfect," Nathan told her, immediately getting up on his knees and stripping his shirt over his head.

He smiled as Bailey giggled. Once upon a time, he'd thought of himself as the nerdy Anderson. But being with Bailey had changed him . . . for the better. He still loved numbers and math, but when he saw the envious looks men shot his way when he was out with Bailey, it felt good. She was his.

When he felt Bailey's hands begin to work the belt on his pants, he grinned. Yeah, his woman knew exactly what she wanted, and thank Christ that seemed to be him.

Blake Anderson slowly worked on unfastening the back of his wife's dress. Earlier she'd insisted they didn't have time to get undressed, and he'd been so ready to officially make her his in body as well as on paper that he would've agreed to anything she asked for.

But now he could take his time.

Worship her.

Show her how lucky he was to be her husband.

"Bradford looked content tonight, don't you think?" Alexis asked.

Blake mentally rolled his eyes. He was not going to talk about her family right now.

"And Felicity and Ryder were really happy."

He grunted in response, concentrating on what seemed like thousands of little buttons that went from her ass up to her neck. They were way too tiny for his large hands, but he diligently kept working, trying to be careful not to rip her wedding gown as he went.

"My mom and dad told me tonight that they've planned a huge after-wedding party for us at their house up in Denver. They've invited all their friends. Expect it to be over-the-top lavish." When Blake didn't say anything, Alexis asked, "Are you listening to me?"

"No," Blake answered honestly.

"Blake!" Alexis exclaimed, sounding very put out.

Finally getting the last button undone, Blake spun his wife around and dropped his mouth to hers. He pushed her beautiful dress over her shoulders roughly. Lifting her, leaving the dress pooled on the floor, he took the few steps over to their huge four-poster bed. Turning her, he bent her over the mattress, which happened to be the perfect height for him to take her from behind. He pulled a stool they kept handy for just this reason over with his foot, even as he unhooked her lacy bra. At almost a foot shorter than he was, Alexis needed the extra height so Blake could take her the way they both wanted. Without a word, Alexis stepped up and spread her legs. She propped herself up on her elbows and looked back at Blake.

"Fuck me, husband."

"With pleasure, wife," Blake returned. Instead of removing the ivory panties, he simply pulled the gusset to the side. He made sure she was ready for him before plunging inside with one quick thrust. They both moaned.

Their coupling was quick. Both reached their peak within minutes.

Later, after he'd taken her twice more and they were both almost asleep, Blake said, "The next time you try to talk about your family in our bed, I'm going to take you over my knee."

"Like *that's* a deterrent," Alexis mumbled.

Chuckling, Blake turned on his side, moving Alexis until they were spooning. One hand cupped one of her breasts, and the other arm was under her neck. She curled both hands around the forearm at her chest and sighed happily.

"Love you."

"Love you too, Alexis."

Logan Anderson watched as his wife fussed over their children. They were still sleeping in a crib next to their king-size bed, but he didn't care. He knew it would be a while before Grace would be able to sleep somewhere other than where her children were. If he was honest with himself, he didn't want to be separated from Ace and Nate either.

The week his son had been missing had been the worst in his life. Worse than the abuse he'd suffered growing up. Worse than some of the missions he'd been on overseas when he'd been in the Army. He hadn't ever known pain like wondering if his son was dead or alive.

And almost worse than that was watching Grace struggle with the same knowledge. She had been hurting, and there was nothing he could do for her except be by her side, loving her.

Grace leaned down and kissed both babies once more, then turned to the bed. She took off the T-shirt she'd been wearing and climbed in next to her husband.

Logan opened his arms and sighed in relief when Grace cuddled right into him. It seemed as if the trauma they'd been through had brought them closer together. Logan knew it could've easily done the opposite. He swore right then and there never to take his wife for granted. Not that he had in the past, but not knowing where their son was, if he was hurt, or dead, just made him all the more determined to make sure Grace and their children had the best lives possible.

"Where do you think he was?"

Logan knew what Grace was talking about. They hadn't really discussed this yet. He was happy she was opening up about it, finally. "I don't know, Smarty. But I believe with all my heart that whoever had him treated him as well as they could."

"Detective Baker said that the fireman who found him thought a woman dropped him off."

Logan nodded against Grace. "Yeah, I think so too. The writing on the note was pretty ornate."

"Do you think she's okay?" Grace asked, lifting her head and looking him in the eyes as she asked.

Logan's heart melted a little more at her question. His Grace worried about other people more than she did herself at times. "I don't know," he answered honestly.

"If Joseph knew her, it couldn't have been good."

Logan had thought the same thing. He knew more about Joseph Waters than his wife or any of his brothers' women did. Joseph had a network of sexual slaves he'd kept around the country. He apparently bought them from human traffickers and kept them locked up in crappy apartments in different cities. He had contacts who were allowed to use the women how they wished in return for their loyalty. It was sickening, and Ryder had said that his handler, the mysterious Rex, had made it his mission to track down and free every single woman Joseph had enslaved.

"I think if she was brave enough to leave Nate at that fire station, she had to have escaped."

"I hope so." Grace moved then. Getting on her knees over him, she straddled Logan's waist and looked down at him. "I love you."

"I love you too, Smarty."

And with that, she began to scoot down his body.

"Grace," Logan managed to get out, but the rest of his words were lost as his wife leaned over and took him into her mouth. It had been a while since she'd done this for him. It had been a rough stretch of time for their love life. Between the worry for their son, and then her paranoia that making love in the same room would somehow scar their children for life, they hadn't been intimate for quite a while.

Logan didn't mind. Whatever Grace needed, he'd gladly give her. Even if that meant not making love.

But lately, his wife had been getting her confidence back. He loved watching her blossom once more. "Grace," he moaned again as she enthusiastically showed him how much she loved him. "If I'd known the effect a wedding would have on you, I would've taken you to one way before now."

He felt her chuckle, and the reverberations rocketed through his dick. He had to concentrate not to prematurely go off in her mouth.

"In fact, I think I'll find a ceremony to take you to every weekend from here on out. I'll check the church's schedule."

Then he couldn't think or talk anymore. His wife shifted and took him inside her hot, wet body, and rode him as if her life depended on it. Looking up at her, lost in the exquisite feelings coursing through her, Logan thought to himself what a lucky bastard he was.

It was late, but Cole couldn't sleep. Being at his best friend's wedding and seeing her finally break free of the hold Joseph Waters had on her for years was a miracle. Felicity deserved all the happiness in the world.

Leaning back against the back of the chair in his home office, Cole reread the e-mail he'd received from Logan earlier. Ace Security was working on a particularly nasty case involving a woman named Sarah Butler. She lived in Castle Rock, and her ex-husband was a grade A asshole. Instead of moving on with his life after their divorce, as Sarah was apparently trying to do, he was showing up at her work and outside her apartment to harass her. Logan had e-mailed, wanting to know if Cole had any spaces in the self-defense-for-women class he'd started.

He didn't, but after reading the restraining order Logan had sent along with his request, Cole's decision to help Sarah was an easy one.

Cole clicked "Reply" and typed out a short response to Logan.

Logan,

Honestly, there isn't any room in my current SD class, but I'm happy to work with Sarah one-on-one. People like her are why I started the classes in the first place. Shoot me her contact info and I'll reach out and make arrangements.

Cole

Miles away, at the Women's Correctional Facility in Denver, Margaret Mason lay bleeding and dying on the dirty kitchen floor of the prison. She'd been tasked to work the morning shift, which meant she had to get up at four in the morning to start preparing breakfast for the hundreds of inmates. She hated mornings.

Life for the former socialite hadn't been easy behind bars. She'd done what she always did and what had worked in the past—tried to boss everyone around. She might've been able to order her husband and daughter around, but the hardened criminals around her didn't take kindly to her attitude.

She'd been in the infirmary more than half a dozen times in the last six months with wounds she'd received from being beaten by the other prisoners. The staff had finally given her her own cell, even though overcrowding was rampant in the prison.

The day she'd been questioned about her missing grandson had been a highlight in her otherwise miserable existence behind bars. When the detective started talking about her son-in-law's half brother, Margaret wanted to laugh and tell the asshole cop that she already knew. Wanted to gloat that she'd known about Logan's half brother long before anyone else in the miserable town of Castle Rock had—including Rose

Anderson. Margaret had been shopping in Colorado Springs one day and had seen Ryder. She'd known with one glance he looked way too much like Ace Anderson for it to be a coincidence.

And since she always liked to have something to hold over other people's heads, she'd spent a considerable amount of money to have a private investigator check him out. The man had gotten a DNA sample from Ace after he'd thrown away a bottle of water that confirmed Ryder was his. She'd loved keeping that secret from them. Knowing something they didn't. That Logan boy thought he was better than she was. That he was smarter. Well, he wasn't. When the detective had told her Logan's son was missing, Margaret couldn't help but laugh. She'd had everything taken from her, and now karma had come full circle and taken what meant the most from him too.

But unfortunately, Margaret Mason hadn't thought about karma affecting her. Not too long after she'd learned Nate Anderson had been found and returned to his family, her luck finally ran out.

The homemade knife had been thrust into her back, hitting her kidney without a sound. By the time Margaret had turned around to see who had shanked her, no one was there.

Whoever had done it knew exactly what they were doing. All it had taken was one thrust, and she was bleeding out internally.

Margaret first fell to her knees, then to her stomach. She lay on the filthy floor, facedown, watching as the other women simply walked around her as they continued to prepare the morning meal. No one cared that she was dying.

Margaret Mason's last thoughts swam through her head. *This is all Grace's fault. If I'd only had that abortion when I found out I was pregnant, I wouldn't be lying here right now. My husband wouldn't be in a prison hospital somewhere, comatose after having a heart attack behind bars, and I would still be living in my beautiful home ordering my servants around. Grace's fault. Everything was Grace's fault.*

It wasn't until the morning head count at breakfast that Margaret Mason was discovered to be missing. And it wasn't until an hour later that her cold, dead body was found in the kitchen. Lying amid the grease and food droppings from the preparation of breakfast that morning.

The man who ran Mountain Mercenaries drummed his fingers against the hard wood of his desk. Rex had done what he could to rescue the women Joseph Waters had held captive, but it still didn't feel as if it was enough. Garrick Watson had gotten an earful from Rex, and the man had sworn up and down he didn't have any idea what his son had been doing.

Joseph had hired a pilot to fly Nate Anderson and him to San Antonio. He'd dropped off the infant and flown back to Colorado. He'd bribed the pilot to go against FAA rules and not file a flight plan. But to make sure the man didn't have any second thoughts about flying a kidnapped child across state lines, once back in Colorado, Joseph had followed him home from the airport and murdered the man and his family. There was no telling how many people he'd cold-bloodedly killed over the years just to get his revenge on Megan Parkins.

Garrick had made the connection between the murders and his son, and had willingly passed the information on to Rex, saying once more that he didn't know anything about his son's sexual slaves he'd kept on the side.

The thing of it was, Rex believed him. Garrick had bent over backward sucking up to Rex to try to make sure he didn't sic his Mountain Mercenaries on him. The fact that he'd killed his own son didn't mean dick to Rex. Garrick would kill his own mother, if the woman was still alive, if it meant keeping Rex and his men off his back.

But Rex wasn't happy. Joseph might be dead, but there were thousands of men just like him still walking around, harassing, stalking, and enslaving women as if they had the right to do so.

The handler picked up a small picture he kept on his desk as a reminder of why he did what he did. Felicity had been lucky. Ryder had been at the right place at the right time to step in and help her. But not all women were fortunate enough to have a champion like Ryder, his former mercenary—someone who was willing to die and kill for them, at the right time and place.

Running his thumb over the woman's cheek in the photograph, Rex sent up the silent apology and promise he repeated every night.

I'm sorry I wasn't there for you, and I swear I'll never stop looking for you.

Taking a deep breath, Rex put the picture frame down and concentrated on the computer screen. It was time for another case. Ryder might have retired from the Mountain Mercenaries, but there were still six more men ready and willing to do whatever it took to rescue women who had found themselves in dire situations.

He kept himself separated from his crew for their own safety. What he did wasn't exactly legal, and if he was taken down, he didn't want his men taken down with him. It was for their own good that he was merely a voice on the phone. His men came first. He'd protect them with his life if need be. He hadn't gotten his reputation by being a pushover either—Garrick Watson would attest to that.

Feeling satisfaction in his gut that he'd had a role in setting Megan Parkins free, and that one of his favorite mercenaries was living a good life, now working side by side with his brothers at Ace Security, Rex clicked on the next case Mountain Mercenaries would be taking on.

It was time to get back to work.

Acknowledgments

Thank you to Colleen for letting me name one of my characters after you . . . sorry about the whole killing-you-off thing. Ha!

Thank you also to everyone who picked up the first book in this series—and kept reading. It's been fun to write about a new group of men and how they find the women meant to be theirs.

As you've probably guessed, the Mountain Mercenaries will get their own series. I want to thank Maria Gomez and everyone at Montlake Publishing for believing in me and always cheering me on. Because of their enthusiasm and support, all of you, my readers, will get more stories in the near future.

About the Author

Susan Stoker is a *New York Times*, *USA Today*, and *Wall Street Journal* bestselling author who loves hot alpha heroes. She debuted her first series in 2014 and quickly followed it up with her SEAL of Protection series and her Ace Security series, which includes *Claiming Bailey*, *Claiming Grace*, and *Claiming Alexis*. She is addicted to writing and creating stories readers can lose themselves in.

Susan considers herself an all-American girl with a heart as big as her home state of Texas. Thanks to her Army husband, she's lived in several different states. Now that he's retired, however, it's *his* turn to follow Susan around the country.

Discover more about Susan and her books through her website, www.StokerAces.com, or follow her on Twitter (@Susan_Stoker) and Facebook (www.facebook.com/authorsusanstoker).

Connect with Susan Online

Susan's Facebook Profile and Page

www.facebook.com/authorsstoker

www.facebook.com/authorsusanstoker

Follow Susan on Twitter

www.twitter.com/Susan_Stoker

Find Susan's Books on Goodreads

www.goodreads.com/SusanStoker

E-mail

Susan@StokerAces.com

Website

www.StokerAces.com

Made in the USA
Columbia, SC
28 November 2021